A Wish in the Dark

A Wish in the Dark

CHRISTINA SOONTORNVAT

CANDLEWICK PRESS

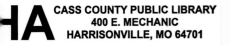

First edition 2020

Library of Congress Catalog Card Number 2020901923
ISBN 978-1-5362-0494-0

21 22 23 24 LBM 10 9 8 7 6

Printed in Melrose Park, IL, U.S.A.

This book was typeset in Adobe Jenson Pro.

Candlewick Press
99 Dover Street
Somerville, Massachusetts 02144

visit us at www.candlewick.com

A JUNIOR LIBRARY GUILD SELECTION

For my mother and father

Chapter 1

A monster of a mango tree grew in the courtyard of Namwon Prison. Its fluffy green branches stretched across the cracked cement and hung over the soupy brown water of the Chattana River. The women inmates spent most of their days sheltered under the shade of this tree while the boats glided up and down and up again on the other side of the prison gate.

The dozen children who lived in Namwon also spent most of their days lying in the shade. But not in mango season. In mango season, the tree dangled golden drops of heaven overhead, swaying just out of reach.

It drove the kids nuts.

They shouted at the mangoes. They chucked pieces of broken cement at them, trying to knock them down. And when the mangoes refused to fall, the children cried, stomped their bare feet, and collapsed in frustration on the ground.

Pong never joined them. Instead, he sat against the tree's trunk, hands crossed behind his head. He looked like he was sleeping, but actually, he was paying attention.

Pong had been paying attention to the tree for weeks. He knew which mangoes had started ripening first. He noticed when the fruit lightened from lizard-skin green to pumpkin-rind yellow. He watched the ants crawl across the mangoes, and he knew where they paused to sniff the sugar inside.

Pong looked at his friend, Somkit, and gave him a short nod. Somkit wasn't shouting at the mangoes, either. He was sitting under the branch that Pong had told him to sit under, waiting. Somkit had been waiting an hour, and he'd wait for hours more if he had to, because the most important thing to wait for in Namwon were the mangoes.

He and Pong were both nine years old, both orphans. Somkit was a head shorter than Pong, and skinny — even for a prisoner. He had a wide, round face, and the other kids teased him that he looked like those grilled rice balls on sticks that old ladies sold from their boats.

Like many of the women at Namwon, their mothers had been sent there because they'd been caught stealing. Both their mothers had died in childbirth, though from the stories the other women still told, Somkit's birth had been more memorable and involved feet showing up where a head was supposed to be.

Pong wagged his finger at his friend to get him to scoot to the left.

A little more.

A little more.

There.

Finally, after all that waiting, Pong heard the soft pop of a mango stem. He gasped and smiled as the first mango of the season dropped straight into Somkit's waiting arms.

But before Pong could join his friend and share their triumph, two older girls noticed what Somkit held in his hands.

"Hey, did you see that?" said one of the girls, propping herself up on her knobby elbows.

"Sure did," said the other, cracking scab-covered knuckles. "Hey, Skin-and-Bones," she called to Somkit. "What do you got for me today?"

"Uh-oh," said Somkit, cradling the mango in one hand and bracing himself to stand up with the other.

He was useless in a fight, which meant that everyone liked fighting him the most. And he couldn't run more than a few steps without coughing, which meant the fights usually ended badly.

Pong turned toward the guards who were leaning against the wall behind him, looking almost as bored with life in Namwon as the prisoners were.

"Excuse me, ma'am," said Pong, bowing to the first guard.

She sucked on her teeth and slowly lifted one eyebrow.

"Ma'am, it's those girls," said Pong. "I think they're going to take —"

"And what do you want me to do about it?" she snapped. "You kids need to learn to take care of yourselves."

The other guard snorted. "Might be good for you to get kicked around a little. Toughen you up."

A hot, angry feeling fluttered inside Pong's chest. Of course the guards wouldn't help. When did they ever? He looked at the women prisoners. They stared back at him with flat, resigned eyes. They were far past caring about one miserable mango.

Pong turned away from them and hurried back to his friend. The girls approached Somkit slowly, savoring the coming brawl. "Quick, climb on," he said, dropping to one knee.

"What?" said Somkit.

"Just get on!"

"Oh, man, I know how this is gonna turn out," grumbled Somkit as he climbed onto Pong's back, still clutching the mango.

Pong knew, too, but it couldn't be helped. Because while Pong was better than anyone at paying attention, and almost as good as Somkit at waiting, he was terrible at ignoring when things weren't fair.

And the most important thing to do in Namwon was to forget about life being fair.

"Where do you think *you're* going?" asked the knobby-elbowed girl as she strode toward them.

"We caught this mango, fair and square," said Pong, backing himself and Somkit away.

"You sure did," said her scab-knuckled friend. "And if you hand it over right now, we'll only punch you once each. Fair and square."

"Just do it," whispered Somkit. "It's not worth —"

"You don't deserve it just because you want it," said Pong firmly. "And you're not taking it from us."

"Is that right?" said the girls.

"Oh, man." Somkit sighed. "Here we go!"

The girls shrieked and Pong took off. They chased him as he galloped around and around the courtyard with Somkit clinging onto his back like a baby monkey.

"You can never just let things go!" Somkit shouted.

"We can't . . . let them have it!" panted Pong. "It's ours!" He dodged around clumps of smaller children, who watched gleefully, relieved not to be the ones about to get the life pummeled out of them.

"So what? A mango isn't worth getting beat up over." Somkit looked over his shoulder. "Go faster, man — they're going to catch us!"

The guards leaning against the wall laughed as they watched the chase. "Go on, girls. Get 'em!" said one.

"Not yet, though," said the other guard. "This is the best entertainment we've had all week!"

"I'm . . . getting . . . tired." Pong huffed. "You better . . . eat that thing before I collapse!"

Warm mango juice dripped down the back of Pong's neck as Somkit tore into the fruit with his teeth. "Oh, man. I was wrong. This *is* worth getting beat up over." Somkit reached over his friend's shoulder and stuck a plug of mango into the corner of Pong's mouth.

It was ripe and sweet, not stringy yet. Paradise.

Chapter 2

Later, as they lay on their backs next to the river gate, Pong tried to remind Somkit how great that mango had been. The sun had started to set, and their golden-brown cheekbones and shins were turning the same purple color as the sky.

Somkit touched his bruised cheek and winced. "Why do I have to be friends with such a loudmouth?"

Pong grinned. "Because no one else will be friends with you."

Somkit reached over and flicked him on the ear.

"Ow!" said Pong, scooting away. "You know, between the two of us, you've actually got the bigger mouth."

"And you'll notice that I keep it shut around the guards and mean kids," said Somkit. "Sometimes you have to go along with things if you don't want to get mashed into pulp. But you? You just never know when to shut up and let things go."

"I know," said Pong, folding one arm under his head. "But we earned that mango. It's stupid that we even have to wait for them to fall. The guards should just let us climb the tree. It's almost like they *want* us to have to fight over them." He put two fingers on the bone in the center of his rib cage. "Stuff like that, I don't know — it just makes me so mad. I get this burning feeling right here."

"It's probably gas," said Somkit. "Look, next year those stupid girls will turn thirteen, and then they'll be out of here. We'll be the oldest ones, and we can eat our mangoes in peace."

Children born at Namwon were released when their mother's sentence was up or when they turned thirteen, whichever came first.

But Pong didn't care about the girls' release date. If anything, it was just one more bit of unfairness that those two would get out first. It would be four more years until Pong and Somkit turned thirteen. Four years. It felt like forever.

Pong turned his face from Somkit and looked past the bars of the river gate. Namwon sat a little upriver from Chattana City. From here, Pong could just see the lights starting to come on, one by one by one thousand, until there were two cities: one on the shore, one in the water, both made of light.

Normally at this time of night, the two of them would take turns sharing their dreams about what sort of life they'd lead in the city after they got out: the food they'd eat, the boats they'd buy. Somkit would have at least three boats: one to live on, one to fish from, and one speedboat with a custom motor that would be good for nothing except driving ridiculously fast. Pong liked to picture himself as a grown man with a good job and a full belly, lounging in the back of that slick speedboat, with Somkit at the wheel.

A single orb of glass swung from the mango tree overhead. Its dim Violet glow couldn't compete with the bright blaze across the river. Compared to the city, Namwon was like a cave. Was it any wonder that life wasn't fair for them? How could fairness find its way to them through all that darkness? But once they got out, under those lights, life would be different. They would eat mangoes they didn't have to fight for. When they asked for help, people would listen.

Somkit turned onto his side with a groan. "Ugh, every bone in my body hurts! You've got to promise me to lie low. At least until after next week."

"What's next week?"

Somkit rolled his eyes and shook his head. "You'll sit and listen to mangoes for hours, but you can't even hear what people are saying when they're standing right next to you! Didn't you hear the cooks today? The Governor is coming here next week for an official visit."

Pong sat up, ignoring the ache in his ribs. "The Governor!"

"I know," said Somkit, licking his lips. "We're actually going to get some decent food for once. The cooks said they're going to grill a bunch of chickens."

But Pong couldn't think about food. He was thinking about the guest. Most people in Chattana looked up to the Governor. After what he'd done for their city, how could they not? The man was a hero. But to Pong, he was even more.

Pong had only ever seen a portrait of him in a textbook, but even from the picture, he could tell that the Governor was someone who would understand him. He would care about the unfairness at Namwon. If he knew how things were, he'd change them. That's just the kind of person he was: someone who made things right.

Pong's wild and secret wish, the one he didn't tell even Somkit about because it sounded so silly, was that one day he'd work for Chattana's great leader. He imagined himself standing at the Governor's side as an assistant or an adviser, or whatever sort of jobs grown people had. Together, they would make everyone's life brighter.

The fact that the Governor was coming to Namwon for a visit couldn't be just a coincidence. It had to be a sign. It had to mean that one day Pong's wish would come true.

"Hey," said Somkit, snapping his fingers in front of Pong's face. "You've got that funny look of yours right now, and I don't like it. Listen, you've got to promise me that you're going to keep your mouth shut from now on. No more trouble, okay?" He leaned closer and bugged his eyes out. "*Okay?*"

Pong squinted at the city, making all the dots of light blur into one. "Okay," he said. "No more trouble."

At the time it seemed like a perfectly reasonable promise.

Chapter 3

Nok crossed her fingers behind her back as she watched her father clean his glasses for the hundredth time that morning. He was nervous — she could tell.

Warden Sivapan was supposed to be in charge of everything and everyone at Namwon, and Nok wished that just for today he could play the part.

"Nok . . ." whined her little sister Tip. "I am going to *die* in this thing!" Tip stuck her finger into the high, frilly collar of her blouse and pulled it away from her windpipe. It snapped back against her throat with a *thwack*!

Tip's twin sister, Ploy, giggled.

"Stop fidgeting," said Nok. She straightened Tip's collar, then Ploy's sash. "Aren't you ashamed of yourselves, whining on a day like today?"

At least the twins got to wear short sleeves. Nok tugged at the cuffs of her itchy dress, fighting the urge to scratch her arms. She longed for the loose comfort of her spire-fighting uniform. In her opinion, any clothes you couldn't throw a punch in were stupid. But of course she wouldn't complain, especially not today, the day of the Governor's visit.

Nok's mother glided toward them, an older version of the twins, in pale-blue silk. "All right," she said. "Everyone ready? Remember what I told you to say. No embarrassments today — got that, everyone?"

Nok's older brother smoothed down his hair. "That's fine for us," he whispered, "but who's going to tell Dad?"

Nok glared at him. Her mother snapped her fingers, and it was time to go. The twins followed Nok, who followed their brother, who had come home from university just for this occasion, who followed their mother, who was really the leader of the family, but who walked behind her husband to keep up appearances.

The family lined up near the river gate, in the shade of the big mango tree. The prisoners were supposed to be standing in orderly lines, too, but the children had run up to the gate to wait for the Governor's boat.

"I feel sorry for them," whispered Ploy, slipping her fingers into Nok's hand. "They have to live in a jail. Isn't that awful?"

"It's not a *jail*," said Nok. "It's a reform center."

Nok and her siblings hardly ever visited their father's workplace. That morning, Nok had made a point to show her sisters the official NAMWON WOMEN'S REFORM CENTER sign on the front gate, but the truth was that no one ever called it anything but a prison.

"Why can't Daddy just let them go?" asked Ploy.

Her twin leaned closer. "You know what Mama says: *Trees drop their fruit straight down.*"

"Huh? I'm not talking about fruit, dummy. I'm talking about kids!"

Nok sighed. "She means that you can't expect children to turn out very different from their parents. And these children have *criminals* for parents. It's best to keep a close eye on them. Besides, where else would they go? Some of them are orphans. They'd have to live on the street. At least here they get good food and they go to school. They're happy here."

The children did look happy, or at least excited. Nok noticed that only two of the boys weren't pressed up against the gate. One scrawny boy with a moon-round face stood on his tiptoes, unable to see over two girls who seemed to be blocking his view on purpose.

His friend, a boy with thick hair that stuck up at the top, also hung back, near the trunk of the mango tree. He wasn't looking at the gate at all, but up into the branches.

The boy tilted one ear up at a low-hanging fruit, almost as if he were listening to it.

How weird, thought Nok. *Who listens to mangoes?*

"Here he comes!" the other kids shouted.

"The Governor's boat! I can see it!"

Nok's mother snapped her fingers and hissed, "Places! To your places! Now!"

The Governor's barge glided toward the prison dock, its teak paneling gleaming in the sunlight. Swags of white flowers swished from the prow.

A soft whir churned the water behind the boat as it swiveled into place at the dock. A glass orb the size of a watermelon hung suspended over the silver prongs of the barge's motor. Its Jade light glowed so bright that it made spots float over Nok's eyes when she blinked.

The river gate swung inward. Uniformed guards disembarked and stood at attention. Nok glimpsed the sheen of the Governor's robes, and then her mother snapped her fingers again. The prisoners pressed their palms together and dropped to their knees.

Nok bowed her head, her stomach flipping somersaults. Was this really happening? If the kids from school could see her now, they would burn with jealousy. She was about to meet the man they all idolized, the hero they learned about in history classes, whose proverbs they had memorized since nursery school. In just a few seconds, Nok would meet the man who had saved their city from the brink of destruction.

It was a story that every child in Chattana knew.

Long ago, Chattana was the City of Wonders. Giants as tall as palm trees waded in the river while singing fish schooled around their ankles. In the floating markets, vendors sold all manner of magical treats: pears that made you fall in love, cakes frosted with good luck, even a rare fruit shaped like a sleeping baby that would let you live for one thousand and three years if you ate it in a single bite.

The people lived blessed lives. Wise old sages traveled down from the mountains to share their wisdom, heal the sick, and grant wishes. But most people in Chattana had all they could wish for — at first.

The city prospered and grew. The houses stacked on top of each other, higher and higher. The canals became crowded. Unfortunately, magic doesn't like a crowd.

As Chattana swelled, the wonders thinned away. The shy giants wandered north and never returned. The singing fish were netted for rich men's dinners. Bakers began frosting their cakes with plain sugar — it was cheaper than luck and just as sparkly. And the wise sages stayed on their mountaintops.

At first the people of Chattana didn't mind. They were successful and too busy to care about those old-fashioned things. The city spread wider. Buildings rose higher. There was more of everything, but it still wasn't enough. Greed made people careless, and that was a mistake.

No one knows how the Great Fire started. In one rainless night, the City of Wonders became the City of Ashes. Every building and nearly every boat burned. Chattana had always been isolated from its neighbors, but the destruction was so great that no one could have helped them anyway. The few who survived the Great Fire suffered miserably. The sun seared down during the day, and at night there was no shelter from the drenching rains. Disease spread. Fights broke out over what little food remained.

The people missed the wonders then. They despaired, sure that the end was near for all of them. But somewhere among the ruins there must have been one luck-frosted cake left. Because out of the forest came a man who carried magic that no one had seen in more than a century.

That one man turned everything around. He brought Chattana back to life.

Chapter 4

Nok kept her head bowed, but she couldn't resist popping one eyelid open. The Governor walked past her, leaving the scent of lemongrass trailing behind him.

Another snap from Nok's mother, and the prisoners sat back on their heels, palms still pressed together at their chests. Nok blinked, hardly able to believe that she stood just a few yards away from Chattana's great hero.

He looked ordinary. Nok didn't know what she'd been expecting. It's not like he would be floating in on a cloud, or anything like that, but the man standing before them could have been any man. He was taller than her father, but not by much. His face was smooth and pale, the color of milky tea. He smiled briefly as her father greeted him, and only then did faint age lines appear at the corners of his eyes.

Her father seemed in awe of him, too. Or maybe he was just afraid of messing everything up. He could hardly meet the Governor's eyes as he stepped forward and cleaned his glasses yet again.

"This is a very special day for us all," her father announced. "His Grace, our Governor, honors us with his presence. As you know, His Grace gives such thought and care to your reform. We are . . ." The warden looked down the line of prisoners, and his eyes became glassy and sad behind his spectacles. His voice drifted off.

Come on, Dad. You can do it, Nok thought, willing him to gather up his thoughts.

Nok's mother cleared her throat softly.

"We — we are so blessed to have you with us today, Your Grace," her father stammered. He was supposed to give a longer speech, but he must have forgotten it. "We will now serve a meal, after which my wife has planned entertainment in your honor."

Nok's mother smiled stiffly. She flicked her fingers at the kitchen staff.

Nok's nostrils filled with the smell of garlic and meat. The cooks carried big steaming pots out of the kitchen to the tables under the pavilion. They set the pots on top of metal stands that cradled Crimson orbs to keep the food bubbling and hot.

The prison children all perked up. The moonfaced

boy even licked his lips. Nok wished they wouldn't look quite so hungry.

The prisoners bowed, then made an orderly rush to the pavilion. Nok herded the twins behind their brother, to wait their turn to be introduced to the Governor. She told herself not to be nervous. After all, she'd been practicing what to say to him for weeks now.

As she waited, her eyes wandered to the boy with the sticking-up hair. He had been near the front of the line, and he was already slurping up the last bits of food from his bowl. She tried not to stare, but she found her eyes drawn to him. He seemed so different from the other children. He looked around, taking in everything. He stared at the Governor intensely, though he kept a respectful distance.

Suddenly, he turned his head and then stood up and hurried toward the boy with the round face, who had tears running down his plump cheeks. A full bowl of chicken and rice lay spilled on the ground at his feet.

Two older girls stood beside him, cracking their knuckles. The boy with the sticking-up hair strode up to the tallest girl and without a word, stomped on her bare foot. Nok gasped.

"Nok!" her mother snapped.

She turned to see her family staring at her. Even

her father looked mortified. With a flush of embarrassment, she realized she was supposed to be greeting the
Governor at that very moment.

Nok's practiced speech flew right out of her head.
Her cheeks burned as she bowed. "I'm very sorry that I
was distracted, Your Grace. It's just that . . ."

"Just that what?" asked her mother, impatience edg-
ing her voice.

Nok pulled down the cuffs of her dress. "It's just that
I think that boy over there is fighting."

Her mother's lips parted, horrified. "*What* boy?"

Nok pointed him out. The older girl was howling
now, clutching her wounded foot.

Nok's mother stormed toward the children. "You
there," she said to the sticking-up-hair boy. "What do
you think you're doing?"

The boy froze. "Oh, ma'am, I, well, I just saw —"

"You saw that we were busy, so you thought you
could misbehave, hmm?"

"No, ma'am, it isn't that. You see, these girls —"

The girl he'd stomped on wailed and hopped on her
good foot.

"Hush!" snapped Mrs. Sivapan. "You dare to start
fights on a day like this?" She looked ready to swallow
the boy whole.

His spine straightened. Nok couldn't believe the way he was looking at her mother — as though he was right and she was wrong.

"My friend has been waiting for this food," said the boy. "And they —"

"How *dare* you talk back to me!"

The Governor glided toward the boy and spoke in a deep, smooth voice. "Allow me to handle this, Madam Sivapan."

The entire courtyard hushed. Nok's mother patted down her hair as she stepped back to make room for him. "Thank you, Your Grace."

The boy swallowed and wiped his palms against the sides of his trousers. He bowed to the Governor. When he raised his head, he had a hopeful, almost happy, look in his eyes.

The prisoners and staff had inched closer to see what was going on. Everyone pretended to eat as they leaned forward, listening.

"Is it true, child?" asked the Governor. "You were fighting?"

"Your Grace, it is the greatest honor to finally meet you," the boy said breathlessly. "I know that of everyone, you will see that —"

"Tut-tut," the Governor chided. "Now is not the time

for flattery. It is the time for truth. Tell me. Did you hurt this girl, yes or no?"

The boy stood wide-eyed, with his mouth open. He nodded.

"Do you know why I'm here?" the Governor asked.

"To . . . to make sure we're being treated fairly?"

The Governor stared at him for an uncomfortably long moment. "I am here to remind you all of the price of breaking the law. Tell me, child, are the nights dark here in Namwon?"

The boy nodded.

"As they should be," said the Governor. "Chattana is a city of light, but that light must be earned. That is why I had this reform center built here, away from the city. To remind the people that wickedness has a price. You see, light shines only on the worthy."

The boy continued staring, speechless, as the Governor took a half step back. He raised his arms, palms up. The air grew thick, the way it does before a storm. The hairs on Nok's arms stood on end and her scalp tingled.

Everyone in the courtyard seemed to be holding their breath. A pinprick of light appeared in the Governor's palm, like a hovering firefly. It shone brighter, then brighter still, swelling to the size of a marble.

The little ball of light was blindingly bright, even brighter than the orb that powered the Governor's boat. But it didn't seem hot. If anything, the courtyard felt a little cooler than it had a moment before.

A chill raced up the back of Nok's neck. She had grown up surrounded by the Governor's magic, but few people ever got to see him actually use his powers. She shivered, thrilled and frightened at the same time. The man may have looked ordinary, but he was far from it.

Everything in Chattana — every orb, every cook-stove, every boat motor — all of it ran on the Governor's light-making powers. Once he arrived, there was no more need for fire, no more danger. The orbs lit the night; they powered magnificent machines; they had made Chattana prosperous again.

The city had transformed in more ways than one. The Governor hadn't just made light. He had made laws. Chattana had become the City of Rules, the City of Order. Now there would never be another Great Fire. The people would never have to suffer like that again.

The Governor reached his other hand into his pocket and drew out a glass orb, clear and thin as a soap bubble. "Light shines on the worthy," he repeated, placing the orb into the boy's hand. "All others fall into darkness. Tell me, child, do you want to remain in darkness forever?"

The boy's throat bobbed as he swallowed. He shook his head.

The Governor closed his fingers over the light in his hand and touched the glass orb. The air between him and the boy wavered and crackled. A second later, everyone in the courtyard gasped.

The Governor's hand was now empty. The light had traveled into the orb, filling it with a Gold glow. Trapped inside the glass, the Governor's light was still bright, though a little less raw and frightening than it had been a moment before.

"Tell me," said the Governor. "Will you be a good boy from now on?"

The boy stared at the light in his hand, speechless. Nok realized this might be the first time he had ever been this close to a Gold orb.

Nok's mother stepped forward. "He will, Your Grace — we will see to that, of course." She turned to the boy. "I hope you appreciate His Grace's generosity! For him to give you that light — and Gold light, no less! — is a kindness I'm not sure you deserve. But, please, Your Grace, allow us to convey our gratitude to you with a song we have prepared in your honor."

She clapped her hands overhead, the signal for the women prisoners to break into the number they had rehearsed for the occasion.

The small courtyard rang with the sound of their voices. Nok's mother beamed. Her siblings smiled perfect smiles. Everything was back on track and going smoothly.

All eyes were on the Governor, who bent down to whisper some last comforting words to the wayward boy before turning to watch the prisoners' performance.

But Nok was watching the boy. He stood staring at his palm. The hopeful, happy look had left his eyes.

The orb in his hand had gone dark.

Chapter 5

"Y ou're no fun anymore," said Somkit. He said this a lot lately.

"I thought you wanted me to lie low," said Pong. "Stay out of trouble."

"Yeah, well, I didn't mean for you to turn into a tree stump. Besides, since when do you listen to anything I say? Seriously, what's up with you?"

Pong shrugged. He knew he'd changed. No more scuffling with older girls, no more arguments with guards. Pong had become quiet. He just didn't feel like talking.

It had been three months since the Governor's visit. Pong had been so excited that day, even though he hadn't dreamed that he'd actually get the chance to tell the Governor how much he admired him. And when the chance did come, everything had gone so very wrong. Pong would have thought it was all a bad dream if he didn't still have the faded glass orb tucked behind his mat in the boys' bunk room.

Every night Pong lay there, with the used-up glass close to his head. He could still remember the orb's beautiful Gold glow — so much brighter than the Violet orbs they had to make do with at Namwon. He could still hear the Governor's words. Not the words of his speech — those famous phrases printed on posters and in schoolbooks. No, the words that haunted Pong were the ones the Governor had spoken in his ear as the prisoners began their song.

"Look at them," he'd whispered to Pong, nodding at the prisoners. "They go free, but they always come back. Year after year, the jails are full. The world is full of darkness, and that will never change." And then the Governor leaned a half inch closer to Pong. He looked into Pong's eyes with his own cold stare. "Those who are born in darkness always return. You'll see. You and I will meet again."

And then the Governor had squeezed his fingers tight, and the orb in Pong's hand had gone dark.

That was when Pong realized how stupid he'd been. Had he really thought he'd grow up to work for the Governor himself? The Governor would never let someone like him even come near. Pong's dreams of a life outside Namwon vanished in that instant. Things wouldn't be any different out there — not for him.

The world is full of darkness, and that will never change. It didn't matter what he and Somkit did or how old they got. They would be in the dark wherever they went.

Pong didn't share his thoughts with Somkit. He closed them inside himself, where they hardened into a physical thing, making a box around his heart. And when night fell and the lights of Chattana blazed across the water, and Somkit chattered on and on about orb motors and the latest speedboat models, Pong stayed silent. He turned his face away from the river gate. If anything, the lights only made Namwon seem darker.

Though the nights had changed, the days for Pong and Somkit were the same. For Somkit, that meant fruit scavenging.

Mangoes were the only fruit the prisoners were allowed to have, and only then because they dropped straight into their arms. But the prison guards, like most people in Chattana, lived for their fruit. Once a week, after payday, they would wait on the boat dock and wave down the fruit boats heading to the floating markets in the city.

The prison children would press their faces against the metal gate and sniff the sweet scent of mangosteens and rambutans, the acid aroma of the pomelos and green oranges. They would suck the fruit-flavored air down their nostrils and roll it around on their tongues. But there was one fruit boat they would not smell.

Durian is called the King of Fruits. It's creamy and rich, more like custard or pudding than something you'd expect to find growing on a tree. Its flavor is musky, buttery — sweet at first, tangy at the end. It makes the back of your neck hot to eat it. It tastes like heaven.

It smells like the opposite.

After flagging down the durian boatman, the guards would carry the enormous spiky-skinned fruit to the wooden table under their shaded pavilion. They hacked the fruit open with a machete, careful not to get the juice on their hands or clothes. They scooped out the yellow flesh inside and rolled their eyes back in their heads with pleasure.

After an hour, the ground all around the table would be littered with piles of durian husks, stinking like a dying mongoose. That's where Somkit came in.

Somkit was the only kid in Namwon who didn't mind the smell of durian. He was happy to gather the stinking, sticky rinds and cram them into the trash baskets by the river dock. The guards rewarded him for his help by letting him scrape up any remaining fruit. The baskets didn't do much to hide the smell, but luckily the trashman would come in his boat that same evening to dump them downriver.

One hot afternoon, the guards had just finished off a particularly ripe, particularly smelly durian, and more husks littered the pavilion ground than usual.

Somkit held one of the rinds, scraping out the last bit of flesh with his fingers. "Hey, Pong, help me take these to the trash."

"No way," said Pong, holding his nose and breathing through his mouth. "That's your thing, not mine."

"Come on, don't be a jerk." Somkit coughed.

Pong's ears tuned to the raspy sound. Somkit had trouble breathing. Running or doing anything active could make him collapse into a fit of coughing. A few times it had been really bad, and Pong had watched him choke and gasp like a fish drowning on dry land.

"Are you okay?" Pong asked.

"Yeah, I'm fine," said Somkit. But he coughed again, three times. His eyebrows shot up with each cough like someone was poking him in the ribs.

Pong was pretty sure it was a trying-to-get-out-of-work cough, but he rolled his eyes and grumbled, "Fine, let's get it over with."

He gulped in a big breath and started picking up the

rinds with the tips of his fingernails. The juice oozed onto his wrists as he followed Somkit to the trash.

The trash baskets sat near the river dock, on the other side of the guards' storage hut. The baskets reeked sweetly, like raw chicken left in the sun all day. Pong opened the lid and gagged at the rotting smell of old durian mixed with old bananas, old orange peels, and old eggshells. He dumped his durian rinds in with the rest.

"I'll go back and get what's left," said Somkit. "Cram all that down to make room, okay?"

"Oh, come on," protested Pong.

"Just do it," said Somkit, making the same eyebrow-cough as he walked away. "I'll be right back."

Pong waited, craning his face away from the durian stench. When Somkit still hadn't come back, he leaned around the corner of the storage shed to look for him. It was the hottest part of the day, and the prisoners lay dozing or chatting in the shade on the other side of the courtyard. The guards, full and happy, reclined on the steps, picking their teeth.

Pong had their schedules memorized, and he knew they wouldn't get up for another forty minutes, when they changed shifts. No one in the entire prison was paying attention.

Pong had never thought about escaping Namwon

before, but now the opportunity lurched up like a mud-skipper and slapped him across the face with its tail. He could get out of Namwon. Not when he was thirteen. *Now*.

Without pausing to think, Pong tipped the basket and climbed inside. He took one last gulp of semi-fresh air and wriggled down under the trash. He nearly threw up as he pushed the durian skins, orange rinds, and banana peels up around him, packing them over his head, covering his face.

He breathed through his mouth as shallowly as he could. With one eye pressed against the straw weave of the basket, he could see a blurry, golden view of what was happening outside.

He froze when he heard footsteps coming closer. Someone swung open the basket lid and held it open for a long time. Pong listened but couldn't tell who stood there. Somkit? A guard? Whoever it was, they shut the lid and walked away.

Surely Somkit would wonder where he'd gone. Surely he would start asking if anyone had seen Pong. But no one called for him. And Somkit never came back.

Pong sat gagging in the basket, stinky juice dripping off his hair and down the bridge of his nose. He didn't know if he could make it until the trashman came back. The whole thing began to feel like a really bad idea. Pong was ready to give up and get out, but now the guards had moved back into position and would see him if he climbed out of the basket. He'd have to wait until sundown for the next shift change.

As the sun began to set, the trashman arrived. When Pong heard him whistling, he was seized with terror. He was sure that when the man lifted the basket, he'd realize it was too heavy.

Pong's nervous stomach writhed like a bowl of eels. What had he been thinking? He was going to get caught any moment. And then what would he say? *I fell into the basket, you see. I tried to call for help, but no one heard me. Please don't put me into solitary confinement. Being inside a basket of durian is punishment enough.*

One benefit of being underfed is that you don't weigh much. The trashman lifted the basket with just a little more effort than usual, hauled it to the river dock, and plopped it into his boat.

Pong couldn't see much of what was happening, but he swore he spotted his friend's silhouette standing at the gate. Suddenly, he realized everything he was leaving behind. *No! Wait!* he thought. *I can't go without Somkit!*

But it was too late. The trashman shoved the boat away from the dock with his bare foot and they were off, down the river.

Chapter 6

Pong crouched inside the basket, one eye pressed against the straw, trying to see the world outside. By now the sun had gone down, and it was difficult to make anything out. Even inside the basket, he felt too exposed, like he was naked. He scooted farther down, wincing as the spiky durian rinds jabbed into his skin.

The zippy whir of the trashman's small orb motor rose in pitch as he steered the boat out into the central channel of the river. If Somkit were there, he'd know what model the motor was just from the sound.

Larger boats with more powerful motors passed by, throwing up waves that rocked the little boat. Pong could make out hazy pinpricks of light beaming from the houses lining the riverbanks. The lights and the boats grew in number as they moved downriver.

Pong's stomach now churned with excitement more than fear. Finally, he was going to see the city up close.

He heard it first. The buzz of the orb lights sounded like a swarm of bees flying toward him. He heard shouting and laughing on the shore, a band playing music, and a woman's voice singing, *"Take my hand, oh, my darling, take my hand and dance with me . . ."*

And then the darkness lit up like the inside of a star.

They'd reached the heart of Chattana.

Homes, stores, and restaurants lined the water's edge, stacked one on top of the other, lit ceiling to floor in a rainbow of orb lights that blurred together through Pong's tiny basket window. He could hear customers shouting orders, people haggling over prices, babies wailing for their mothers. He smelled sizzling catfish skin and vegetable dumplings and the human odors of too many bodies living too close together.

A herd of bare feet pounded against wood planks. Children shrieked as they ran down one of the gangways that lined the river. Pong heard their laughter, then a dozen splashes close to the boat.

"Hey, you kids, get outta my way!" shouted the trashman, cutting off his motor. "Lazy brats! When I was your age, I already had a job!"

The trashman used his oar to turn the boat down a canal that led away from the main flow of the river. Chattana was a city built on water, with canals serving the place of roads. People got around by boat or used the crowded gangways and bridges that crossed the canals.

The trashman turned them down another canal, then another, picking up more baskets of rotting garbage before returning to the wide highway of traffic on the river. The boat dipped up and down on the wake of barges as they crossed to the western shore. The West Side of Chattana was also lit up bright as a sunrise, but with a difference. Unlike the rainbow chaos of the East Side, the charged orbs of the West Side were all Gold.

Pong's heart ached at the sight. He realized that this side of town was what he and Somkit had seen from the river gate every night when they dreamed of someday walking free under all those lights. And now here he was, almost close enough to touch them.

The West Side was so quiet. The orbs hanging off the trees barely hummed, and the music played softly. Even the smells were sweet and clean. Canals branched out from the main river, just like on the East Side, but here, the sidewalks weren't nearly so crowded. Pong could just make out the tidy rows of buildings through his pinprick window in the basket.

The trashman also got very quiet as he pulled alongside one of the docks. Servants loaded baskets into the boat without a word. The trashman kicked up his orb motor and they were off again, downriver.

The boat rocked up and down, and up and down. Pong felt those eels in his stomach writhing again, but this time it was seasickness.

Don't throw up. Don't throw up, he told his stomach. Sadly, his stomach didn't listen. He clutched the sides of the basket, lost in a woozy fog.

Back and forth the boat went, crossing the river as the trashman made his way south to all his stops. Pong's mind clouded over in a haze of seasickness, and he didn't notice until too late that the boat had stopped.

His eyes popped open in time to realize that his basket was being picked up and tipped over the side. Rotten durian rinds showered over him as he tumbled into the black water.

Pong, who'd lived his whole life inches from the river, didn't know how to swim.

His feet kicked and his hands clawed at the dim glow of the surface. He managed to fight hard enough to get his face above the water. He sucked in a breath of air and a pint of river as his head went back down. Pong didn't care about getting caught and taken back to prison anymore. In fact, he was splashing and glugging and waving his arms as high above the water as he could.

But the trashman was eager to drop off his cargo and get back to the lights of the city. He revved his motor and sped back upriver. He didn't see or hear Pong's pitiful splashes.

According to law, the trashman had to dump his baskets outside the city limits, where the river made a wide bend. Here, the current was slow and the water clogged with trash of all sorts: fruit rinds, broken boxes, torn fishing nets, empty rice sacks, nine-year-old prison escapees.

Pong was so exhausted that he gave up trying to swim. But the trash wedged itself under his armpits and the balls of his feet, as if it wanted to be useful one last time before sinking into the silt at the bottom. Pong's fingers gripped the edge of a sheet of plywood. Ready to sink, he found instead that he was floating, buoyed up by the garbage.

The current carried him around the bend, where the river narrowed again and flowed a little faster. Pong held tight to his wooden life preserver as he drifted downstream. Seeing his chance, he kicked and wiggled his body, aiming for the bank.

By the time he reached the shore, he'd floated out of sight of the city. He climbed up the long muddy bank, out of breath and shivering in the wet clothes clinging to his body. He looked up at the stars, dim and tiny compared to the lights of Chattana.

Pong had done it. He had escaped. He was out in the world for the first time.

He knelt in the mud in the dark in the trash and cried.

Chapter 7

Pong woke up to a chicken pecking his foot.

"Ah! Get away!" he shrieked, kicking the scrawny bird.

The chicken squawked and fluttered into the brush. Pong cradled his injured foot in his lap. To be fair to the chicken, Pong's skin was so wrinkled and white from lying in the soggy mud that it did look like a maggot.

Pong stood up and looked out across the gray-green water. The other side of the river was thick with trees. He looked up. This side of the river was thick with trees. There was no city, no buildings, nobody. In truth, Pong had drifted only a few miles south of Chattana, but to him it seemed as if he'd entered an impenetrable wilderness. He imagined tigers ripping the flesh off his bones and pythons strangling him slowly.

What was he going to do? Where was he going to go? The sides of his empty stomach smacked together. *Somkit must be having breakfast right now,* he thought.

He'd never been without his friend for more than a few minutes. To realize how far away they were from each other gave him an itchy, panicky feeling.

A horn sounded upriver, and a large cargo barge floated slowly into view. Pong flattened himself onto the mud. As he waited for it to pass, his eyes went to his left wrist. He rubbed his thumb over the bright-blue ink of his prison mark, as if that could make it disappear.

All prisoners in Chattana were tattooed with the name of their prison. Pong and Somkit had gotten theirs when they were babies. The ink was permanent, set with the light from a powerful Gold orb owned by the Governor's office. No one could make it disappear except maybe the Governor himself.

If anyone saw it, they'd know immediately that he'd run away. When a prisoner was released, the prison crossed out their mark with a line and added a little star symbol. Without that bright-blue symbol, Pong was a fugitive. If he got caught, they'd take him right back. Worse, they might take him to Banglad, the men's prison. From the stories the guards told, Banglad made Namwon seem like a fancy hotel. The Governor's words pounded in Pong's temples: *Those who are born in darkness always return.*

Pong shivered and rubbed his bare arms. His journey in the trash boat might be the closest he'd ever get to walking free under Chattana's lights. Now he'd be lucky if he could manage to avoid being arrested.

Heavy clouds hung overhead. The rainy season would arrive any day, swelling the river and washing out the roads. He needed to get moving. But where to?

He couldn't go back to the city, but if he followed the river downstream, he knew it would eventually lead to the sea. The Governor, the police, the warden, none of them had any power over him once he stepped off the sand. He could get on a boat that would take him out of their reach forever, where no one would have heard of Namwon or know what his tattoo meant.

Pong had seen a picture of the ocean once, in a book. In the picture, the water wasn't gray-green, like the river. It was blue. That color of blue filled Pong's mind as he put his head down and started walking south.

He kept to the ditch along the river road so that he could duck out of sight whenever a rare oxcart came rumbling by. The day turned hot and sticky. Sweat rolled down the side of his nose and dripped into his mouth.

Now he begged the rains to start, so he could have something to drink. He did manage to find a clutch of hard green bananas growing along the road, but by midday, his hunger hurt so bad he thought he would faint from it.

All morning he had been drawing closer and closer to a cluster of small mountains — lumpy and green at the top, with sheer gray sides where the rock was too steep for the jungle to cling to. The road made a bend to the right, then back to the left, and then all of a sudden the mountains loomed right above Pong. Here, the road split. The main road turned inland, away from the river. A narrower track, barely wide enough for an oxcart, continued on, straight toward the mountains.

Pong frowned. Could this be right? Those dumb mountains seemed to be perched right along the river, standing smack between him and the sea. He didn't like the idea of climbing a mountain with nothing but green bananas in his belly. But what if the main road never led him to the sea at all? What if it led to a town? What if people stopped him and asked questions? If anyone saw his tattoo, he didn't think he'd have the strength to run away.

Pong chose the mountain track.

Good decision, he told himself as he huffed up and up the track, as it wound around the mountain, as the river got farther and farther below the gray cliffs.

Very good decision, he thought as night fell, as he curled into a ball under a bush, half on the road, half off it, as the clouds finally cracked open and released a river of rain.

Chapter 8

Pong opened his eyes. He was hungry, wet, muddy, and cold, in that order. The rain had stopped, and the sky was just beginning to lighten. He sat up. He smelled something.

Cooked fat.

That smell drew him in like a fish with a hook in its nose. He followed it up the road, around a curve, to a small wooden house set among the trees. The house was little more than a shack, but Pong stared at it in wonder. The front was lit by a soft, golden glow.

The only orb lights they'd had at Namwon were Violet (for the courtyard and classrooms) and Crimson (for cooking and boiling the laundry). On his journey past Chattana City, Pong had gotten a brief view of the other colors, too: Blue, Amber, Jade, and — on the West Side — Gold.

But the light in front of the house behaved strangely. It seemed to shift and dance around. It was soft and warm at the same time, with no buzz. Instead, Pong heard a different sound: a crackle.

He crept a little closer, hiding behind a plant with leaves shaped like elephant ears.

A short man with a round belly stood in front of the house with his back to Pong. He flipped his wrists and something sizzled. Then Pong noticed the smoke drifting up into the dark sky. His jaw fell open.

The man was cooking over a fire.

Pong had never seen one before. After the Great Fire and the arrival of the Governor, flame of any kind had been outlawed in the city. Pong's schooling at Namwon was fairly pitiful, but one lesson was drilled into the prison children over and over again: the greatest danger in the world was fire.

Pong watched entranced as the flames licked the sticks of meat. He opened his mouth and let the pork-flavored air settle on his tongue.

"Don't just stand there!" shouted a woman's voice. Startled, Pong ducked farther behind the bush. "You'd better get going or you're going to miss them!"

"I'm hurrying as fast as I can!" said the potbellied man. "Here, hand me that dish. I think it's ready."

Pong peered through the elephant ears. The man picked up the skewers of meat off the smoking grill and piled them onto a wooden dish. Greasy bits dripped down and sizzled on the coals. Pong gasped to see the man putting his hand just inches from the flames.

A woman with a face caked in half-wet baby powder came out of the house. She dressed the dish with some green onion and herbs and then slapped the man's back. "Go on, get. The monks will already be back at the temple. You'll have to take this straight there."

"Yes, yes, I'm going, I'm going," said the man as he slipped on his shoes.

He shuffled out of his yard and up the dirt road. Pong waited a few seconds, then followed behind, staying in the bushes.

The tall pile of meat teetered on the man's dish as he huffed up the mountain. Pong wished with all his might that one of the skewers would fall off. But the man was like a juggler, never dropping any of it. The dirt lane wound through the jungle and met up with a larger road. There were houses here, but not many, and Pong was able to stay hidden in the vegetation and the early-morning shadows.

The trees and the road opened up all at once to reveal the grounds of a temple. The cluster of buildings all had stacked-tile roofs that sloped steeply to the sky. Pong had never been to a temple before, but based on what he'd seen in books, this one was on the plain side. Only the roofs were painted, and there weren't any statues or fine carvings around the grounds.

Pong caught the scent of incense cutting through the glorious pork smell. The man puffed up the steps of one of the temple halls. Pong stayed at the bottom of the steps and watched him.

The man set his dish of meat on a low table in the center of the hall, next to other bowls of food donated to the temple monks: garlicky vegetables, fried chicken, and mysterious morsels wrapped in shiny banana leaves. The monks must have already been on their morning walk through their village and brought the food back here.

The man bowed low and respectfully, even though no one was there to see. Pong could hear the deep voices of men chanting farther back in one of the other buildings.

The man stood up with a groan. He jogged back down the steps and disappeared down the dark road. Pong's mouth watered. The monks would be taking their morning meal soon. He didn't have much time.

He leaped up the steps and snatched two skewers of meat off the dish on the table. With one in his hand and one in his teeth, he whirled around to find a face caked in baby powder staring at him in shock.

The old woman stood frozen, the basket of sticky rice her husband had forgotten swinging from her fingertips. The baby powder flaked off her cheeks as her shock turned to outrage. "Are. You. *Stealing* that? From the monks?"

Pong took the skewer out of his mouth. He held his left arm behind his back and waved the other stick of meat out in front of him, like a wand. Lies tumbled from his lips. "No! No, this isn't what it looks like! I didn't steal this. The monks said I could have it!"

A quizzical look spread over the woman's face, and for a moment, Pong thought she believed him. But then he spotted a group of monks walking toward them, holding their saffron-colored robes gathered in the crooks of their arms. His stomach dropped.

The old woman leaned over Pong, scowling deeply. "We'll see about that, you little thief!"

Chapter 9

Pong tried to dart around the woman, but she blocked him with her stomach and whacked him on the head with the basket of sticky rice. Bare feet padded across the temple floor as the half dozen monks rushed toward them and clustered around them in a semicircle.

"What's going on, Mrs. Viboon?" asked one of the younger monks.

Mrs. Viboon bowed respectfully to each of them. "My husband forgot to bring the rice when he brought your breakfast this morning," she said, swinging the sticky rice and nearly clocking Pong in the face with it again. "When I got here, I caught this boy taking this food, the meal we prepared for you. And when I questioned him, he lied to me. He told me that you gave it to him!"

The monks stared at Pong, tilting their shaved heads at him in confusion. They parted to let an old monk with a walking stick stand in front of them. His robes were darker, a reddish brown, and his bald head was speckled with moles.

Mrs. Viboon bowed again, even lower this time. "Father Cham, I am very sorry for disturbing your morning prayers. But this boy! He said you told him he could have this food. I can tell he's lying! Can you imagine? Stealing and lying inside the temple!"

The old man looked at Pong curiously. Pong had never spoken with a monk before, but he knew that monks fasted each day from noon until sunrise the next day. They prepared no meals themselves and depended on other people to feed them. Mrs. Viboon was trying to shame him, but he didn't plan to stick around long enough for that.

He searched for an opening where he could make a quick run for it. Just as he was ready to bolt, the old monk stepped in front of him, blocking his way with the walking stick. It was such a quick motion for such an old man that it startled Pong, and he dropped the precious pork skewers onto the dusty floor.

"Now, now," said Father Cham calmly. "You didn't do what I asked, did you, child?"

"What — what?" squeaked Pong. "I d-don't know what you mean!"

"I told you to make an offering plate for the grave-yard first. *Then* you may take food for yourself. But I see that you haven't made the offering yet, have you?"

Pong blinked up at him, confused. He tried to squirm away, but the old man somehow got in front of him again.

Father Cham clucked his tongue and shook his head at Mrs. Viboon. "I did tell him he could eat this food, but clearly he was in too much of a hurry to listen to all my instructions."

"Oh," said Mrs. Viboon. "I see. Well, I . . ."

"Thank you for alerting me, Mrs. Viboon. I will see that he learns his lesson." The monk looked down at Pong, his dark eyes stern. "Because of your mistake, you will come with me to pray that you learn to listen. And you will be the last to eat."

"I — but what . . . ?"

"Don't argue with Father Cham!" scolded Mrs. Viboon. "You're lucky that he wants to teach you to be a good boy. If it were me, I would have whipped you!"

The old monk took hold of Pong's shoulder as he smiled at her. "Thank goodness we have you to look after us, madam. Thank your husband for this food. Tell him to come to the temple tomorrow for a special blessing. Come along, my boy."

He led Pong past the other monks, who seemed as confused as Pong himself. Pong shuffled his feet, trying to keep up with the old man. Father Cham hummed as he led Pong away from the hall and up the steps of another open-air building.

The monk settled himself in a low chair at the front of the room and shut his eyes. Pong looked over his shoulder. He could still see the other monks, and Mrs. Viboon, who had started serving food to them. They were busy now. Pong could break away from this old man if he had to, and no one would catch him. But instead of running, he found himself kneeling down in front of Father Cham.

Pong pressed his hands together and bowed his forehead to his thumbs. He cracked one eye open and looked around. Behind Father Cham, a gold statue of Buddha glowed in the light of dozens of little flames that danced on top of thin sticks. More fire.

Pong's pulse galloped as he waited for the old monk to finish his prayers. What was going to happen now? Why had Father Cham lied about the food to that woman? Pong had always been taught that monks never lied.

Finally, the old man opened his eyes. He settled his hands in his lap and smiled. "What is your name?" he asked.

"P-Pong, Father, sir."

"Did they tell you your last name at Namwon?"

A shiver ran across Pong's shoulders. He hid his hand behind his back, even though it was much too late for that now. "I know what you're thinking," Pong blurted out, rubbing his thumb over his tattoo, "but you're mistaken. My mother and I were both released, fair and square. But there was a mix-up, and the warden forgot to fix my tattoo. My mother was going to take me back there to have it fixed, but we got separated. I'm on my way to the sea to meet up with her now . . ."

The lies kept coming, pouring out of Pong's mouth like water from a pitcher. Father Cham listened quietly, nodding, as lie after lie tumbled forth. At no point did he stop Pong, even when the lies turned wild and outlandish.

A hot, angry knot started forming in Pong's stomach. He was a runaway and a thief and a liar, and if there was a word for someone who disrespects a monk in his own temple, he was that, too. It had all happened so fast. In the span of a few days, Pong had become exactly what the Governor said he was.

He jumped to his feet and took a step back. Standing up over a seated monk was the height of disrespect, but Pong was too far gone for that to matter now. "I know what you're going to do," he said, his voice trembling.

"You're going to call for the police to send me back. But it won't work. I'm never going back to Namwon, and no one can make me!"

"Send you back?" said Father Cham calmly. "Of course I wouldn't do such a thing. You said yourself you've been released fair and square, so it would be a waste of time to send you back."

Pong paused. "I don't believe that."

Father Cham shrugged. "What you believe is up to you. You are free to go and meet up with your mother, of course. But I would prefer to send you on your way with a full stomach and a blessing."

Pong stared at the monk. Father Cham didn't look like anyone else Pong had ever met. For one thing, he was older than anyone Pong had ever seen — even his ears were wrinkled. But there was something else that Pong couldn't quite name. Something bright and serene danced in his eyes, like the strange flames on the sticks near the altar.

"A blessing?" Pong asked.

Father Cham smiled, his wrinkles deepening. "Yes. It will bring you good luck on your journey to meet your mother."

Before Pong realized what he was doing, he had sunk to his knees again on the carpet.

Father Cham reached for a small lacquered set of drawers. He opened one of the drawers and took out a roll of white string and a pair of scissors.

The old man measured out a length of string and cut it. He held it between his palms and said a prayer. Then he tied the string around Pong's left wrist. As he did so, he said, "May you never step in a snake's nest."

Father Cham blessed and tied a dozen more bracelets around Pong's left wrist, plus a couple on his right to balance it out. The old man's blessings were varied and strange: "May you never get food poisoning from raw chicken" and "May wasps never sting the palms of your hands or the bottoms of your feet," and others, all very specific and related to things that seemed unlikely to ever happen in the first place.

"There," said the old man, sitting back on his heels with a satisfied smile. "You see? Lots of good luck."

Pong turned his arm over. A thick cuff of white string bracelets circled his left wrist. His tattoo was completely concealed.

"You say you are meeting your mother at the sea?" Father Cham asked.

Pong nodded sheepishly, wondering if the monk suspected that he'd made that up.

"Well, it's several weeks' walk to the sea from here.

Without a boat ticket, you'd have to walk around the mountains. It could be a difficult journey for someone so young."

Pong frowned. Walking around the mountains meant taking the road. It meant passing through villages and people asking questions.

"Or," said Father Cham, looking as if he'd had a sudden idea, "you could stay here at the temple. We could try to get word to your mother, telling her to meet you here instead."

Pong looked up into the old man's eyes.

"And . . ." Father Cham nodded to Pong's left wrist. "While you are here, if any of those bracelets pop off, I can easily give you new ones to replace them. But the choice is up to you. I would never make the decision for you."

Pong ran a finger over the bracelets. He tried to get that image of the blue ocean back in his mind, but he couldn't picture it for some reason.

He suddenly felt overwhelmingly tired and hungry, hungrier than he had ever been before. It would be safe here. He could rest and eat and then keep heading south in a few days.

"Maybe I could stay," he said softly. "For a little while."

"Excellent!" Father Cham tapped one finger to his

chin. "I told Mrs. Viboon that you would learn a lesson. I think I know the perfect lesson to start with."

"What's that, Father?"

The old man grinned. "How to choose the best dipping sauce for grilled pork."

Chapter 10

One day turned into two, and two days became a
week, which stretched into months as Pong found
more and more reasons to stay in the village of Tanaburi
and its temple, Wat Singh. He kept telling himself that
soon he'd return to the road and make for the sea, even
as his head was shaved and he took his vows.

Pong became a "baby monk" and began training
under Father Cham's guidance. The other monks never
saw his tattoo or heard the story he'd made up about his
mother. And Father Cham never asked about her again.
He kept Pong's bracelet supply up, always replacing the
frayed ones just before they snapped. Everyone assumed
that Pong must be some distant relative of the old man.
Why else would he bestow so many blessings on one
quiet, ordinary boy?

It would also explain why Pong never complained
about being hungry, even though monks didn't eat

anything after noon, or about being bored, even though a monk's daily routine is long and mostly uneventful.

They couldn't know that Pong was eating better than he had in his life, fattening up on Mrs. Viboon's barbecue, which was worlds better than the cold turnips and rice the prisoners were served at Namwon.

The monks couldn't know that Pong's practice of paying attention to mangoes and watching out for the swing of a guard's baton had prepared him to sit in long hours of quiet meditation.

Yes, in those ways, life in the temple was similar to what Pong was used to. But otherwise, it was completely different. At Wat Singh, he had the kinship of other monks, who called him Brother. Pong was cared for, and he was expected to care for others. The biggest difference, though, was Father Cham.

At Namwon, everyone was respected according to their rank or their age. But Father Cham treated everyone the same. Pong had never seen anything like it. When beggars came to the temple from down the mountain, Father Cham received them as if they were visiting nobles, feeding them and chatting with them for long hours. He never talked down to children. And Pong was given as much respect as the oldest monks at the temple. For the first time in Pong's life, a grown-up was concerned for him, caring for him, teaching him, and always repeating to him, "You have a good heart, Pong."

But did he?

At night he lay on the floor of his tiny room, listening to the rains drenching the jungle. His mind, which had been so quiet all day, began to whir with the thoughts of all the bad things he'd done.

He'd run away from prison.

He'd left his best friend behind, alone.

He'd lied to the monks.

It was as if in trying to run away from the Governor's words, he'd instead made them come true. He was a fugitive, taking advantage of the kindness of the monks. If anyone ever found out, he'd go back to prison. Worse — Father Cham might even be in trouble for hiding him. The thought made Pong sick to his stomach.

Pong resolved that he would build up a mountain of good deeds to overshadow his bad ones. He swept the temple twice a day. He walked the meditation paths in the forest until they were worn to rock. He read the Buddha's teachings again and again, until he had memorized every word.

The Governor's words never left Pong. The box they had formed around his heart had settled in deep, and when he sat very still, he could hear them in the back of his mind: *Those who are born in darkness always return.*

Even so, Pong grew and thrived at Wat Singh. And by the time four years had passed, he'd stopped dreaming of the sea.

He'd started to forget about the warden and the prison, and he'd convinced himself that he had been forgotten, too.

Chapter 11

Pong spent most of his time inside the temple grounds, but when he turned thirteen, Father Cham began taking him along more often on his visits to the village and surrounding countryside.

The old monk's walking stick clacked in time to his steps as he called to the people who came out to greet them. "Ah, hello, Mrs. Treesuwan! You look very happy today. I hope this means your brother is doing better? Good day to you, Mr. Prasert. I heard your son is graduating this year. How time flies!"

As they passed on through the village square, meeting and chatting with the villagers, Pong's senses were dialed all the way up. Tanaburi was a small, ordinary village, and it was the ordinary things that he liked to watch the most: people hanging their wash out to dry, sweeping porches, chatting with their neighbors, cooking breakfast. Walking beside Father Cham, surrounded by this everyday life, made Pong feel safe. It made him forget about his tattoo and all those things he'd done wrong. He was just a boy in a village, following his teacher.

They turned onto the road that led down the other side of the mountain. "You said we're going to the school today," said Pong, slowing his steps to match the old man's stride. "Are you giving a talk to the students?"

"Not today. Today we have a special errand," said Father Cham. "There is a baby we need to see about."

"A baby?"

Father Cham nodded and clucked his tongue. "Yes, an orphan, poor thing. One of our farmers found her, wrapped in blankets near the crossroads at the base of the mountain."

"Who'd be so heartless to leave their baby alone on the road?"

Father Cham didn't answer. He tilted his chin down and appeared to be thinking very hard about the gravel at his feet.

"Teacher, not even you could excuse such a thing as leaving a baby alone to die by the side of the road," said Pong. "I can't imagine anything worse."

Father Cham scratched his nose with the pad of his finger. They walked in silence for a while. Pong knew what this meant. When Father Cham didn't want to talk, nothing in the world could get him to say a word. This is what he did when he wanted his students to do the talking.

Finally, Pong sighed and said, "Well, maybe the parents were starving or something."

"Ah," said Father Cham, nodding as if Pong were the one who'd thought this through and not the other way around. "You make a very good point. There are starving and desperate people in this world, aren't there?"

Pong looked down at the road as they walked. "And maybe they had other children. Children they couldn't feed."

"Can you imagine the heartache of having to choose which of your children you are able to keep alive?" said Father Cham sadly.

"And I guess . . ." said Pong, thinking as he talked, "they knew that someone from our village would find the baby and take it in."

Father Cham nodded. "They did leave her in the morning, when the farmers drive their rice carts down the road. And our village does have a reputation in this area for taking in orphans."

"It does?"

"Oh, yes, a long reputation," said Father Cham, looking up into the trees with a faraway gaze. "In the years after the Great Fire in Chattana, things were very bad. Food was scarce, and many people died. Our fishermen began finding baskets floating down the river with babies inside. The little notes tucked in with them were heartbreaking. The parents who sent them away had nothing to feed them. Instead of watching them starve, they sent them on and hoped that someone would find them. For a little while our fishermen caught more babies than fish!"

Father Cham stopped in the road, leaning heavily on his walking stick. He pretended to inspect the bottom of his staff while he caught his breath. Pong offered his arm to help him stand up again.

"So I sent word out all over the province that our village would care for any children from Chattana or anywhere else, no matter what the circumstances," said the monk. "We also spread the word to leave them at the crossroads, not send them down the river. Too many crocodiles for that!"

"Did people listen to you?"

"Oh, we took in dozens and dozens of babies!" The old man smiled and pointed down the road. "That's why we ended up building the school. To hold all those babies." After a little while, he patted Pong's shoulder and smiled widely. "Thank you, my boy."

"For what?"

"For teaching me that desperate people deserve our compassion, not our judgment."

Pong started to protest that he certainly hadn't taught his teacher that lesson, but the old man was off and walking down the road again.

"The Great Fire was so long ago," said Pong. "But the babies are still showing up here?"

Father Cham turned and gave him a surprised look, as if Pong had questioned that objects fall down when you drop them. "Of course they're still showing up," said the old monk sadly. "The people are still desperate."

They rounded the bend in the road, and the low plaster building that made up the Tanaburi Village School came into view. Most villages had craft schools, where boys and girls learned how to weave cloth, carve wood, and master other skills that would land them steady work when they grew up. Father Cham had insisted that Tanburi's school also teach literature and mathematics. It was a much better education than Pong had gotten at the prison and even rivaled some of the private schools in Chattana.

"Ah, Father Cham, you've come!" said the headmistress, bowing when she saw them come through the gate. "It is an honor to have you here, as always."

"I got your message at the temple," said Father Cham.

"We would've gotten here sooner, but my friend is a slow walker." He winked at Pong. "Where is she?"

The headmistress smiled. "In my office. Right this way."

Pong followed behind them as they passed the classrooms. He glanced inside at the children bent over their workbooks. He would never join them — it was too big a risk that his tattoo would be seen — but he liked watching them from a distance. He always searched the boys, expecting to find Somkit's face grinning back at him, even though he knew it was impossible.

They entered the headmistress's office, and Father Cham leaned on his staff as he lowered to the floor in front of a woven laundry basket.

"Oh, my goodness, look at you!" the old man cooed in a high voice that Pong had never heard him use before. "What a sweet little melon! Coo-curoo! Ja-ka-jee!" he squealed as he tickled the baby's foot. She gurgled happily.

Pong and the headmistress both laughed to see the old man so natural with the baby.

"Poor thing, she was very dirty when they brought her in," said the headmistress. "We had to give her a bath right away."

"Well, she looks clean as anything now, ma'am," said

Father Cham with a smile. "Not fat enough, but we will change that. Yes, we will." A look of worry rippled over his smiling face. "Have you found someone who can take her?"

"Yes, you'll be happy to know that a farmer in the next village wants to adopt her. He and his wife haven't been able to have children."

"Ah, the Srinavakool family — yes, I know them. She will be happy there. Well, let's see, what do I have for this special girl? Oh, yes. The most vulnerable among us always deserve the greatest blessings, don't you agree?"

Father Cham reached into a pouch he kept tied at his side and pulled out a long woven cord. This one was far more special than any bracelet Pong had seen the old man use before. It was braided from red and gold threads, and it was quite thick.

The old monk leaned over the basket and looped the braid around the baby's wrist. As he began to tie it, he recited the prayers and blessings that Pong had heard him say a hundred times at the temple, but then he ended with another blessing, different from the ones he usually gave: "May you walk in peace wherever you are in the world."

The baby, who had been fidgeting and kicking just a moment before, became very still and very calm. She looked into Father Cham's wrinkled face with her shining black eyes.

Outside, children's voices rang out over the soccer field. The headmistress turned her face away from the basket to see what was going on outside the window.

"Children!" she called. "What have I told you about wrestling . . . ?"

Pong started to follow her gaze when he noticed something odd out of the corner of his eye. A wavy glimmer of light rippled on the ceiling. He looked up at the spot where the golden light danced, and he tracked the shimmer back to Father Cham and the basket. Pong gasped. A light as bright as sunbeams shone out from the place where Father Cham's fingers tied the bracelet on the baby.

The headmistress turned at the sound of Pong's gasp. "What's wrong?" she asked.

He looked at her, then back to the old man. The strange shimmer was gone.

"What . . . ?" whispered Pong. Bright spots danced in front of his eyes, as if he'd stared at the sun too long.

The baby gummed her slobbery mouth on her new bracelet. Pong stood bewildered. He looked at the headmistress. She blinked a few times but didn't seem to have noticed anything out of the ordinary.

Father Cham leaned against his walking stick with a

groan. He faltered and nearly slumped to the floor. Pong rushed over to help him stand.

"Are you all right, Father Cham?" asked the headmistress with concern.

"I'm fine," he answered with a wide smile. "Just an old man's old bones." He patted the baby's head. "She is going to make her new family very happy. Thank you for letting us meet her. We should get back to the temple now, shouldn't we, Pong?" He leaned heavily on Pong's arm.

"My groundskeeper has an errand to run back in the village," said the headmistress. "I'll have him walk with you."

She gave Pong a look that said the groundskeeper was only going along to make sure that Father Cham didn't fall again. But the old monk waved his hand at her. "Don't trouble him on my account! My friend here can barely keep up with me as it is." He tapped Pong's leg with his walking stick.

Before they bid goodbye to the school, the headmistress motioned Pong aside and whispered, "You should keep a good eye on him. He's not young like he used to be. He tries to fool everyone that he's not getting old, but I notice these things. I'm more observant than the average person."

* * *

When they were back on the road, Pong cleared his throat and said, "Father Cham, about that —"

"Not yet, Pong," said Father Cham, puffing with each step.

Pong fell quiet, and the two of them walked on in silence until they were well out of sight of the school.

"Please, Father," said Pong, unable to keep the words from bursting out any longer. "Back at the school . . . with the baby. I thought I saw . . . something."

Father Cham tilted his chin very slightly. "Oh? What did you see?"

"I . . . don't know exactly," said Pong, still a little dazed. "I thought I saw a light. A really bright one. It didn't last very long, and when I looked closer, it was gone."

Father Cham stopped and tugged Pong's arm to halt his steps. "You saw that?"

Pong nodded.

Father Cham searched Pong's face for a long moment before smiling again. "The other monks say you have a gift for noticing which trees will bear fruit first. I have a feeling they're mistaken about what your gift is for."

Before Pong could ask what he meant or what had actually happened in the schoolroom, they heard the commotion of a large group of people. They had now reached the edge of the village, where almost half the town had gathered in the street around a horse-drawn coach. Pong stared. No one in their village could afford horses.

"It seems we have a visitor," said Father Cham, pointing ahead with his staff. "And a very fancy one at that."

The carriage door swung open and out stepped a man with an official government uniform, followed by a woman wearing a gold-flecked dress. A girl with chopped-short hair and a sharp black gaze climbed out after them. She wore a spire-fighting uniform.

Pong's heart shrank to the size of a peppercorn.

Warden Sivapan and his family had arrived on the mountain.

Chapter 12

When Nok Sivapan climbed out of the carriage in the village of Tanaburi, she didn't recognize Pong at all. Having regular meals had filled out his once hollow cheeks, and he was three inches taller than her now. That sticking-up hair of his had been shaved off, and his monks' robes also helped to hide him.

Nok, on the other hand, had just grown into an older version of the sharp-eyed girl who Pong remembered visiting Namwon from time to time. She hadn't sprouted up the way he had. She was small, though her regular spire-fighting practice kept her strong. Her hair was still chopped straight across her shoulders, and she wore the same wary, serious gaze.

Even if Pong hadn't been dressed as a young monk-in-training, Nok would probably have glossed over him.

She was distracted.

Her family rarely traveled outside of Chattana City, and the small mountain village was a curious sight. They had left the twins at home and had taken a barge downriver to the base of the mountain, where they had boarded a horse-drawn carriage.

"Horses!" her mother had gasped when the carriage rolled up to the dock. She lifted her sleeve to cover her nose against the musky green smell. "Haven't you told them who you are? They should send an orb-powered coach for someone in your position!"

Nok's father sighed. "They don't have orb coaches this far from the city. We'll be inside. You won't have to smell anything."

At that, one of the horses lifted its tail and plopped out a contradiction to his statement. Nok offered her mother her arm to help her into the carriage. The driver clucked once, and they began to roll slowly forward.

Nok's mother patted the sweat off her nose with a handkerchief and looked worriedly out the window. "We'll never get there by nightfall at this rate! I told you we should have left earlier. I don't want to be caught in the country in the darkness."

Nok's father reached over and patted her knee. "It couldn't be helped. There's only one barge that stops at Tanaburi, and we were on it. We can stop at the temple and still get to our house with plenty of time to spare."

"Don't call it *our* house," said Nok's mother, pushing his hand away. "It's a rental. One without running water, don't forget!"

"It's the nicest house on the mountain," said Nok's father patiently, sneaking a smile at Nok. "The one reserved for visiting officials. Besides, what can we do? It's the country. They don't have the same luxuries that we do in Chattana — though that should change after this visit."

The family was in Tanaburi because someone from the Commission on Law and Light Regulation had finally noticed that no one in the village had ever bought an orb. At least there was no record of anyone from Tanaburi visiting one of the Charge Stations, where most of the country people could purchase small amounts of light from the vast stores produced by the Governor.

Were the villagers using fire? Nok's father had no interest in making arrests, but he did plan to give the village leaders a talking-to. Sure, Tanaburi was a scrap of a town with one school and a tiny temple, but they still had to follow the same rules as everyone else. It was high time that someone official educated the poor villagers on the benefits of orbs and the powers of the Governor. That was one part of the reason Nok's father had decided to come.

Part, but not all, as Nok knew well.

"Imagine," grumbled her mother. "The Governor's own Law Commissioner going to the bathroom in an outhouse! If we wanted that sort of treatment, we could have stayed in a slum on the East Side."

Nok listened to her parents go back and forth about how short or long their visit to Tanaburi would be. Outside the window, the fields of tall sugarcane gave way to lined rows of papaya orchards, and then to forest, as the carriage rumbled slowly up the mountain road. If her parents would have stopped chattering, it would have been very quiet.

Nok liked it quiet, and this would have been a peaceful and pleasant outing if she didn't know why she was there. But she did know, even though her parents had worked hard to keep it hidden.

Like most parents, Nok's were terrible at keeping secrets from their children. For example, they never told Nok or her siblings when their father was switching jobs, and if they did, it was always called a "promotion," even when everyone knew it was no such thing.

A promotion should have meant more money and

prestige, not less. The first "promotion" happened four years ago, when Nok was nine and her father was still warden of Namwon. A boy disappeared from the prison that year, and it was a complete mystery what happened to him. Another little boy had sworn that he'd seen the missing kid climbing the mango tree onto a branch out over the river. Maybe he fell in. The child's disappearance was ruled a drowning, but everyone whispered about Nok's father behind his back. What kind of warden lets a child slip through his fingers?

The incident brought the prison under review. The Governor's officials looked into the record books and found that Nok's father ran Namwon half-heartedly. He hardly spent any time there, as if he didn't even want the job in the first place.

So Nok's father was "promoted" to a desk job at the courthouse. Nok thought the quiet courthouse was actually perfect for him. He liked to read and study and be by himself. He belonged behind a desk, not running a big operation like a prison. He could have been happy there if Nok's mother had let him. But courthouse lawyers don't make good salaries. Nok's brother was at an expensive university. Her sisters, the twins, would join Nok at private school soon. So Nok's mother wheedled and cut deals with her society friends, and by a sheer miracle, she landed Nok's father an even better gig: Chief Law Commissioner.

He had no staff and few responsibilities — just touring around the province and checking the court record books. Best of all, it came with a fat paycheck. Nok's family moved to a bigger house in one of the West Side's best neighborhoods. Her mother was back on the invite list for fancy parties. With everything going so well for the family, her parents should have been happy.

But something was the matter.

Nok's mother had been watching her. Even now, as the carriage creaked slowly up the mountain, Nok could feel her mother looking, her eyes disappointed and full of sadness.

It was as though Nok had done something wrong. But that was impossible. She had never once in her life done anything wrong. Nok was the perfect daughter. That wasn't bragging, not when it had been such hard work.

She was at the top of her class at school, beating every other girl her year by miles. And last month she had won the citywide spire-fighting championship for her age group. Everyone from the city had come out to watch the competition. That was when Nok noticed her mother's stare for the first time.

It had been the best night of Nok's life. Her opponent

was a tall boy with a loud mouth named Bull. *More like Mouse*, thought Nok as she swept her leg behind his knee and toppled him backward onto the mat. He sprang back to his feet quickly, his staff ready to strike. But Nok could see the uncertainty in his eyes, the horror that he was about to get beaten by someone smaller than him in front of everyone he knew.

She, on the other hand, was the quickest she'd ever been. It was as though she could see his movements seconds before he made them. She blocked his attacks easily, holding her staff steady while his quivered with every clack. Nok felt the strength of all her years of training surging through her muscles, gathering into her core in a ball of energy.

Bull staggered back from one of her blocks, and she knew the time had come to finish him off. She raised her staff and brought one end down hard, onto the floor, performing a feat that no one except the most skilled spire-fighting masters could do: The ball of energy flowed out through her arm, into her hand, and down the staff. It radiated out, shook the floor, and threw Bull off his feet and onto his back. The force of the blow blew back the hair of the spectators in the first three rows. The crowd sat in shocked silence for two heartbeats, and then they jumped to their feet, roaring her name.

Later, Nok stood between her parents, holding the trophy, feeling both drained and giddy, while her father's colleagues came up to congratulate them.

"Thank you, thank you!" said her father, shaking their hands. "Wasn't she amazing? Yes, she's worked so hard for this, so hard. She trains every day for hours!"

Nok almost laughed. She'd never seen her father so talkative. His glasses sat skewed on his nose, and he was smiling so big she could see his molars.

"Good fight, little Nok!" said one of his friends from work. "You are making your parents so proud."

"Yes, a hard worker, just like your father," said another, patting her shoulder. "And his spitting image, too!"

Nok had quickly looked down at her feet to discourage more comparisons. No one could deny she had inherited her strong chin and dimples from her father. Nok's older brother and her sisters also shared those traits, but they looked like their mother, too: slim as herons, with long limbs and graceful fingers. Nok, on the other hand, was short, with muscles thickened from all the spire-fighting practice.

"Perhaps she resembles some distant relative," other family members had started to say. "Far back in the bloodline."

"Yes, far back," her mother had said. *So far that no one need bother looking.*

But her mother was looking. Looking all the time and thinking something Nok could only guess at.

And then, a few nights before they were to leave for Tanaburi, Nok had overheard her parents talking as she lay in bed. Her father's voice was a low, steady *hum-hum*. And there was a higher-pitched sound she didn't recognize.

Nok got up from her bed and tiptoed out of her room and into the hallway. Spire fighting was an ancient practice, and one of its elements was the "Nothing Step," a way of walking so quietly that nothing — not even the dust — knows you are moving.

She crept closer to her parents' door. Their lights were still on, and she couldn't make out their words over the buzz of the orb lights until she was just outside the doorway. As she leaned her ear to the door, she realized what the high-pitched sound was.

Her mother was crying.

"There, there," said her father soothingly. "Please don't make yourself so upset. We've lived with it for this long, and we can wait it out. No one knows."

"They do, they do," sobbed her mother. "I can see it

when we go out together. Everyone can tell. It's so obvious to everyone but you!"

"My darling," said her father gently. "You know how sorry I am. But I can't change the past. We have had this conversation so many times. You were in agreement with me when we made the decision. It was the right thing to do. You wanted to do it as much as I did."

"Yes, I did . . . I still do. But imagine what this is like for me. . . ." Nok's mother took a deep, shaking breath. Her voice calmed and she spoke more measured and low. "You have to think of your son. Next year he'll graduate and be out in society. He's primed to make a good match with a girl from a good family. But no one will come near him if the truth comes out. No one will want to take on that kind of scandal!"

Nok heard footsteps pacing the room — her father's. "So what are you saying? That we turn our family upside down because of gossip? What was the point of everything we went through if you just want to rip everything apart now?"

"Please don't be dramatic," said Nok's mother. "No one is ripping anything. I love her as much as you do. But someone has to think about what is best for the whole family. If our reputation is destroyed, it won't be any good for her, either. We can set her up in a comfortable place away from all the chatter. She can grow up happy and healthy and someday marry a nice boy from the country, someone respectable but not connected to anyone in town. Your next official trip is to Tanaburi. I heard that the village school is actually quite good. She could come home for holidays. It wouldn't be forever. Just a little while."

"I don't know. . . ." said Nok's father.

The wood floor shook as her mother got to her feet. Nok could imagine the scene on the other side of the wall — her tall father, trembling before her slim little mother. "This is your fault, and you have to make it right," her mother demanded. "If you love your children, you'll do what's best for them."

Nok didn't wait to hear his answer. She flew back down the hall on her Nothing Steps and into her room. She knelt on her pallet in the darkness and clasped her hands together on her knees. Her thoughts galloped wild in her head.

Nok had realized long ago that she was not her mother's daughter. But she was her father's — she was sure of that. It wasn't just because they looked alike. She knew it from the way he smiled at her tournaments and beamed so proudly when she brought home her reports from school. She was his perfect, golden girl.

Nok's parents had never once spoken about her birth, and she had never asked. She didn't feel the need to know any more than she already did. This unnamed secret was something passed silently among the three of them, like a pebble one of them always kept tucked inside a pocket. It was enough to know it was there — she didn't need to hold it up for a closer look.

But based on what she'd just overheard in the hallway, their little secret had clattered out onto the floor. Every week, Nok's mother's society friends gathered around her family's dining table for cards, dealing out gossip as they dealt out their hands. It didn't take much effort to imagine those same gossip sessions happening at some other dining table, with her own family as the subject.

Well, she'd just have to give them something else to whisper about. She needed to do something so impressive that it would overshadow any rumors about her birth — something so incredible that no one would dare speak ill of her family.

Nok squeezed her fingers tight together. She took another breath and let it out slowly, reminding herself of the words that had given her strength over the years, words she'd heard spoken by the Governor himself:

Light shines on the worthy.

Yes, light and love and pride, and everything that had shone on her from time to time, like that night at the spire-fighting championship. Nok clung to those words.

"I can do this," she whispered to herself. "They just need a reminder of how much I bring to this family. Then nothing else will matter."

And so when she came face-to-face with Pong, she was distracted, racking her brain, wringing it out to think of what she could do to prove to her parents — to *everyone* — that she was worthy of being called their daughter.

That was why she didn't notice that the young monk-in-training trembled as he hid his left hand tight behind his back.

Chapter 13

All afternoon, Pong's throat seized up as if he'd swallowed a fish bone. The Sivapan family had followed Father Cham back to the temple to pay their respects. They sat before the old monk in the prayer hall, chatting and drinking chilled tea while Pong pretended to repair a bench just outside. As afraid as he was of being recognized, he had to figure out why they had come.

He learned that Warden Sivapan was now the Chief Law Commissioner, a position that reported straight to the Governor himself.

"Orbs provide more than just light," said the Commissioner, raising his cup to his lips. "When your villagers buy them, they'll help pay for police and hospitals, and for officials who could ensure that the laws of the province are being obeyed."

The old monk smiled. "Commissioner, I like you very much, so please don't take offense, but we don't need an official to tell us whether our neighbors are taking good care of one another."

Commissioner Sivapan took a sip of tea and sloshed some on his shirt. His wife cringed and looked away. "Father Cham," he said, brushing the fabric dry, "your village is charming, but the law is the law. Fire is dangerous, and it's a danger you don't need. Everyone in the province uses orbs. I'm afraid I can't make an exception just for you."

"Why not?" asked Father Cham innocently.

"Well, because . . ." Commissioner Sivapan straightened his glasses. "Because then everyone will expect me to make exceptions for them."

"What's wrong with that?"

The Commissioner fluttered his lips. "Because then law and order would completely break down."

"I see," said Father Cham, nodding slowly. A pained look spread over his face. "It seems you take very good care of the laws in Chattana City."

"That is my job," said the Commissioner. "What could be more important?"

Pong didn't hang around to hear the rest of their discussion. He swept the temple grounds, his palms sweating as he waited for the moment when one of the Sivapan family would come charging across the courtyard, finger pointed at him, shouting, "There he is! The one who escaped!"

But incredibly, the family didn't recognize him. The entire afternoon passed without incident, and as evening approached, the Sivapans finally got into their carriage and left for the house where they were staying in the village.

Pong was so relieved when they left that he felt dizzy. He needed to talk to Father Cham right away. But what would he say? Surely his teacher wouldn't have invited Commissioner Sivapan to the temple if he knew he used to be the warden of Namwon. Should Pong tell him? Or keep quiet and just try to hide until the family left?

No, that wasn't going to work. He'd have to figure something else out. In the meantime, he needed to find out what the Sivapans were doing in Tanaburi and how long they were planning to stay.

Pong found Father Cham in the prayer hall. He slipped off his sandals and walked up the steps, then paused, knowing that he shouldn't disturb his teacher in the middle of his meditation.

Without opening his eyes or turning his head, Father Cham smiled and said, "Ah, Pong, I'm glad you're here. I wanted to talk to you."

The eels in Pong's stomach wriggled. "You did, Father?"

Father Cham opened his eyes and leaned back in his chair. "Yes, come up."

Pong walked farther into the hall and knelt in front of Father Cham. Had Commissioner Sivapan said something about him after all? He tried to act normal, but he couldn't stop sweating.

Father Cham reached out to the shiny black set of drawers. He pulled out a white string and held it up for Pong. "I noticed you're about to lose one," he said, nodding at the dingy white bracelets around Pong's left wrist. "Let me replace it for you before it snaps."

Pong sighed, relieved. "Yes, Father, thank you."

He held out his wrist so the monk could tie on his bracelet. He stared down at the strings and thought about all the blessings that had accompanied them over the years. *May you sleep through the sound of snoring* and *May you never spill hot tea on your friends.* They were little blessings, funny sometimes. Small as they were, every single blessing the old monk had given him had come to pass.

The villagers all had stories to tell about Father Cham's "gift," about the wishes that came true. There was the fisherman who Father Cham had wished would never get a hole in his boat. When a sudden storm battered the other boats at the dock, his had been the only one spared. And what about the poor widow who had only one hen? Father Cham had told her, "May that bird always provide for you." Thirty years later, the widow claimed the chicken still laid an egg every day.

These stories were so well known to Pong that they felt as ordinary as the village itself. But maybe Father Cham's gift was less ordinary than he thought.

Pong recalled the baby at the school. He remembered the blaze of light that only he had seen, the special cord tied to the baby's wrist, and what Father Cham had said just before he blessed her:

The most vulnerable among us always deserve the greatest blessings.

Pong's fingers trembled where they pressed together in prayer. He lowered his hands to his lap, and the next words he spoke slipped out before he could stop them.

"How do you choose?"

Father Cham raised one eyebrow. "Choose what?"

Pong swallowed. "How do you choose which blessings to give to which people?"

Father Cham's face remained calm, but he didn't answer.

"All your blessings come true, don't they?" pressed Pong.

The monk nodded. "They do."

"The big ones as well as the small ones?"

Father Cham looked into Pong's eyes a long moment before nodding again.

"And so the baby that you blessed today," said Pong. "You wished for her to walk in peace. That will come true."

Father Cham smiled. "It will. But I hope it would have come true anyway, without me."

"Why that blessing, though? Why not wish her to be a wealthy woman? Or to live a long life?"

The monk's forehead creased into dozens of crinkled folds. "Now, Pong, surely I've taught you better than to think that wealth is a greater gift to bestow on someone than peace. Wealth can be as much a curse as a blessing, and no guarantee of happiness. And a long life? It can also be a difficulty, if you are in pain or if the people you love have already passed on. You don't understand now because you are young." Father Cham's smile lessened for a moment. "You can't imagine yet that one day you'll be ready to bid this life goodbye."

Pong took a deep breath and let it out again. Father Cham didn't understand what he was trying to say. "If happiness is the goal, then you could wish her to be happy."

"Is happiness the goal of a person's life?"

Father Cham was talking in riddles. It was so frustrating. Today Pong wanted straight answers. "I don't know. I — I just don't understand why you didn't give her something that she really needs. Something she might need one day very badly."

"Pong, you are talking around and around the thing you want to say, and we both know that's my job." Father Cham's smile left his face. His brow creased again. "Why don't you come out and tell me what you really want to know?"

Pong felt trapped — squeezed by the walls of the temple, by the walls around his heart.

He held out his left wrist. "All these blessings and prayers," he blurted, pointing at the bracelets. "What are they for? They're to protect me, right? They're supposed to cover up my mark so no one will see it. But why not just wish the mark away? Why not erase it completely instead of making me hide?"

Pong was trying hard to keep his voice level, but he couldn't hold back the angry crackle in his words. He burned with shame to hear himself speak like this, but he also couldn't stop.

"I could be out there," he continued, "walking in the

world without worry. You could have wished me to the sea. You could have wished for me to be free. You said that the most vulnerable among us deserve the greatest blessings. But *I'm* vulnerable, aren't I? All these years I've been here, scared every day that someone will discover who I am and take me back to jail. When all this time..."

All this time you could have stopped it, Pong thought.

A deep sadness washed over Father Cham's face. "Oh, my boy. My dear boy. I have considered erasing that mark for you. But what if someday you need it? What if I do more harm than good?"

Pong knew he couldn't speak without sounding even more disrespectful than he already had been, so he kept silent. Who could believe he would ever need his wretched tattoo?

Father Cham sighed heavily. "I have been doing this a very long time. There was a time when I was a younger man, before I learned my lesson, when I *did* grant the types of blessings you are talking about. I wanted to use my gift to help people, to wish away all the pain and suffering in this world. But it was arrogant of me to think that I alone could save the whole world. And my gifts went awry."

"How?"

Father Cham looked out the open doorway. "In ways that were more complicated and unexpected than you can imagine. I learned the hard way that it's not up to me to save people or to force the world to bend to my desires, even if I have good intentions. That's not what my gift was meant for."

Pong looked down at the carpet. More philosophy, more teaching. He was asking for something so small. Let Father Cham talk about saving the world some other day. Pong needed this now.

When he looked up, the old monk had his eyes closed and his lips shut in a straight line. His brow was wrinkled and tense.

"Father Cham," said Pong. "Please, I'm begging you . . ."

"We can finish this conversation another time," the monk whispered hoarsely. "I must complete my meditation now."

"Father, I may not have another time —"

"It's time to go, Pong," said Father Cham more sternly. The conversation was over.

Pong's eyes filled with hot tears. He bowed low and left.

* * *

Pong went straight to Brother Yam's quarters. He knocked softly on the door, even though he knew that Yam was out. He swung open the door and stepped into the small room.

Brother Yam kept a schedule of the boats that docked at the base of the mountain in case a sick villager needed to be transferred to the hospital in the city. Pong found the schedule and scanned it. There would be one southbound and one northbound cargo barge the next day, both departing the dock at two o'clock.

As soon as the morning meal was over, Pong would make his way to that southbound boat and head for the sea.

Chapter 14

Nok had already lain awake for an hour before she decided to give up on going back to sleep. The sky was still dark. Maybe she could get in some spire-fighting drills before her parents woke.

As she Nothing-Stepped down the staircase, she heard the sounds of their housekeeper in the kitchen. Nok peeked her head inside and bowed to the old woman. "Good morning, Mrs. Viboon," she said.

The woman gave a little cry and wheeled around. "Oh, Nok! You scared me. You're up much too early. Young ladies like you should sleep late."

"I'm not up any earlier than you are. Can I help you?"

Mrs. Viboon scratched at the talcum powder caked to her neck. "Thank you, but I'm just finishing up making some fish and rice for the monks. I'll take it to the village square, then I'll come back and start your breakfast. Your mother told me that you two are going to visit the school today. That should be fun."

Nok's stomach clenched. Her mother hadn't said anything about visiting the school. *It could be a charity visit,* Nok told herself. Her mother was always going to places like schools and shelters and giving them money. But if that were the case, she wouldn't take Nok with her. No, the only reason would be to introduce her to her future teachers. *Well, maybe I just won't be here when she wakes up, then.*

"Mrs. Viboon, why don't you let me take the food to the monks this morning?" Nok asked.

"Are you sure?" asked the woman as Nok stepped into the kitchen. "If you don't mind, that would be helpful."

"I don't mind at all," said Nok, taking the covered dish. "I never get to do this at home. And besides, I'd like to see Father Cham again."

Before the sun rose, Nok walked up the road to the village, the fresh smell of green herbs and steamed fish rising up from the dish. It was true, she did want to see Father Cham again. He'd talked with her father for a long time when they arrived, and even though the two of them disagreed about almost everything, Nok liked the old monk right from the start.

By the time she got to the village square, the sky was pale gray and the monks had almost finished their walk through. Nok slipped off her shoes and joined the villagers standing in line. They all held dishes of food, and as the monks came to them, they spooned it into their wooden bowls. Father Cham wasn't there, so Nok gave the fish to the other monks.

Afterward, she stood beneath a tree, watching the villagers. It was a market day, and people had come from the surrounding countryside to buy and sell goods on the main street.

Nok's eyes wandered to the row of shops along the road. In the center, a grocery store sold vegetables and takeaway meals wrapped in banana leaves. The shop owner had just finished setting up a tidy pyramid of fresh-baked sweets: golden egg-flour cakes, the insides probably stuffed with sweet beans or pineapple jelly.

Nok's mouth watered. She started to get up, planning to buy some to take back to Mrs. Viboon, when she saw a brown five-legged spider crawling on the display. It took her a minute to realize it was a hand. The hand belonged to a barefoot little boy.

His fingers curled around one of the cakes and slipped it off the pile. But in his hurry, the boy sent the rest of the sweets rolling off the table, onto the ground.

The shop owner ran out of his store, puffing and cursing. "Blast! My sunrise cakes! They're covered in dust and dirt!"

Nok watched as the people standing nearby came to help clean up the mess. The boy was long gone. It seemed that no one but her had seen what happened. *And there you have it,* she thought. *Thieving, out in the open. When people don't live with rules, this is exactly what happens.*

Nok crossed the square, following where she'd seen the barefoot boy disappear to. If she caught him, it would help her father make his case to Father Cham about the need for orbs and laws. She held her hands at her side, ready to spring out and grab him. But when she rounded the corner, she saw that someone else had beaten her to it.

One of the monks knelt beside the boy, who still clutched the sticky cake in his hand. The boy stared back wide-eyed, nodding tearfully. The monk was young, just a novice. Nok Nothing-Stepped closer to hear what he was saying to the little thief.

"You know better than that," said the young monk sternly. "So we're agreed. First thing tomorrow. Okay, then, you'd better keep your promise. Run on."

"Run on?" blurted Nok, closing the remaining distance between them. "Are you seriously letting him go?"

Both the boy and the monk twisted to look at her, startled.

"Excuse me," Nok started again, bowing to the young

monk this time. "But you must not have seen what just happened. This boy stole a cake from that shop, and in the process ruined the entire batch."

The monk turned his head away from her and looked down at the ground. "I did see it, miss."

"Well, then, I'm sure you'll agree that we can't just let him run off with a cake in his hands," said Nok, trying her best to sound respectful. "He needs to at least go back and pay for it."

The little boy's lip started to shake.

"He can't afford it," whispered the monk.

"Well, he should have thought of that before he took it."

"I'm sorry . . . I'm sorry . . ." whimpered the little boy. He'd crushed the cake into a sticky mush in his hand.

"He knows what he did is wrong," said the monk. He tapped the boy on the arm. "Don't you?" The boy nodded, sniffling.

The monk kept his face turned away, avoiding looking into Nok's eyes. She supposed this was because she was a girl. She took a step back to try to make him feel less awkward, but she wasn't going to back down.

"That doesn't really help that baker," she said. "He's now got forty ruined cakes on his hands."

The monk stood up, keeping his chin tucked down. For a moment, Nok thought he was backing off. He took a step back, then forward again, as though he couldn't decide what to do.

In the end, he planted his feet and then spoke quietly, so only Nok could hear. "Look at him," he said, nodding at the snot-soaked boy. "He hasn't stolen anything before. And he won't do it again — that's for sure. There's no sense in shaming him further. That man, the baker — he's got a bad temper. If you go tell him what happened right now, he'll blow up and maybe have the boy whipped. Or worse, make the family come into town and pay for the cakes, and they can't. They're very poor. He promised me that he'll come every day for a week to volunteer at the shop to make up for it. Right after school. That's good enough, don't you think?"

Nok's shoulders tensed.

School.

The same school that her parents wanted to drag her to this morning. The one they wanted to leave her at. She was running out of time to do something to save herself. Bringing this little boy to justice was hardly the impressive feat she needed to accomplish, but she was feeling desperate.

"I'm sorry," she said firmly. "But it's just not the way we do things in Chattana. The boy needs to come with me. Don't worry: I'll make sure he isn't whipped." She reached out for the child. "Come on, let's go —"

But before she could take the boy's hand, the monk stepped in between them. "Go on, run!" he whispered to the boy over his shoulder.

The little boy didn't need to be told twice. He shot off into the forest, leaving the crumbled cake on the ground.

"Stop!" called Nok. Too late. He was gone. "What was that boy's name?" she demanded of the monk-in-training.

"What boy?"

Nok realized that he hadn't used the boy's name the entire time on purpose. Now the monk did glance up at her, just for an instant. It was long enough for her to see a flicker of defiance in his eyes. It was so striking that Nok took a step back. She'd seen eyes like that somewhere before.

"Do I . . . do I know you?" she asked.

"Brother Pong!" called a voice, far away but growing closer.

Pong. Had she ever known a boy named Pong?

"Brother Pong!" A lanky monk whirled around the corner and stumbled toward them, panting. "There you are!" he gasped. "You've got to come . . . quick!"

"What's wrong?" asked the monk-in-training.

"It's Father Cham. . . . He's fallen!"

Chapter 15

Pong knelt beside the other monks outside Father Cham's living quarters. The doors were shut, and he could hear the low murmur of Brother Yam speaking inside. The rest of the temple complex was silent, but Pong's thoughts swished like the wind through palm leaves, filling his head with noise.

Nok had recognized him — he was sure of it.

The way she looked at him, with those keen blackbird eyes. He was sure that if Brother Daeng hadn't come running up, Nok would've confronted him right there in the village square.

As the sun rose higher in the sky, he felt drawn thin and tight as a fishing line. Why couldn't he have done what Somkit used to tell him and kept his mouth shut? He should never have gone into the village at all, but he'd wanted to see it one last time before he left forever. When he saw the little boy take the cake, he should've just ignored it. When Nok had wanted to turn the boy in, he should've ignored *that*. But the old familiar heat had flared up inside him and he couldn't stop himself. And what good had it done?

Where was she now, that bird of a girl? Telling her father? Gathering up some police? He kept imagining he could smell her close by: the scent of lemon flowers and wood shavings. A voice inside Pong's head broke through his thoughts. *You need to run now. Before she gets to the temple, or it really will be too late!*

He had missed his chance to hitch a ride on the southbound cargo barge. The barge would leave the dock beneath the mountain in little over an hour. It would take Pong more than twice that long to get down the twisting mountain track, but he couldn't leave before learning how Father Cham was.

The door to the room opened and Brother Yam came outside. Pong could read the verdict on his face before he spoke.

"Brothers," said Yam, clearing away the catch in his throat. "It's time to say farewell to our teacher. Go in and pay your respects. Don't linger too long. Father Cham is very weak. Brother Daeng, come on, you first."

As Daeng went into the room, Mr. Viboon, who had come to take care of the cleaning, approached

Brother Yam. Pong could just make out his hushed words.

"Commissioner Sivapan and his family are here," he said to Yam. "To pay their respects."

Yam sighed and rubbed the space between his eyebrows. "Can you tell him there isn't time? Or stall them somehow? I don't think that all the monks will even get to say good-bye before Father Cham leaves us."

The monks continued to file into the room, one after another, and another. Mr. Viboon choked up and nodded. "Yes, I will. But the Commissioner also says he has something important to talk to *you* about."

"After," said Yam firmly. "Tell him that as soon as we're done here, I'll come out and speak with him. Pong?"

Pong's body jerked. "Yes?" he managed to get out.

"Little Brother, are you all right? You look like you're going to be sick." Yam bent down close to him. "You know that Father Cham is merely leaving this life behind and going on to the next. You shouldn't be so sad." He added, more gently, "But I understand how you must feel. You two had a special bond. If it's too much for you to go in right now, you don't have to do it."

Pong looked in the direction of his living quarters at the back of the temple, near the forest edge. He could pretend to go to his room, then run away before Yam or anyone else knew what was going on. This was his one chance to escape.

It was also his one chance to say goodbye.

"I want to go in."

Yam nodded. "All right. It's your turn now, then."

Pong rose and walked into the room. The door closed behind him, shutting out the daylight. Father Cham lay in the center of the room on a mat. Candles flickered on a small altar, and the woody smell of incense floated in the air.

Pong knelt at the side of Father Cham's mat, not sure if he was awake. But the old man opened one eye and smiled his old smile. In the candlelight Pong couldn't see any wrinkles on his face. He looked fresh and healthy, not at all what Yam had prepared him for. For a moment, Pong thought perhaps the old man was fooling them all and would live for years and years longer.

Father Cham crooked a finger at him and Pong moved closer. The old monk raised his hand and cupped it over Pong's left wrist, on top of the bracelets.

"You have been here a long time, Pong," said Father Cham, his voice smooth and steady. "I've kept you close during that time. Too close maybe."

"You've taught me so much," whispered Pong.

"I taught you some, but you have taught yourself

even more. You're a good boy. A kind boy. Your heart is right."

Pong wanted to stuff his fingers in his ears so he couldn't hear. He wasn't good. He was a liar and a thief and a runaway. Plus he'd lashed out at the one man who'd cared for him. Pong was so ashamed that he had to fight off tears.

But he did fight them. He wanted his teacher to feel at peace when he left the world. "I'll use your teachings and carry on as you would," he whispered. "We'll keep your good work going in the temple after you're gone."

Father Cham grimaced. For some reason, Pong's words were having the opposite effect. "I think I made a mistake," whispered the old man. "I kept you hidden to protect you, but now I wonder if that was the right thing to do." He coughed, and it took him a long time to get his breath again. He pointed to a low table along the wall. "The small box there. Bring it to me."

Pong looked behind him at the door, ready for it to burst open any moment with the Sivapan girl behind it. His skin prickled with urgency, but he couldn't leave Father Cham, not now.

Pong picked up the little wooden box and brought it to the monk's bedside. Inside there was one length of braided cord — red and gold, just like the one Father

Cham had given to the baby girl at the school.

"You have a gift," said Father Cham softly. "You notice things that other people miss. I've always wondered if that's because you are looking for something."

"Looking for something?" repeated Pong.

But Father Cham went on without explaining. "I think I finally understand what it is. And now that I know, I realize you can't stay here any longer. Come closer, Pong. I have one final blessing for you."

Pong leaned forward, unsure what the old monk could mean. The candlelight flickered in Father Cham's eyes. His eyes seemed too bright, too full of fire for the old body they belonged to, and they stared at Pong, full of meaning that he didn't understand.

Pong held his wrist out over the monk's chest. Father Cham's papery hands trembled as he tied the cord around Pong's left wrist beside the other bracelets. His lips moved quietly, murmuring the words of a prayer.

Pong shut his eyes.

"My wish for you is that you find what you are looking for," the old man whispered.

Behind his closed eyelids, Pong saw a wash of golden light, as if the sun had flown past his face. Startled, he opened his eyes, but the room was dark as before.

The door swung open. Pong looked up to see Brother

Yam. "I'm sorry," he said to Pong. "But Commissioner Sivapan says he must speak to me, and he won't wait. May I have one moment with Father Cham first?"

"Of course."

Pong rose, still blinking away the bright spots that danced in his eyes.

He felt weighted down with sadness, as if there were stones tied to the hem of his robes. He bowed low to his teacher for the last time, and then he walked out of the room.

Chapter 16

Nok and her parents stood in the temple courtyard, a sprawling jackfruit tree shielding them from the afternoon sun. Nok rolled a pebble back and forth across the dirt with the toe of her shoe, trying not to count the minutes. As sad as she felt about disturbing the last moments of Father Cham's life, she was anxious to get all of this underway. Her family had decided to wait, out of respect, but it was taking longer than expected.

Nok looked at her mother. She seemed nervous, too, but pleased. Of course her mother remembered the boy who'd nearly ruined their lives. "His name was Pong," she had reminded Nok, her voice edged with bitterness. "It must be him."

Yes, Nok agreed that it must. She had looked at the young monk's left wrist as he'd walked away from her in the village, but it was completely covered with string bracelets. That didn't matter. She didn't need to check for a tattoo to know it was him.

She knew that Pong had recognized her, too. She wondered if right now he was begging the other monks for forgiveness or trying to lie his way out of this. It wouldn't do him any good. He was caught, and now he'd have to face the consequences.

Nok's pulse beat faster as she thought of how news of the arrest would spread across the province. She pictured her mother's friends, flicking their cards back and forth to one another across a polished dining table.

Did you hear the latest about the Sivapan girl? She caught a fugitive hiding in plain sight!

Thank goodness she was there! He might have gotten away with it forever.

Her parents must be so proud. . . .

Nok paced beneath the tree, letting her eyes wander the temple grounds. Even at the height of the afternoon, the air was cool and breezy. The temple was so peaceful. It was hard to imagine that a dangerous runaway had been hiding here for the past four years.

The groundskeeper, Mr. Viboon, shuffled toward them and bowed to Nok's parents. "Brother Yam is ready to see you, Commissioner."

"Finally," muttered Nok's mother.

As they followed after Mr. Viboon, a parrot flew out from the forest, chittering as it glided overhead. Nok tracked it over the temple buildings. It was a lucky bird, a nice thing to see on a day like this. It landed on the archway above the temple gate.

Nok paused. She'd been the last one inside, and she remembered shutting the gate behind her. Now it hung open. A thin swirl of dust hovered inches above the ground.

Heat rose up the sides of her neck and pulsed into her cheeks. She grabbed her staff from where she'd left it leaning against a wall and sprinted out the gate.

"Nok?" called her father. "Nok, where are you going?"

Nok didn't slow down. If she waited for her parents to rally the police, it would be too late. If she wanted Pong to be captured, she would have to do it herself.

The forest formed a tunnel of green around her as she sped down the mountain road.

I'm faster than him, thought Nok as her feet flew. *There's only one road down the mountain, and it won't be long before I catch up to him.*

Nok jerked to a stop. She *would* catch up to him eventually, and unless he was a complete fool, he knew it, too. Nok didn't think Pong was a fool. A fugitive didn't evade capture for four years by making stupid mistakes like that.

She retraced her steps, walking backward slowly, so

silently that not even the dust knew she was there. She calmed her breath so she could listen. For a moment, she heard nothing but distant birds. Then she heard the crack of a branch. It could be an animal.

Or it could be a boy.

Nok scanned the forest to either side of her. Now that she was paying attention, she saw that she had run right past a path that led into the trees. Behind her, back at the temple, she could hear the hubbub of voices. She heard her father call her name again.

She left the road and took the forest trail. She Nothing-Stepped down a well-worn path through the trees. This must be one of the trails the monks used for their walking meditations. It began to wind down so steeply that she had to dig her staff into the ground to keep from skidding. Ahead, she heard a heavy crunch, like two feet stumbling. Nok froze.

Then she heard a body crashing through leaves, as if someone no longer cared about being quiet.

Nok ran down the slope, using her staff to brace herself. Her heart pounded excitedly. This wasn't some spire-fighting drill at the gym. This was the real thing.

But even though Nok's many years of training should have prepared her for this moment, she was scared. She was alone with a dangerous criminal. If something went wrong, there would be no teacher to stop the drill, no referee to step in and call a time-out.

Nok was so distracted that she failed to notice that the forest path led straight into a sinkhole. She wheeled her arms, stopping herself just in time to keep from falling in. She looked up at the thick trees, then back down into the hole. This area was known to be full of caves. Pong must have gone down there. There was nowhere else for him to go.

As Nok climbed down after him, she tried to steady her nerves.

You can do this, she told herself. *You've taken down much bigger boys than him before.*

Nok dropped onto the dusty floor of the cave and quickly took up her defense posture. Her eyes flicked side to side, taking in her surroundings.

She stood inside a huge limestone room with a high ceiling. An enormous stone statue of the Buddha sat cross-legged and serene near one wall of the cave. If Nok hadn't been on her guard, she would have bowed in reverence. It was a breathtaking statue, carved in the old style by people who had lived here before the village, maybe even before the temple. Above the Buddha's head, a wide hole in the cave's ceiling opened to the sky.

Nok suddenly realized where she was. This was the famous Tanaburi Cavern. The mouth of the cave opened out above the river. At noon, sunlight would pour in through the hole and make the Buddha statue appear to glow. It was past noon now, almost two o'clock, so the statue was already in shadow.

Nok tore her eyes away from the statue and looked to the mouth of the cave. A boy's form stood silhouetted with the blue sky behind him.

"Stop right there," called Nok, her voice startling her as it rang off the limestone. She held her staff in front of her and took slow steps forward.

Pong backed away, toward the cave mouth. He held his shoulders hunched forward and his hands out in front of him. He looked scared.

He should be. The drop down to the river below was more than fifty yards. There was nowhere for him to run.

With a little leap in her stomach, Nok realized she truly had him caught.

"Stay where you are," she said, more confident now. "If you come peacefully, you won't be hurt."

"Back to the temple?" asked Pong. "Why? So you can put me in handcuffs?"

Nok straightened her staff in front of her. "Only if necessary."

Pong took another step back. "And then you'd take me back to Namwon, wouldn't you?"

Nok advanced slowly, confidently. Even though she was smaller than Pong, she felt like a giant. It was a rush, this feeling of being the bearer of justice. She wished that her parents were there to see her.

"Not Namwon," she said. "You're too old to go back there now. You'll have a trial, and afterward they'll send you to the men's prison. To Banglad."

Pong shuddered. Suddenly, he leaped forward, trying to run past her. But Nok was too fast. She swung her staff down in front of him. It whistled, a pale blur, and then hit the stone with a loud *crack*, blocking his way. Flecks of loose limestone crumbled off the cave ceiling and rained onto her shoulders. She spun her staff again, forcing him back toward the ledge. As a girl, she wasn't supposed to touch a monk, much less attack one. But Pong was a fake. The rules didn't apply to him. Nok was prepared to do what she had to, even if it meant wrestling him to the ground.

Pong's eyes flickered wildly. "I'm not going to Banglad," he said, panting. "I'm not going to any prison. I don't belong there. I didn't do anything wrong."

"You escaped," said Nok, holding her staff steady. "You broke the law."

"A law that says kids have to live in a jail? You'd blame me for breaking a law like that?"

"Do you realize that if you would've just stayed where you were, you'd be released by now?" she said. "You'd be free if you'd just followed the rules."

"The rules are stupid!" Pong cried, so loud that it made Nok take a step back. "And unfair!"

"Call them whatever you want," said Nok, steadying her feet and her voice. "You still have to follow them. Otherwise, what good are they?"

Pong was breathing hard. His head was bent and his shoulders curled in, as if he'd already been put in handcuffs. He looked at her from under his hairless brows. "That's so easy for someone like you to say."

Nok narrowed her eyes. "What's that supposed to mean?"

"It's easy for you to follow the law," said Pong flatly. "It was written for people like you. For families like yours."

"How dare you talk about my family!" Heat rushed to her temples. Her voice was rising, too. She sounded out of control and she didn't like it. She tried to calm herself, but the words tumbled out of her mouth too fast. "Yes, we follow the law, because that's what good people do. Good people obey the rules, and if they don't, they accept their punishment. You don't get to break the law just because you think it's not fair. You don't get to just decide for yourself what's right and what's wrong!"

"Then who does?"

It was a stupid question, a question for a classroom or a philosophy discussion, not a question to be asked in the middle of an arrest. But Nok didn't have an answer for it. Her tongue pressed against the roof of her mouth while it waited for her brain to come up with words.

Behind her, in the woods above the cave, she heard voices and the sound of people crashing through the brush outside the sinkhole.

She exhaled and held her staff steady. "Give yourself up peacefully," she said, her voice calm once more.

Pong stood in a half crouch, his knees bent, like an animal ready to spring at her. Nok raised her staff. She let the nervous energy inside her pool into a ball, but then she paused. If she struck the ground with her staff, she might damage the statue. She might even cause the ceiling to cave in.

"Give yourself up," she repeated. "And you won't be harmed."

She heard familiar voices behind her.

"Nok!" called her father. She turned her head to see

him climbing down the opening at the back of the cave, with villagers following behind.

"I'm here, Father!" She smiled, relieved to see him, proud that he was seeing her like this. "I've got him!"

Nok turned back to Pong just in time to see him leap off the edge.

Chapter 17

A far drop, farther than it looked from the top.

A hard smack, harder than you'd think water could feel.

A bubble of air, trapped by monks' robes, lifesaving, but disappearing fast.

Desperate treading, gurgling, clawing for the surface.

A barge, right on time, swinging its back end wide, near enough to throw up waves, but too far to reach.

A crusted rope, stained green from months of trailing off the barge's hull, forgotten.

Frantic grasping. Catching! And then climbing, hand over hand, lungs on fire.

Grateful breathing. Weakly clinging to fraying nets.

Hopes sinking, like the waterlogged gold-brown robes.

This barge is the wrong barge.

This barge is not bound south, for the sea.

This barge is headed north, back to Chattana.

Chapter 18

As soon as Nok's eyes opened that morning, she knew her father wasn't there. He woke early, as she did, and she'd become used to hearing his shuffle across the wood floors, the sound of his pen scratching across paper, and his regular cough, kept soft as he tried not to wake her mother.

Nok lay on her pallet for a long while, looking up at the ceiling while the sunlight warmed the room.

She usually woke earlier than this, but it had been a late night. By the time she and her father and a group of villagers got down to the water, the sun had already begun setting behind the mountain. They found Pong's robes floating near the shore, but no body. She'd stayed up with her father, watching the villagers drag the river with nets and bamboo poles.

Mrs. Viboon had stood with them, sobbing. "He can't swim! Oh, why, why didn't we teach him to swim?"

Nok kept her distance so no one could see her scowling. She liked Mrs. Viboon, but she wished the woman would hush up. The more she wailed about Pong drowning, the less likely the villagers would listen to Nok and start searching the riverbanks.

"There's no point," said Mr. Viboon, holding an empty net and nearly in tears himself. "We won't find him there or anywhere else. He's gone."

Nok's father looked into the dark jungle lining the shore and nodded. "There were boats in the water when the boy jumped, weren't there?"

Mrs. Viboon wailed again.

"It's most likely that he was run over by the barge, sir," said Mr. Viboon. "The robes we found were shredded. Trapped under a big boat like that? No one would survive."

Nok was so frustrated. Why couldn't anyone else think it possible that a boy who had tricked everyone around him his whole life was tricking them all at this moment? She didn't know what was worse — that no one would listen to her, or that the entire village was racked with grief over a criminal's supposed death.

Nok was angry at everyone and everything, but mostly she was angry at herself. She had been so close to catching Pong, and she'd failed.

She slipped out of bed and went to her window. A servant was sweeping the empty driveway with a frayed broom. The carriage was gone. Nok wondered if her mother was gone, too.

She walked to the dresser. Her mother had packed her a dress, the way she always did, even though she knew by now that Nok would never wear it. As she reached out for the dark fabric of her spire-fighting uniform, the sunlight fell across the scar on her arm.

Nok traced her fingers over the puckered skin that ran from the base of her palm almost to her elbow. She knew the scars so well. If they suddenly rose up into a terrain full of valleys and peaks, she would be able to travel them blindfolded.

She had been only three at the time of the accident. She didn't remember getting hurt, but she did remember being tended to afterward. It had been late at night. She recalled the crush of servants around her, fussing over her, and her father's voice shouting for the doctor.

"Come quick! She's in here!" And then his face, leaning close to her, his smile masking his worry. "It's all right, Nok. You're very brave. You're such a tough girl."

She knew she must have been crying. What three-year-old wouldn't cry after getting burned? But when she thought back on that night, she couldn't remember making any sound. She could only remember the people crowded around, telling her how tough and how brave she was.

Most of all, she remembered her mother holding her close and sobbing. She could feel her mother's tears wetting her own hair. She could smell her mother's perfume, the scent of tuberoses that followed her still wherever she went.

"I'm so sorry," her mother had wailed. "Oh, I'm so sorry. So sorry. Nok, baby, sweet baby, I'm so sorry."

Nok's mother's maid rubbed her back. "An accident, ma'am," she kept repeating. "It was an accident. You aren't to blame."

The doctor had rushed in, wearing pajamas under his coat. "Tell me what happened," he said, kneeling in front of them as he opened his bag.

Nok remembered glimpsing her mother's dressing table through a gap between the servants' bodies. A shiny jar of some sort of medicinal cream lay on its side, the lid on the floor. The candle on the dressing table had been blown out already, but its wick still smoked. Her big brother stood in the doorway to the room, wide-eyed and scared.

Her parents looked at each other, but it was the maid who answered the doctor's question. "The baby was playing with her mother's creams. She got some on her arm, and when she got near the candle, it caught her."

The doctor sighed. All the wealthy West Side women kept secret candles to burn for good luck, even though it was against the law. But he made no judgment. He couldn't very well scold one of his best clients.

"I'm so sorry!" her mother wailed.

"Hush, ma'am," said the maid, almost sternly. "It was an accident."

Nok traced her fingers over her scars again. No one in the family talked about that night. Even though the doctor kept their secret, fire was still forbidden. It wasn't worth talking about such things and getting the whole family in trouble. Best to forget about it entirely.

Normally, Nok would have been happy to do just that. She would much rather think about the future and leave the past behind. But this was one memory she wanted to hold on to: no pain, just her mother holding her close, rocking her back and forth, and the smell of her perfume in her hair.

The memory faded as Nok pulled on her uniform. The long sleeves slid down over her arms, all the way to the wrists.

* * *

Downstairs, she was surprised to find her mother awake in the sitting room, her hands folded over her lap, looking out the window. She glanced at Nok when she heard her come in, then turned her face back to the glass. In the harsh light of the morning, her cream-colored powder looked caked and dry.

"Everyone says the country is so quiet," said her mother, "but these birds are deafening. What can they be saying to each other?"

Nok walked farther into the sitting room and took a seat across from her mother. "Where did Father go?"

"The carriage took him down to the pier early this morning. He ordered a fast boat back to Chattana. I'll go on a slower barge later this afternoon."

Nok noticed there was no mention of her. She looked at her mother and waited.

When her mother turned her face, it was set as though she'd been sitting at the window composing what to say and how she'd look when she said it. She glanced down at Nok's arm and sagged. Her face softened and she sighed, and Nok could tell that the words that came next weren't the ones her mother had practiced.

"Nok, your father and I have been talking, and we think it could be good for you to stay here in Tanaburi for the rest of the school year."

Even though Nok had known this was coming, she still felt the words like a punch.

Her mother shifted in her chair. "Tanaburi is close enough to the city that we can come visit easily. And I went to the village school yesterday and met the teachers. It's actually very impressive. You'll have a good education here."

"I'm already getting a good education in Chattana," said Nok, finding her voice again.

"The countryside is healthier for children," replied her mother. "The city is too harsh a place to live."

Nok kept her voice calm. "It isn't harsh for me, Mother. I like it there."

"You don't know how hard it can be because you've been sheltered. But soon you'll see. The way gossip runs wild in the city. It can cut worse than a knife."

"I don't care about gossip," said Nok.

Her mother shook her head. "You will if —"

Nok held her breath, waiting for her mother to finally say it out loud: *If people find out you are not mine. You are an embarrassment to this family.*

Instead her mother cleared her throat and straightened the rings on her fingers. "You'll understand when you're older."

Now it was Nok's turn to forget the words she'd

practiced. She had made the case to her mother in her head, over and over again. She'd wanted to be very grown up and logical, but she couldn't stop her voice from sounding whiny and childish.

"I'm not trying to have that kind of life, Mama. The kind where it matters what people say about you. I don't want to be in society and do things like go to parties. I want to join the police. No one cares about the police enough to gossip about them."

Nok's mother looked out the window again. It was a look that said Nok didn't know what she was talking about.

"I've researched everything," Nok added. "About what it takes to join the police force. Anyone can do it as long as they pass the exams and the physical tests. You can try out when you turn eighteen. Just let me try. If I fail, then I'll come back here and stay in the country, like you want."

Nok's mother sighed again. She seemed to be considering.

Nok pressed her case. "I know I'll make it. And Father could get a recommendation letter from the Governor himself."

"The Governor?" said Nok's mother, whirling to face her. "Do you know why your father has left so suddenly?

I made him go. I wanted him to explain the situation before the Governor gets wind of it. Do you know how all of this looks? Before, it seemed that your father merely lost a boy under his care. Now it's clear the boy escaped! And not only that, but he fooled a monk and was hiding right under your father's nose. Escaped — twice! Even if they can prove the boy drowned, this whole thing has made our family look like incompetent fools!"

Nok sat frozen, stung by the words. She didn't know which hurt worse: the accusation that she'd brought shame on her family or the way her mother kept saying "your father," making it sound as though they were a duo, separate from the rest of the Sivapans.

Her mother stood up in front of Nok. "You are going to stay here and go to the country school. This is the right place for you. It's a good village full of good people."

"But, Mother . . ."

"I don't want to hear a word about it! You will respect our wishes as your parents." She took Nok's hand and pulled her up to stand. She looked down at her daughter's arm, covered by the sleeve of the spire-fighting uniform. Suddenly, she hugged Nok close.

"I know this isn't what you think you want," she whispered. Nok was surprised to hear her voice quiver. "But sometimes life doesn't give us what we want. We don't get to do everything we wish, and we have to deal with what we're given in the best way we can. I know you're angry. But you'll forgive me one day. It's amazing what the heart is able to forgive." She pulled away and cupped Nok's face in her smooth hands. "I love you. Don't ever forget that."

And with that, she walked out of the room.

Chapter 19

Police Officer Manit took deep breaths and rolled his shoulders back, trying to wake himself up.

I'm getting too old for the night shift, he told himself as he strode down the walkway along the shore. The Gold lights of Chattana's West Side twinkled across the river. Manit thought about the officers assigned to that side of the city. Talk about a cushy job. An officer could walk around with their eyes shut over there and never miss a thing. Not like here, where the streets were getting more crowded and rougher all the time.

Manit passed the piers where the big fishing boats docked under hazy Amber orbs. As he walked on, the Crimson and Amber lights gave way to Blue, and then to Violet. The loud *vrumm!* of orb motors faded, replaced by the splashes of bodies diving into the river. Dozens of people, many of them children, treaded water, checking crab traps and hoisting river prawns up to their parents and friends, who waited up top with buckets.

Night fishers.

There were so many more of them now than there had been years ago, when he started this patrol. For Manit, it was a hard thing to watch. Most of the parents had once been fishermen — not crabbing around the docks but out on the river, with boats and nets of their own. But the big fishing trawlers, with their fancy, fast motors, had put them out of work. To compete with the big boats, you needed a big motor and an orb to go with it. To get orbs, you needed money. To make money, you had to have a fast boat, and so on and so on. No wonder he saw so many doing the dangerous work of swimming in the churning water of the river at night.

Manit turned away from the Violet-lit shoreline and headed up a dark canal. After a few minutes of searching, he found a familiar figure leaning over the edge, staring down into the black water below.

Now he remembered why he kept turning down that cushy West Side job. There were people here that mattered to him, people who deserved someone to look out for them.

Somkit was one of those people.

Manit slowed his steps and checked his pockets for

change. He always tried to give Somkit some money if he could. He had no idea how the kid survived. Where did he sleep? What did he eat?

Despite his plump cheeks, Somkit was spindly as a stick bug — that never helped when you were living on the streets. And he had trouble breathing, which was why he couldn't hold his own night fishing with the others on the better section of the river. Manit always found him setting his traps in these stagnant back canals. Poor kid. On top of that, he was a Namwon orphan. Most of the time, those kids ended up right back in jail.

Well, that wouldn't happen to Somkit. Not if Manit could help it.

"Hey, Somkit!" he called. "Just the guy I needed to find tonight."

The boy jerked up his head. When he saw Manit, a look of panic flashed over his face. He quickly pushed something — a crab trap, perhaps? — down under the water.

"Oh, uh, Officer Manit! I, uh . . ."

Manit worried for a second that something was wrong. "You okay, kid? You look like you just saw a ghost."

Somkit smiled his easygoing smile. He waved the fingers of one hand, gripping tightly to the rope of his crab trap with the other. "Me? Oh, yeah, totally fine! Living the dream, as usual."

Manit smiled. "Good. So, listen, I need some advice. The motor on my boat chugs when it starts. Sounds like it's going to rattle into pieces."

"Hmm . . . you've got a good connection between the orb and the motor? Because if the connection's bad, it can —"

Something gurgled and sputtered in the water below. Manit leaned over the edge of the jetty and saw a boy's face come up to the surface for air. "Who's that?" he asked, pointing to the water.

"Oh, him? That's just my cousin," said Somkit.

Cousin. So that's how Somkit made do. He must have family in the city who'd taken him in after he got out of Namwon.

Officer Manit started to ask the cousin what his name was, but before he could say anything, Somkit leaned over the water. "You find any crabs?" he shouted to the kid.

The boy gasped for air, clutching onto the rope of the crab basket. "What? No. I — I can't brea —"

"Well, try again!" yelled Somkit. "You think they're just gonna jump into your hands? You gotta catch 'em!"

Somkit reached down and pushed his cousin's head, sending him back underwater.

Somkit shook his head at Officer Manit. "He's lazy. I'd do it myself, but the guy's gotta learn somehow. So, anyway, make sure the motor connection is clean. If that's not the problem, it could be you just need a new starter . . ."

The cousin reemerged at the surface and took a big gulp of air. He managed two more gasping breaths before Somkit shoved him back underwater.

"You can get a starter for cheap at the Light Market, bottom level," continued Somkit. "If you tell them I sent you, they'll give you the wholesale price."

"Hey, that's just what I needed to know," said Manit. "Here, this is for you." He held out the coins from his pocket.

"Oh, nah," said Somkit. "You don't need to do that . . ."

"Go on, take it," pressed Manit. "You just saved me a bunch of time and money. This is the least I owe you."

Somkit bowed his thanks and took the money. The good-for-nothing cousin came up for air, empty-handed again. Somkit rolled his eyes. "I'll be needing this money if my lazy cousin keeps coming up with no crabs!" He reached down and shook his fist at the boy in the water before pushing him under again. "Get back there and don't come up again unless you've got a crab in each hand!"

Manit laughed and turned to go. "You tell him, Somkit. I've got to finish my rounds." He called over his shoulder, "Hey, you and your cousin watch out for yourselves, okay? We just got word at the police station that there's a dangerous criminal on the streets. He's a runaway from prison, and he was hiding out in a temple down south. You see any weird people around, you let me know, okay?"

Somkit nodded gravely. "Sir, if I see anything out of the ordinary, you'll be the first to know."

Chapter 20

In the hours after Pong leaped from the cliff at Nok's feet, he had clung to the cargo barge as it puttered slowly upriver, making stop after stop at every tiny village dock. Even if Pong had known how to swim, he had been too terrified to make a break for the shore in the daylight. He had nestled deeper into the nets hanging from the boat's hull and waited.

Night fell. The barge glided past a tall tower that beamed blinking Gold light into the dark — the first orb light Pong had seen in years. The river widened, and then he caught sight of what he thought were the rays of daybreak.

Chattana.

The city was even brighter than he remembered. This time, though, the sight of the lights filled him with terror, not wonder. He kept seeing Nok's furious face. Her words drummed in his brain: *You'll go straight to Banglad.*

They echoed the words that had haunted him for four years: *Those who are born in darkness always return.*

Pong shuddered. The only thing that gave him any hope at all was touching the red braided bracelet. Surely this was just a little detour. He would find the sea and his freedom. He had to — Father Cham had wished it.

Finally, the barge docked at Chattana to unload. Before anyone could see him, Pong swung himself under the planks of the pier. He spent the next few hours under the loading dock, dodging the fish blood and shark guts that dribbled down through the cracks and trying desperately to come up with a plan for hitching a ride on a boat heading south to the sea. He was starving. Worse, he was freezing. Even the warm, soupy water of the Chattana River would make a person cold if he was in it too long. Pong's fingers had shriveled like dried plums. He had to get out of the water.

But by then, the river was full of swimmers. He heard boys' voices and the splashes of them diving in and popping back to the surface again. The shore teemed with their families. There were too many people for Pong to get out where he was.

Teeth chattering, he crawled out from under the dock. Using the old tires and slimy ropes hanging off the shore, he pulled himself along, keeping in the shadows as much as he could, until he came to a narrow canal that branched off the main river. It was dark back there. Maybe if he went that way, he could climb out without being seen. But he was so weak, and the sides of the canal were so slippery. A wave of desperation washed over him.

"H-h-h-help ... p-p-p-please ..." he called feebly, not caring who heard him now.

"Over here!" called a voice from above. "There's a rope there, near you! Grab on!"

Pong's fingers found the rope. He clung to it and looked up.

A face wide and round like the moon gaped down at him. It was a face Pong never thought he would see again. It filled him with an indescribable joy.

And then it reached a hand down and shoved him under the water.

After the police officer left, Somkit hauled Pong up onto the dock beside him. It was an awkward maneuver, with lots of grunting, and Pong nearly pulled Somkit over the side. Finally, Pong knelt on the slippery wood boards, heaving and shaking. Somkit draped a thin towel over his shoulders.

"All right, I think Manit's gone," whispered Somkit,

looking over his shoulder. "Man, that was close. Sorry about pushing you underwater so many times! I just didn't want him to see you. Thank goodness it was Manit and not —"

Somkit turned back to Pong, startled all over again, as if he were fully realizing who Pong was for the first time. He placed his hands on the sides of Pong's chattering jaw and turned his face one way and then the other, as though he weren't quite convinced the face really belonged to his old friend. He let go and smiled the same wide smile that Pong remembered. "Man, when you popped up out of the water like that, I was sure you were a ghost!"

Pong tried to smile back at his rescuer, but his teeth were chattering so hard that it made his entire skull shake. "I — I — s-s-so c-c-c-cold," he stammered.

Somkit's smile faded as he eyed the fuzz of Pong's shaved head. "We've gotta get you out of here. We can wrap this towel around your head, and — whoa, I did not need to see that!"

Pong was nearly naked, wearing only the thin cotton underwear from the temple, which was almost transparent when it got wet.

"Uh, okay, it's all right," said Somkit, averting his eyes as he wound the towel around Pong's head like a turban.

"Just carry the crab trap over your — you know — your stuff, and if anyone asks, we'll say your clothes floated away in the river."

Pong followed after Somkit in a daze, holding the crab trap over his groin, trying to keep the crabs from pinching his underwear, as they made their way through the busiest, brightest part of the city.

Chattana had more canals than streets, and in a few months, when monsoon season hit, it would have hardly any streets at all. Most people got around on boats that traveled the canal system, winding through the different neighborhoods, out to the main flow of the river, and back into the city again. Those on foot squeezed onto the narrow wooden gangways that hung suspended over the water on either side or the skinny alleys that crisscrossed the tracts of land between canals. Tall apartments rose overhead, their open windows overflowing with orchid plants, laundry, and chatting neighbors.

People pressed against Pong on all sides, hurrying in both directions. He did his best to keep up with Somkit. At least having to hustle was helping Pong to warm up — that, and all the lights.

After years of living in the quiet solitude of the mountain, Pong had forgotten what it was like to see the artificial light of the orbs, hear their buzz, and smell their metallic tang. And here in the city, there were thousands — no, millions — of them. Even though the rains were weeks away, that many orbs made the air feel thick and pressurized, the way it does before a thunderstorm breaks.

The boys dove into the rowdy throng of the entertainment district. Pong had never felt more exposed in his life, but there were so many people and so many distractions that nobody gave him a second look. Somkit pressed farther into the city's belly. Away from the clubs' thumping drumbeats, the alleys became more dingy, with fewer orbs.

They crossed a bridge filled with people sitting on the ground, holding up signs and open palms. It took Pong a moment to realize they were begging. He stared, shocked at how many outstretched hands reached toward him. Beggars had come to Wat Singh, but never as many as this. Pong had never seen so many needy people gathered together.

Somkit reached into his pocket and pulled out the handful of coins that Manit had given him. He dropped them into a woman's tin cup. "Come on," he whispered to Pong as he pulled him over the bridge. "And try not to look like such a country bumpkin, okay?"

Somkit swerved suddenly to the left and led Pong

down a dimly lit alley. Strands of tiny Violet orbs swayed overhead, strung between the rickety buildings.

"Where are we going?" asked Pong.

"Shh," said Somkit. "Whatever I do, just go along with it."

At the end of the alley, a faded cloth banner swung over an open doorway. The banner had the image of a fish printed on it and said MARK'S SEAFOOD EATS.

The banner swished aside and a short man with glasses emerged wearing a grumpy scowl. "It's about time you showed up, Somkit!" he shouted. "But where's your haul? Don't tell me you're coming empty-handed and expecting to be paid again."

"Calm down, Mark, calm down," said Somkit, nodding behind him. "My cousin's got a full crab trap. And we need full bellies to go with it."

Somkit leaned in close to Mark and whispered something to him quickly. Mark glanced at Pong and his eyebrows shot up. He nodded, then reformed the scowl. "Yeah, yeah, I remember your cousin," he shouted. "All right, take the crabs to the kitchen. Make a plate and then go. And no refills! Got it?"

"We got it," said Somkit. "Come on, cousin."

Pong followed Somkit into the restaurant. He patted the towel tighter on his head and tried his best to shield his half-naked body from the customers. Mark followed them inside and said in a loud, grouchy voice, "Kids these days got no manners. Showing up wet, with no clothes, expecting a meal."

The diners in the packed restaurant had their heads bowed over their plates, spooning curried crab into their mouths or slurping fat, jiggly oysters out of their shells. Pong's mouth watered. He hoped that they were about to eat.

Somkit ducked into a kitchen full of steam and smoke. The cooks leaning over Crimson orb burners stopped their work for a minute to nod a hello to him and looked curiously at Pong.

"It's okay. He's cool," Somkit said to the cooks, who went back to their chopping and sizzling. "You can put the crabs there," he said, pointing to the corner and motioning for Pong to follow. They ducked under a curtained door, into a green-tiled bathroom.

"Come on, behind here," whispered Somkit. He slid a stack of fish-sauce crates to the side, revealing a hidden passage.

"But that guy Mark said we were supposed to make a plate and go," said Pong.

"Nah, that was all just for show. You go in. I'll close this back up after."

Pong stepped inside the dark passageway. He heard Somkit behind him, sliding the crates back into place.

"We'll get you something to eat," said Somkit. "But first we gotta get you clothes. I'm tired of looking at your butt crack, okay?"

Pong followed Somkit down the dark hall. Gradually, the darkness gave way to a lavender twinkling light.

"My friend," said Somkit, slapping Pong on the shoulder, "welcome to the Mud House, the finest burned-out tenement building in the whole city."

Chapter 21

P ong and Somkit stood in the atrium of a cavernous building. The house's wooden walls and floor were as dark and slick as the inside of a turtle's den. Strands of Violet orbs swung overhead. Pong counted six stories, each one open to the central hall on the ground floor.

"Somebody here told me this used to be a government building, where the old Governor worked," said Somkit. "You know. Before the Fire."

Pong nodded as he looked around. That would explain the blackened color and the building's strange layout. Each floor was ringed with rooms that must have once been offices. The Great Fire had burned away the entrances to each room, leaving behind a warren of square cubbies.

Just like the rest of Chattana, the Mud House was packed with people. They leaned over the railings on every floor, chatting to their neighbors or hanging laundry up on lines strung between the orb lights. Children played games on the stairs. On the ground floor, people sat at rows of long tables, eating or studying together over stacks of books.

Pong could smell the sizzle of food cooking back in Mark's restaurant. His empty stomach gurgled.

"Clothes first," said Somkit, reading his mind. "My room's this way."

Pong followed him up the stairs to the third floor, stepping around children who giggled and pointed at his butt. Somkit drew back the curtain of one of the cubby rooms.

"Welcome to my humble castle! Make yourself at home."

Pong stepped into a room not much bigger than his tiny one back at the temple. There was a mat and a pillow in one corner and a shelf along one wall covered in coils of wire, tin snips, pliers, and little glass jars filled with sorted pieces of metal.

"Go on, take a seat," said Somkit, motioning to the mat. He turned his back to Pong and started rifling through a pile of clothes. "No . . . no, too short . . ." he said, holding up a pair of pants. "Why'd you have to get so tall? We used to be the same size!"

"We were never the same size," said Pong. "I was always bigger than you."

"Had a bigger mouth, you mean," said Somkit. He turned and grinned, tossing the rumpled clothes to Pong. "Here. These should fit. The pants'll be too short, but we'll find you some better ones tomorrow."

Pong slipped on the shirt and pulled on the baggy pants over his now-dried underwear. The shirt showed his belly button, and the pants bulged around his hips and barely covered his knees. "How do I look?" he asked.

"Completely ridiculous."

They both laughed, and for a moment it felt as if it had been only four hours, not four years, since they'd last seen each other.

Somkit seemed the same, but also different. He was still scrawny for his age, and his cheeks were still round and chubby, just like Pong remembered from Namwon, but there was something unfamiliar in Somkit's eyes. He looked back at Pong with a sadness that didn't match his happy-go-lucky grin.

Somkit ran his hand over his hair, and Pong noticed his friend's tattoo. It had a bright-blue line running through the letters and a tiny star — the mark of someone who has been officially released.

Not a day had passed at the temple that Pong hadn't prayed for his friend and wished he could know what he was doing. What had it been like after Pong left Namwon? How had Somkit managed? And what did it feel like on the day they opened the gates and let him go free?

Now here was Pong's chance to ask his many questions, but he couldn't speak. He looked down at the floor, guilt twisting its way between his ribs. He'd left Somkit behind. What kind of a friend does that?

The room felt stuffy, the way it does when people go too long without saying anything. And Somkit rarely went for long without saying anything.

He slapped his belly. "Well, I'm starved. And if I'm hungry, you must be double hungry. Let's go down and eat."

By the time the boys got downstairs, most of the people sitting in the atrium had cleared away. Somkit went back into Mark's kitchen and came out with dishes of fish meatball soup and fried eggs and scallions over rice.

Pong inhaled almost his entire meal before he stopped and held one hand over his mouth.

"What's wrong?" asked Somkit.

Pong choked down his bite. "I'm not supposed to eat anything until sunrise," he croaked.

Somkit looked again at Pong's shaved scalp. "A dangerous criminal hiding out in a temple. I don't guess that has anything to do with you?"

"I can explain . . ." started Pong.

The weight of his situation fell on him hard. He thought of Father Cham, by now gone from this life, and the temple that he'd never see again. He thought of Nok, her piercing blackbird eyes and the vengeful way she'd looked at him before he leaped from the cliff into the water.

"Oh, Somkit," he whispered. "I am in so, so much trouble."

Somkit looked at him. He reached for the jar of dried pepper flakes and sprinkled some into his bowl, then Pong's.

"Trust me," he said. "You're safe here. This is the one place in the city where *that*"—he eyed Pong's left wrist—"doesn't matter. No one here is going to turn you in. And no one from the outside is ever going to find you, either."

Somkit picked a meatball out of his soup with his chopsticks and held it up to Pong. "Go on, you better take it. If you wait till sunrise to eat it, it's going to smell super bad."

Pong smiled and took the meatball with his own chopsticks. He turned back to his soup bowl and shut his eyes, willing himself to feel as light as the steam rising into his face.

You're safe here. No one is ever going to find you.

Chapter 22

Nok swung the cottage gate shut behind her. She had her suitcase in one hand and her bamboo staff in the other. It was a four-mile walk up through the village and down the other side of the mountain to the school. She had told Mrs. Viboon to go home after her mother had left the day before. The poor woman was still so distraught over Pong that she didn't do much besides weep, anyway. That left no one for Nok to say goodbye to.

She had just set foot on the path when an oxcart appeared, slowly rounding the corner. A thin-faced monk sat behind the brown ox. Nok tried to remember his name. Was it Brother Yam?

She bowed and he smiled at her. His face was drawn and tired. With a pang of sadness, Nok remembered that Father Cham had passed away the night Pong disappeared. She'd never had the chance to see him again. She told the monk how sorry she was to hear the news.

"Thank you," said Brother Yam. "I'm going to the village at the bottom of our mountain to let them know about the funeral and to bring up the elderly who can't make the trek. Everyone loved Father Cham." He smiled sadly. "And your parents? Are they gone?"

"Yes, my father had to hurry back to the city for . . . for work. Otherwise, I know they'd go to the funeral and pay their respects."

"I know this hasn't been the peaceful visit you likely imagined," said Brother Yam. "I hope your family will come to visit us again and make happier memories. Can I give you a ride to the dock?"

Nok blinked at him. "A — a ride?"

He looked behind him at the dusty cart. "It won't be anywhere near the style you're used to riding in, I'm afraid."

Suddenly, Nok realized that Brother Yam didn't know that she wasn't supposed to go back to Chattana with her parents. In fact, other than the headmistress, no one else in the village knew she was expected at the school.

Nok had never told a lie in her life. Oh, maybe she'd lied as a little girl about going to sleep on time, or to get a second helping of dessert, small things like that, but not since she'd gotten older, and never about anything that mattered. She had certainly never, ever even considered lying to a monk.

She thought about Pong. He was alive; she knew it. She could feel it in her bones that he had escaped. And if she could prove it — if she could catch him this time — it would more than make up for the failure of letting him go. It would save her family's reputation and convince her parents that they didn't have to be ashamed of her. Nok looked down the mountain road. If she were a fugitive, trying to disappear from the eyes of the law, there was one place she'd go. There was one place in the entire province where you could fade away without anyone asking questions.

"Thank you, Brother Yam," she said, swinging her suitcase into the back of the cart. "I think I'll take you up on your offer. And I don't mind riding in the back."

"Wonderful," said Brother Yam, snapping the ox's reins. "Let's get you to Chattana."

Chapter 23

L ast one in the door is the first one to clean the toilet," said the old woman, handing Pong a mop and bucket with a smile that was more gold than teeth.

"He just got here, and you're going to make him scrub the bathroom?" said Somkit. He hooked an arm around the woman's shoulders. "Please, Auntie Mims, can't we give the poor kid a break? I just fished him out of the river a couple of days ago!"

"It's okay," said Pong, bowing to the old woman. "I don't mind. I've cleaned toilets before. Everyone's got to do their part."

Just as he'd done when he arrived at the temple, Pong had fallen into the daily rhythm of the Mud House. With so many people living under one roof, there was a lot of work to do, and Pong was kept busy cleaning or helping to prep food in Mark's kitchen. Pong didn't know if Mark ever slept. The man ran his own restaurant and kept all the residents fed. Technically, no one was supposed to be living in the building, so the restaurant served as the perfect cover-up for all the people coming and going.

Some of the grown-ups who lived there worked in Mark's kitchens, but most of them had one or two jobs in the city. They'd leave early in the morning and come home late, looking wilted and tired. Children and sick family members stayed behind, trying to find ways to stay busy. This section of town had no schools, so Pong often found himself playing tutor to the Mud House children.

There were so many of them, these families with nowhere else to go. Pong would look at the kids playing on the stairs and sometimes think about Tanaburi Village School, and about the basket babies whose families must not have had a place like this to turn to.

He knew everyone in the house must have a story, but he never asked, because he didn't want any questions coming back at him. After almost a week of living there, he realized he had nothing to worry about. No one ever asked him where he came from or tried to figure out anything about his past.

"It's Ampai's rule," explained Somkit. He'd already told Pong about Ampai, the leader of the Mud House, but Pong had yet to meet her. "No questions asked. Everyone comes in the door with a clean slate."

"Everyone? Even a murderer?"

Somkit rolled his eyes. "Ampai wouldn't let someone like that in here. She knows how to tell good people from bad."

"She doesn't know me yet," said Pong.

Somkit elbowed him in the arm. "She's going to love you because you're my friend and she loves me." He lowered his voice a little. "And like I told you: she'll be able to get you on a boat. As soon as she comes back, it's the first thing I'll ask her. Promise."

After that first night, Pong had told Somkit his entire story over a bowl of lychees. He told him everything about Tanaburi, and Father Cham, and Nok, and the cliff. And because Somkit was Somkit, as soon as the story was over, he'd popped a lychee into his mouth and said, "Man, we gotta get you on a boat."

So Pong was willing to wait until the mysterious Ampai returned. She'd be his ticket south. His ticket to freedom.

In the meantime, he mopped the bathrooms while Somkit sat nearby, jabbering away.

"All right, what gives?" asked Pong one hot afternoon. He leaned against the mop handle and wiped the sweat from his forehead. "How come everyone around here works except you?"

Somkit smiled and raised his eyebrows. "Oh, but I do."

"Yapping your mouth all day doesn't count as work."

Somkit hopped off the edge of the table he'd been sitting on. "Friend, I keep this place buzzing." He pointed overhead to the purple lights that swung from the balcony railings.

"What do you mean?" asked Pong.

Somkit's eyes twinkled, and Pong knew he'd been waiting to be asked. "Follow me, good sir, and I shall show you."

Pong set his mop aside and followed Somkit up the stairs to the top floor. Somkit slid open a paper-paneled door and climbed another narrow flight of dusty steps. At the top, he rested a long time, catching his breath before pushing back a rippled metal hatch. Sunlight flooded the stairway. He popped his head out for a minute, then looked back down to Pong.

"We're all good," he said. "You can come on up."

Pong followed Somkit onto the roof, blinking against the blinding light. A flock of pigeons startled and took off, swooping over their heads in a wide circle before landing back in the same spot again.

Pong walked slowly across the tar rooftop. "Whoa, this is unbelievable."

From where they stood, he could see most of the East Side, a patchwork of sheet-metal roofs of different shades of rusted brown, silver, and black. Past the edges of the buildings, the gray-green river snaked north to south, dotted with boats zipping up and down the invisible lanes of traffic.

"Okay, that's enough sightseeing, buddy," said Somkit, pulling Pong's sleeve. "It's pretty safe up here, but until your hair grows out a little more, we should still try to keep you out of sight. Come on, I'll show you my workshop."

"*Your* workshop? Up here?"

"Don't be so impressed. It's nothing fancy, more like a cramped closet than anything else."

Somkit led Pong to a narrow structure that looked like a garden shed at the far end of the roof and swung open the door. Cramped closet was right. The little shed was lined to the ceiling with shelves full of nuts and bolts, wires, tools, jars filled with shards of glass and broken bits of sheet metal. A wood slab of a desk was also covered in the same array of junk.

"Hot in here," said Somkit, reaching up to slide open a window. "That's better. I mostly come up here in the early mornings. By noon the place is hotter than a rice cooker and I can barely breathe."

Pong leaned over the desk and tried to make some sense of what he was looking at. He thought back to their days at Namwon, when Somkit would hoard any little bits and bobs they could fish out of the river through the prison gate. He was always keeping his eyes out for scrap metal and saving things like nails and screws. Back then, they never had tools to do anything with Somkit's stash, but now it seemed like his friend had enough supplies to fill a hardware store.

Pong picked up a strand of small orbs, the same kind that hung from the rafters inside. Each glass ball was cradled in a cone of tinfoil. "You said you keep the Mud House buzzing," said Pong. "You mean you keep all the orbs charged up?"

Somkit sat on a stool in the corner and shook his head pityingly. "You really don't know how orbs work, do you?"

Pong shrugged. "I told you. In Tanaburi we didn't have them."

Somkit took a deep breath and set his hands on his knees. "Okay, I'll try to explain. The Governor makes all the light in Chattana. All of it. Got that?"

Everyone knew that, of course, and Pong had seen the Governor's magic with his own eyes. But when he stopped to consider the million lights of the city, that statement seemed almost unbelievable. One man made *all* that light.

"The Governor puts his light into orbs that are shipped in from the glass-blowing factories down by the sea. When an orb's light fades away, only the Governor's magic can fill it back up again," said Somkit. "But the Governor isn't going to waste his time charging up each orb one by one. Instead, he fills up the Charge Stations. He does it a couple times a year — more often now that the city is growing and getting bigger. You've seen them, right? The great big towers with the blinking Gold lights on top?"

Pong nodded. "The barge I rode on passed one of them on the way up the river."

"Right, exactly. So if you want light, you have to buy it from a merchant who gets it from those towers. You have to go to the Light Market."

"The Light Market?"

Somkit spread out his arms. "It's amazing. Orbs everywhere — every color, every size, millions of them! And food and music. And the best part . . ." He gazed up at the ceiling dreamily, as if he'd just spooned dessert into his mouth. "The ground floor is one big open space full of nothing but orb motors! Just gorgeous machines in every direction, as far as the eye can see. It's my favorite place in the whole city."

Pong smiled. The only thing his friend loved more than fruit was motors.

"Anyway, about my job," continued Somkit. "The brighter an orb, the more expensive it is. The Mud House can only afford Violet orbs. They're so dim that they'd be useless if I didn't give them a little help." Somkit pointed to the tinfoil cones cupped around the lights. "Those things help reflect the light. I do the same for the Crimson orbs in the kitchen, so we can get more soup out of each one."

"Crimson is stronger than Violet, right?"

Somkit took a deep breath, and then, very carefully, as if he were talking to a toddler, he began to explain the levels of orbs. "Violet's the weakest. That's what we have at the Mud House. Blue is a bit brighter. Crimson, yes, that's red. It gives off good light and it gets hot — good for cooking. Amber is even brighter — the nicer shops use it for lighting — and it's good enough to power small machines. But for big motors, like the ones on boats, you've got to use Jade. It's the strongest and most expensive."

"Except for Gold."

Somkit nodded. "Gold orbs give off the brightest light, but they never get hot. You can even hold them in your hand without getting burned. They're strong enough to power any motor, but they're way too pretty for that. They're the best, and they cost a ton. If you put all the Mud House money together in a pot and added what's in Mark's cash register, you might have enough to buy one."

Pong remembered the lovely Gold orb he'd held in his palm once, long ago. "That's why no one on this side of the river has any, right?"

"Anyone who can afford Gold orbs isn't going to be living over here," said Somkit. "But I wouldn't say *no one* has any. There is . . . me."

Pong eyed his friend. "You?"

Somkit couldn't contain the grin spreading over his face. He picked up a small glass orb from his workbench. "I'll show you."

Chapter 24

Sunlight streamed down through a jagged hole in the roof of the shed. It was baking hot now, and sweat rolled down the sides of Pong's nose. Somkit picked up a small black metal box and held it in the beam of sunlight.

"This was the hardest part to figure out," said Somkit. "I call it the Catcher. You put it in the sun, like that. This one has already been sitting out all morning, so it should have soaked up some good juice."

"Juice?"

Somkit laughed. "Light juice." He pointed to two thin strands of copper wire connected to the black box. "The Catcher grabs the sunlight and it flows down through these wires to this." He pointed to a thick glass jar filled with cloudy liquid and a shaft of metal stuck in the middle. "This thing is really complicated, so I won't — hey, don't touch!" Somkit swatted Pong's hand away. "That stuff'll give you a nasty burn if you're not careful, okay? Anyway, I won't go into how that works, but basically, the light juice gets stored in that, and when you attach these . . ."

Somkit took two more wires with little metal clamps on the ends that looked like tiny bird beaks. He gently clipped one onto a flap of metal sheeting that he'd fused to the switch on top of the orb. "You ready?"

Pong nodded, backing away. The mention of getting burned had scared him. Somkit clipped the second clamp onto the metal sheet. Instantly, the orb glowed with a warm Gold light.

Pong's mouth hung open. "Whoa," he whispered.

"Pretty good, huh?" said Somkit. "But look — this is the best part." He unclipped the orb from the metal bird beaks and held it up in his palm. It still glowed. He passed it to Pong.

Pong held the orb out warily, then brought it closer. The light was bright, but the glass was cool to the touch. He thought about that day in the courtyard of Namwon, when the Governor had stood before him and handed him a Gold orb just like this. That had felt different somehow. When the Governor made light, the air had crackled with pressure. There was something tense about the Governor's orbs, something that made Pong nervous. But the one that Pong held now wasn't like that.

It didn't buzz at all. Even though it glowed just as bright, it felt more natural.

As Pong leaned closer, the orb blinked once, then went out.

Somkit took the dull orb back from Pong. "It didn't have time to soak up much juice. If I leave it connected all afternoon, the orb will burn bright for a few days — even longer if I keep it switched off."

Pong shook his head at his friend. "This is amazing. And you can do Gold light, even? The most powerful one?"

Somkit laughed. "The sun is bright, man! It lights up the whole sky. Lighting up a little ball of glass is nothing."

Pong stared at his friend, awed by how much his life had changed. Somkit had been the most bullied kid at Namwon, teased relentlessly for being weak and small. But here he was well liked — important, even. It filled Pong with a mixture of relief and pride and envy to see how well things had turned out for him.

"You can make light," said Pong with a smile. "Just like the Governor."

"I don't make it. I just catch it. What the Governor does — that's magic, pure and simple."

"How long have you been doing this?" asked Pong.

"I actually figured it out just before you showed up," said Somkit, carefully putting away the Catcher and jar. "I haven't shown anyone, not even Ampai."

"So now you can replace all the Mud House orbs with Gold," said Pong. "It'll look just like the West Side in there."

"Eventually, maybe," said Somkit with a sigh. "But I have to wait until the orbs we have fade out first, and that could take a month. You can't double-charge an orb. I tried, and it didn't turn out so good." He nodded at the shards of glass swept into a pile in the corner. "Besides, I have to get more wire and sheet metal first, and it's not exactly easy to come by."

Something about the sheepish look on Somkit's face made Pong suspicious. "You didn't steal that copper wire, did you?"

"Of course not!" said Somkit, throwing his hands up. "Don't even joke about that. Ampai doesn't tolerate stealing. But . . ." Somkit scratched behind his ear and lowered his voice. "The way I got it isn't exactly on the books, either. I get it from a friend at the Light Market. In fact . . ." Somkit tapped his chin and leaned toward Pong. "I'm supposed to go tonight. You wanna come?"

"Leave the Mud House? No, I couldn't do that."

"Please?" said Somkit. "I really want to show you

the market. And we could get you a disguise so no one would recognize you in a million years."

Pong shook his head and touched his string bracelets. "No, that'd be a bad idea. I'm sure there are police there."

"Not too many. And they're looking for a monk, remember? We'll get you all covered up. And there are so many people at the Light Market that no one would notice one kid. It's actually the safest place you could go."

Pong rubbed his hand over his fuzzy scalp. The last few days in the Mud House had been almost unbearably stifling. The thought of seeing something beyond the dark walls of the building was tempting, and Somkit made the Light Market sound like heaven.

"I guess if I wore a hat or something . . ."

Somkit grinned. "Oh, sure. I can definitely get you a hat."

Pong narrowed his eyes at his friend. "What's with that look?"

"I have no idea what you're talking about," said Somkit. "Trust me. This is going to be the best disguise you've ever seen."

Chapter 25

*T*his is your amazing disguise?" asked Pong, tugging at the handkerchief at his neck.

Somkit swatted his hand away. "Yes, and quit messing with it. Now I'll have to fix your tie again. Junior Patrol members always pride themselves on their knot-tying skills."

Pong wore a snot-green shirt with matching shorts. Colorful embroidered patches covered the shirt's sleeves and front pockets. It was the uniform of the Junior Patrol, a club for boys who did good deeds and marched around in formation, singing songs. At least, that's what Pong thought they did. Boys like him didn't exactly get invited to sign up. Many Junior Patrol members went on to join the police academy when they got older.

"I just feel like this is a really stupid idea," grumbled Pong. "What if somebody asks me questions?"

"Who would question a boy with that many patches on his shirt? Besides, it was the only disguise I could find that came with a hat." Somkit slapped a floppy cap on Pong's head. "Just stand up straight and try to look like a real goody-goody. All right, into the boat!"

Pong rolled his eyes and climbed into the shallow-bottom boat Ampai kept tied up in the canal behind the Mud House.

"If I fall in, don't push me underwater before you rescue me this time," said Pong, gripping tight to the sides.

Somkit grinned. "No promises."

They each took an oar and paddled out to join the bustling traffic on one of the main canals. Other boats, selling vegetables, sandals, fried rice, and fizzy drinks, glided past. Somkit steered through the maze of boats, turning down one canal and then another. None of the waterways had signs, and Pong marveled at his friend's ability to know where they were going. Finally, they rounded a bend, and Pong's ears popped from the pressure change. A giant multistory building bathed in a rainbow came into view.

There was no sign, but their destination was unmistakable. In a city clothed in lights, the Light Market was the jeweled tiara. Twinkling orbs of every size and color dangled from banyan trees in the courtyard.

Vendors on bicycle carts sold shaved ice that sparkled like gems under the orbs. A four-piece band was playing a swingy number for couples dancing on the wooden deck. Over the music and the laughter, the buzz of the building throbbed in Pong's temples.

It was so beautiful that it made his heart ache. When he and Somkit were little boys, lying on the concrete of Namwon's courtyard and gazing across the river, they had dreamed of this very thing: walking under the glow of a million lights. And now here they were.

Somkit tied up the boat and pinched Pong's elbow. "Snap out of it — and try not to look so weird," he whispered. "Come on. We have to start on the top floor."

The boys filed into a line of customers waiting for a lift that would take them up through the lit branches of a banyan tree to the main entrance at the top of the building. Pong's stomach did a small leap when the lift took off.

The doors swished open and the crowd spilled onto the fifth-floor terrace. With a lurch in his stomach, Pong saw a trio of police at the building's entrance, surveying the crowd and checking bags and satchels as people wandered inside.

Pong's right hand instinctively flew to his left wrist.

Somkit tapped Pong's hand. "It's okay," he whispered.

"Just smile and walk on through, like the upstanding young man you are."

Right. Pong took a breath and puffed out his patch-covered chest. When they passed the policemen, one of them made eye contact. Pong froze. The officer glanced down at Pong's uniform and winked.

Pong tried to wink back, but it was more of a twitchy sort of spasm.

"Told you that disguise was genius," whispered Somkit, pulling him inside. "Now, pay attention. You're finally about to get a good education."

Somkit provided nonstop commentary as they made their way through the cavernous building.

The Light Market was stocked with every color except Gold, which was sold only on the West Side. The market's top floor was one of the only places on the East Side where they used Jade orbs for lighting. The powerful spheres were usually reserved for motors and big machines, but up here, tiny Jade orbs twinkled in the windows of fancy shops and cafés. Pong and Somkit walked past expensive-looking restaurants, where diners sipped drinks under an emerald-green glow.

They passed lovely shops full of lovely people before descending a staircase to the next level, which was bathed in Crimson and Amber light. It was like stepping inside a tangerine. A singer on a bandstand in the center of the hallway crooned, "*Take my hand, oh, my darling, take my hand and dance with me . . .*"

Shops selling orbs in every shade of red and orange lined the hall. Vendors hawked strings of Amber orbs the size of pomegranate seeds next to enormous ruby-red orbs big enough to cook soup for an army. Pong broke out in a sweat under his scratchy uniform from all the heat.

They descended another stairway and walked down peaceful aisles washed in Blue. Here, away from the loud music, Pong could hear the orbs buzzing more distinctly. He realized for the first time that each color of orb buzzed at a slightly different pitch. The Jade lights had hummed low, like a dog snoring. Crimson and Amber buzzed at a higher tone. Blue was higher still, an uneven *zhh-zhh-zhh.*

They walked on, passing stall after stall of orb shops. Pong noticed that the customers changed along with the prices. Up above, shop owners had purchased Crimson orbs for their businesses. Tidy nannies bought Amber orb-powered toys for children in fresh-pressed school uniforms. The Blue floor was filled with people just off work from desk jobs, their starched shirts rolled up to their elbows.

By the time they descended into the Violet hall, the only people who hadn't peeled off to shop at the upper levels were the working classes. The Violet orbs were lovely in their own way, but dim. All together, the orbs glowed well enough, but one single orb would provide barely enough light to see with — certainly not enough to cook with or read a book by.

Back in Namwon, when Pong had dreamed of walking under the city lights, he'd assumed those lights were the same for everyone. But life outside the prison walls wasn't much fairer than life inside it. The best lights were only for the people who could afford them.

"Wait here just a second," said Somkit. "I'm going to check the prices in that shop real quick."

Pong waited outside the stall, looking over a table covered with Violet orbs of all sizes.

"See something you like, sweetie?" said the woman standing behind the table. "I've got a good deal going for these here." She held up a tray of purple orbs. "Two for the price of one."

Pong leaned over the tray, listening. How strange. All the orbs were the same color, but they didn't all buzz at the same pitch. One egg-size orb buzzed much higher than all the rest. It flickered once, very faintly.

"Come on," said the saleswoman impatiently. "This

offer won't last all day. You want that orb, I'll give it to you for half price."

Pong ignored her, entranced by the orb's shrill whine. It buzzed higher and higher. He leaned back, afraid it might shatter. Instead, it blinked once, then went out.

"Oh, ha-ha — now, how did that happen?" said the saleswoman, quickly whisking the faded orb out of sight. "Must be a defect or something."

Somkit came back out and pulled Pong away from the table. "Never buy orbs on discount," he said. "These scammers try to sell old ones that are already about to fade. You never know if they're going to last you a week or an hour."

"What happens to orbs after they fade?" asked Pong.

"You're supposed to take them to a recycling depot. They'll pay you for the glass. Not much, but at least it's something."

Finally, they reached the bottom level of the Light Market. It had no musicians or decorations. The floor was gray tile, and the giant space smelled like the inside of a metal can.

Somkit rubbed his palms together happily. "You got two sections down here," he said, pointing them out. "Motors on one side, the Jade orbs that power them on the other. Isn't this place just the greatest?"

Pong followed Somkit down the aisle that divided the room in two, squinting against the bright green glare. Down here, surrounded by all the metal and grease, the Jade orbs seemed less fancy and more powerful than they had up above. The boys made their way to the back, where the smaller motors for sleek water taxis were being sold and repaired.

Somkit paused, holding Pong back by the elbow. "This is the place where I get my supplies. Let me do all the talking, okay?"

The people working behind the repair counter called out to Somkit as he approached.

Somkit raised a hand. "Hey, guys!"

A man behind the counter with his hair cut short in front and long in the back shook hands with him. "Where you been, kid? We haven't seen you in weeks!"

"Sorry. I've been away. I've been really busy."

The guy with the short-long haircut leaned over the counter and said, "Hey, I talked to my boss. You know, about the job thing."

Somkit straightened. "Oh, yeah? What'd he say?"

Short-Long shook his head. "Sorry, man. He said we can't take the risk of hiring someone with a record."

Somkit's face sank without losing hold of the smile. "A record? But I got out of Namwon with a clean sheet.

You told him that, right?" Somkit held out his wrist and pointed to the crossed-out tattoo. "I could show him myself, if that would make a difference."

"It won't," said Short-Long. "He's got a strict policy about hiring guys who've been in jail, and he won't make exceptions. I'm really sorry."

Somkit's spine sagged ever so slightly, but he flashed that easy smile of his. "Don't worry about it, man. I understand. I got my hands full already, you know?"

The guy ran his fingers through the long lock of hair in back. "You know that if it was up to me, I'd hire you in a second. You're an ace with motors, that's for sure. In fact, we've got a Model Nine that came in for a repair last night, and none of us can figure out what to do with it."

"I could take a look at it if you want," said Somkit.

"Really?" said the guy, perking up. "I'll give you a sheet of tin and a bundle of copper wire if you can fix it."

"Now you're talking," said Somkit. "Show me the way."

Pong fumed as he watched Short-Long lift a section of the counter so Somkit could pass into the shop. His friend couldn't help where he was born. What did that have to do with fixing motors, anyway?

Somkit crouched in front of the broken Model Nine while the shop workers stood back, scratching their heads. Some leaned forward, trying to watch what Somkit was doing, but his brown fingers worked too fast to follow. Within minutes, Somkit stood up and slapped the motor's metal case. It kicked on, sputtered twice, and then settled into a steady hum.

The men standing by slapped one another's shoulders and cheered.

"What'd I tell you?" shouted Short-Long to the other guys. "Somkit did it again!"

He handed Somkit a stack of tin sheets and a bundle of short copper wires. "Come drop in and help us out anytime, and I'll give you more where that stuff came from."

Somkit bowed his thanks, then took the supplies and raised his eyebrows at Pong, a sign to follow him out.

They climbed back up the levels of the Light Market to exit the same way they had come in. Even the pretty Jade orbs on the top floor seemed less grand the second time through, and Pong was ready to get away from all the light and the noise. As the lift swooped them back down through the banyan branches to the courtyard, Somkit was quiet — a sure tip-off that something was wrong.

"They should have paid you with actual money for helping them," said Pong, guessing at his friend's thoughts. "Not with just some wires and pieces of metal."

Somkit shrugged and rubbed his tattoo against the hem of his shirt. "You heard them. They're not going to give me a job. Anyway, wires aren't such a bad payment. It's what I need to make more sun orbs."

"Well, if it makes you feel any better, I think you're worth ten of those guys."

Somkit rolled his eyes. "Listen, Junior Patrol, you're not earning your compliments badge tonight, if that's what you're after."

Pong pretended to look shocked and said in a very upper-crust voice, "I beg your pardon, but it's the Junior Patrol creed to give out at least three compliments every day."

Somkit laughed. Out in the courtyard, they bought a snow cone and split it. Sticky and giddy from their successful trip, they sang made-up Junior Patrol songs, complete with arm motions, all the way back to the boat.

It wasn't until they rowed back onto the canal that led behind the Mud House that Pong felt an old familiar unease creep up his spine. He looked over his shoulder.

"What is it?" said Somkit. "Still worried about the police? They didn't even look twice at you."

Pong shook his head. He didn't think anyone in the Light Market had been suspicious, but years of living in fear of getting caught had made him extra sensitive to being watched. The air around him pressed in a little tighter. The skin between his shoulder blades tickled.

"I just have this weird feeling that someone is following us," he said.

"Let's get inside quick, then."

They left the boat tied up behind Mark's restaurant and made for the back entrance to the Mud House.

The moment they opened the door, Pong felt the darkness stir behind his left shoulder. He pushed Somkit into the Mud House and started to scream, but no sound came out. A hand clamped hard over his mouth and yanked him into the shadows.

Chapter 26

Nok loved the smell of her spire-fighting gym. It was the scent of lemon blossoms, fresh-scrubbed floor-boards, and the sweat of hard work. She'd put plenty of her own hard work into her last training session, and the blisters on her palms where she gripped her staff were proof.

Nok blew on the tender skin as she walked out of the studio and down the hall toward her room.

"Hey, good fight tonight," called a voice behind her. It was Dee. She was a nice girl, a year older than Nok but two levels below her in training.

"If you keep that up, you'll beat Bull again next year for sure."

"Thanks."

"Hey, it's just us here, so you can tell me." Dee leaned a little closer. "What's your secret to being so good, huh?"

"My secret?"

"Oh, come on. You're better than some of our teachers! You must know something the rest of us don't."

Nok blinked, not sure how to answer. She'd kept to herself for so long that it was hard to remember how to make conversation with someone her own age. She had never had many friends before. Most other kids were either jealous of her or found her perfectionism annoying.

Nok wrapped her arms around herself and shrugged. "If you just keep practicing, you'll get there, I'm sure."

"All right, fine. Be that way," said Dee, sticking out her tongue playfully. "Do you want to walk home over the bridge with me?" Dee's family also lived on the West Side, but thankfully they almost never crossed paths with Nok's parents.

Part of Nok longed to say yes. She imagined strolling with Dee back home, maybe even stopping at an ice-cream cart along the way. She pictured them talking and laughing, making plans for sleepovers.

The vision was fleeting. Nok shook her head. "Can't, sorry," she said. "I'm staying overnight the whole week. Our house is getting painted, so my mom thought it would be good timing for me to get in extra practice."

"Gosh, no wonder you beat the pants off the rest of us," said Dee, laughing. "If I lived at the gym, too, maybe I'd be as good as you."

Nok twisted the hem of her tunic as she watched Dee walk away, taking their imaginary future friendship out the door with her. She let out a breath and shook her shoulders. She didn't have time to think about silly things like ice cream and girlfriends. She needed to get going.

Nok was indeed sleeping at the gym. By her calculations, she had a little over one week to track down Pong — *if* he was still alive. Her parents would go back to Tanaburi to visit during the upcoming holidays, and she'd have to be there. In the meantime, she had some money, but not enough to pay for a guesthouse room for a week. Her gym was on the East Side, in what used to be a good part of town, near the bridge that connected the east and west banks. There were simple sleeping quarters at the top of the building, where students traveling from other towns could stay during competitions.

The only downside of staying at the gym was that she needed to spend at least half of each day training, to make it look convincing that she was there for a reason and not just to have a place to crash while she hunted down the runaway monk.

In her room, Nok changed from her sweaty uniform into a fresh one. She took out her notebook and unfolded the map of the East Side that she'd bought the day before.

She'd suspected that it would be hard to find Pong in Chattana, but it wasn't until she got to the city that she realized how difficult her challenge was. Chattana was like a pile of pebbles: if you stepped on it, it would shift and change until the surface was the bottom and the bottom was the top.

She'd already spent several fruitless days searching, but she wouldn't give up. Not yet. She would stick to her plan of moving through the city methodically, neighborhood by neighborhood, scoping out the streets and canals. Pong couldn't stay hidden forever. As an orphan and a runaway, he wouldn't know anyone who would take him in and feed him. He'd have to surface sometime to get food or he'd starve.

Nok folded up her map and stuck it under her mattress. Leaving her staff behind, she stepped out of the room and slid her bedroom door shut behind her.

Out in the city, Nok wound her way from the quiet neighborhood of the gym into the gritty heart of downtown. Mobs of children ran down the gangways on bare feet, squealing as they launched off the sidewalks and dove into the river. And on a school night! They'd be useless in class the next day. Nok suddenly realized she couldn't recall seeing a school on the East Side before. But that was silly. There had to be schools here. How else would the children learn to read or write?

These were the neighborhoods she'd been warned about by her parents, the places good girls from the West Side didn't dare set foot in. It was thrilling and a little scary to be there alone. But even without her staff, she didn't worry about taking care of herself. Dee had guessed right — she did have a spire-fighting secret.

It wasn't that she didn't want to share it with Dee. Well, maybe that was partly true. But mainly she didn't want to talk about it because she couldn't figure out how to explain it without sounding weird.

A year ago, Nok had traveled with her father on a work trip across Chattana's northern border, to the town of Lannaburi. The journey was long, and her father's meetings were unbearably boring, but the last meeting of the trip took place in a library. Chattana had few books left from the days before the Great Fire, so Nok devoured the titles, reading as much and as quickly as she could before they had to leave. The last book she found was about the history of spire fighting.

According to the crumbling book, it was an old, old art form that had begun back when Chattana was little more than a sleepy fishing village. It started as a self-defense practice used by the wise men and women who lived on the neighboring mountaintops. The name *spire* probably referred to the bamboo walking sticks the old sages carried with them.

According to that book, the principles of spire fighting stated that everyone has a light deep inside them. The book said it was like an ember, or a tiny piece of glowing coal. Just as an ember can start a raging fire if it's fed the right fuel, a person can fan the flame inside them and use it to do all sorts of extraordinary things — like knock a loudmouth named Bull flat on his back, for example.

Nok's teachers had never mentioned anything about this during her lessons. Perhaps that part of the sport had been long forgotten. But as soon as Nok read it, something clicked. Spire fighting wasn't about strength or how well she memorized the moves. It was about finding that hidden light inside herself and letting it pour out. From that moment forward, she had been able to fight better than anyone else her age. Even her teachers said she was becoming as good as the old masters. But she could never explain what she had learned to anyone, not even her teachers. Just thinking about it — all that talk of flames and fire — felt sort of illegal.

Nok shook her head and forced herself to focus

on her route. She had absentmindedly let the crowd carry her along like a current, and they had pulled her away from the main canal, onto a narrow street. The air formed hazy rings around the Blue orbs that hung between shops.

Nok avoided eye contact with the other people around her as she tried to retrace her steps. She turned down one alley, then another, but the streets grew dim instead of brighter. The Blue orbs gave way to Violet. It was so dark that Nok stumbled and put her foot into a deep puddle of mucky water. At least she hoped it was water.

She was lost. People passed this way and that through the purple shadows, but Nok didn't dare ask for directions. *Stay calm,* she told herself. *Just keep walking and you'll find your way out eventually.*

But then, up ahead, on a narrow wooden bridge, she spotted the shine of a bare scalp. All her anxiety about being lost vanished, and her heart hopped in her chest. Could it really be him? Using the Nothing Step, she stalked closer, then closer. She regretted leaving her staff behind now, but she wouldn't let that stop her. She would drag him back with her bare hands if she had to.

He stood with his back to her, leaning over the rail of the bridge. Nok silently threaded the gap between the crowd and lunged at him. She grabbed him with both hands. "In the name of the Governor, you're under arrest!"

The boy spun around.

He wasn't a boy at all. He was an old man, thin with hunger. His sunken eyes searched her face. "Can you spare anything, miss?" he asked hoarsely. "Any change? I haven't eaten today. . . ."

Nok dropped her grip on him and lurched back, nearly tripping over a mass of blankets and bones. Another person. "Please, miss." A woman coughed, holding up her hand. Her other arm cradled a baby. "Do you have any money? Anything at all?"

More outstretched fingers reached for Nok. She spun around. The bridge was full of people: the elderly and sick, men and women in rags, leaning on canes. Tiny children curled around their legs with dark, weary eyes that caught Nok's own and tore at her heart.

"Please . . ."

"Please, miss . . ."

"Anything? Anything at all . . . ?"

They reached for her the way a drowning man reaches up at a passing boat. Nok backed up, but more people gathered behind her, blocking her way. She wanted to say something but couldn't get out the words.

Nok tore herself away from them and ran.

She ran on, not caring which way she went. She just wanted to get away. She ran down one alley, up another, and another, until she came to a dead end. A monstrous building blocked her way, its top half scorched black. Fish-flavored steam billowed out the open door on the first floor.

Nok bolted into the shadows and collapsed against the wall of the blackened building. She slid down to her knees and covered her face with her sleeve. She couldn't get those voices out of her head. *Please. Please, miss.* Nok's pocket jangled with the money she'd brought to buy herself dinner. She could have given it to them. She imagined going back and turning her pockets inside out, even though she knew there wasn't enough money in them to go around.

She squeezed her eyes shut and shook her head. Of course there was suffering in the world. Everyone knew that. But Nok had never seen it so close before. It had knocked the wind out of her, and she was a girl who rarely got the wind knocked out of her.

Light shines on the worthy.

Usually when the Governor's words popped into her head, they gave her strength. But tonight they did nothing to banish the sad things she'd seen. They were words that belonged in a sunny classroom, as useless here on the East Side as her mother's fancy dresses.

Nok might have sat there all night, unable to gather herself and find her way home, but she was pulled out of her thoughts by a trio of people who seemed to be walking straight toward her. She shrank against the wall, willing herself to melt into the shadows. At the last minute, they turned sharply and went around the back of the building. Nok watched them go.

What a strange group they made: a broad-shouldered man with a neck like an ox, a small man with a broken nose and a scuttling swagger, and a woman wearing a man's jacket who tossed a tangerine peel over her shoulder. It tumbled across the ground and landed at Nok's feet.

Once they were gone, Nok reached out and picked up the peel. She put her nose to the rind and breathed in.

It smelled sharp and bright, like sunlight and clean water, and something else that Nok couldn't name. She clung to the rind and inhaled again and again.

Chapter 27

Strong hands wrapped around Pong's shoulders and shoved him through the back door of the Mud House. He tried to wriggle free, but the big man behind him gripped him tight.

"Somkit!" cried Pong, turning to look for his friend in the dark hallway.

"Shut up!" said the big man, squeezing Pong's arms.

"Hands off him, Yai!" said Somkit. "He's my friend."

Confused, Pong twisted around and tried to get his bearings.

A short man with a crooked nose sneered at Somkit. "Since when are you friends with the Junior Patrol?"

Somkit returned the short guy's glare. "Since when do *you* care who I'm friends with, Yord?"

"Everyone be quiet," snapped a woman's voice. Pong heard the clink of an orb switching on, followed by its distinctive buzz. Violet light seeped from an orb lantern and illuminated a long, narrow face with lively eyes. The woman wore a man's jacket with the collar popped up. She inspected Pong from under heavy bangs that hung down past her eyebrows. "Somkit, your little friend here looks like he's about to throw up."

To Pong's surprise, Somkit rushed at the woman and threw his arms around her.

"Ampai! Finally! Your trip lasted so long, I thought you were never coming back!"

"Hey, no hugs for the rest of us?" asked the little guy with the broken nose. His big friend snorted.

"I need to talk to you," Somkit said to Ampai. He scowled at the two men. "*Alone*, please."

"In a minute," said Ampai, without taking her gaze from Pong. "We have supplies and money we need to hand out first."

Ampai sent the big man, Yai, back into the alley to retrieve their rucksacks. As soon as they entered the main room of the Mud House, Ampai was swarmed by people. The rucksacks held food and medicine, which Yai and Yord doled out. But most of the commotion focused on welcoming Ampai home.

The people swirled around her, thanking her again and again for the supplies. She called everyone by name and asked about their families. She reminded Pong a little of Father Cham, making time to speak with everyone, even the children. After a while, she caught Yai's eye and gave him a short nod.

"All right, all right," boomed Yai, forming a one-man wall in front of her. "You said you were going to cook up a feast, didn't you? So go get cooking. Ampai's got a lot to catch up on from being gone so long."

She slipped away, up the stairs, and motioned for Somkit and Pong to follow. Yai and Yord clomped up after them. On the second floor, they followed Ampai into one of the few rooms in the Mud House that still had a full set of walls and a door, which Yai shut behind them.

The room was an office of sorts, with a large desk in the center and shelves along the edges crammed with supplies: toilet paper, bandages, shrimp paste, coconut milk, coils of rope and pulleys, and a hundred other random items.

Ampai sat on the edge of the desk with one leg folded underneath her. "Set those medical supplies over there with the rest," she said to Yai. "Then you two should go back downstairs and see that the food gets doled out evenly. Keep an eye on that new cook and make sure he doesn't skimp on filling the bowls."

"Right, Auntie," said Yai with a short nod.

As he and Yord started out the door, Ampai cleared her throat and asked, "Aren't you forgetting something?"

Yord turned around and gave her an oily gap-toothed smile. "What do you mean?"

Ampai held out her hand, palm open. "The wad of bills that's in your pocket. It stays here."

Yai rocked nervously on his feet, but Yord stretched his smile even wider. "Oh, that. I was thinking since me and Yai took such a risk to get all this loot, we should get to keep a little something for ourselves. Like a finder's fee."

Ampai glared at the two men. "Everyone here takes risks," she snapped. "Not just you. You know my rules. That money we collected isn't for us."

Yord's smile thinned as he reached into his shirt pocket, pulled out the stack of money, and placed it in Ampai's hand. He held the smile as he and Yai slunk out the door and shut it behind them.

Somkit stood leaning against the desk next to Ampai with his arms crossed. "Those guys," he said with disgust. "I wish you'd left them behind."

Ampai shrugged. "They come in handy sometimes. Yord's a little slimy, but that helps if you have to deal with slimy people. And it's always a good idea to have Yai's muscles standing behind you. Especially the places I've been going."

Ampai rubbed her palm over her face and down the side of her neck. Because she was small and had a girlish haircut, Pong had thought that she wasn't much older than a teenager. But here, with a Violet orb hanging directly overhead, he saw the dark circles and age lines framing her eyes.

Ampai reached into her coat pocket and pulled out a tangerine. As she peeled it, she looked at Pong from beneath the bangs that hung over her eyelashes. "You still haven't introduced me to your friend, little brother," she said to Somkit.

Pong blushed as he bowed to her. "My name is Pong."

Ampai nodded and popped a segment of tangerine in her mouth, offering one to Somkit, too. "Pong. That's the name for a protector. You protect my little brother here?"

Pong looked at Somkit, who beamed every time Ampai called him "little brother." "So far he's the one who's been protecting me," Pong answered.

Somkit took a deep breath and twisted his mouth from side to side. "We were at Namwon together, but Pong left before me, and . . ."

"He *left?*"

Somkit swallowed and nodded at Pong. "Go on, show her."

Pong reflexively clamped his left arm down at his side.

"It's okay," said Somkit. "You can trust her."

Strangely, Pong did trust her. He raised his left arm and gently hooked a finger under the string bracelets. They were fraying and thin now. A couple had already snapped off. Pong felt a stab of sadness for Father Cham. He'd be getting no more new bracelets now, no more kind words of wisdom. He held out his wrist to Ampai and stepped toward her.

She took his hand in her slender fingers. Up close she smelled like oranges and boat varnish. Ampai stared down at his wrist, but she seemed more interested in the bracelets than his tattoo. "Where did you get all these?"

Pong reached up and pulled off his cap, exposing his fuzzy scalp. Ampai dropped his hand and crossed her arms. "Word on the street is that the police are looking for a monk who ran away from Tanaburi. I don't guess that has anything to do with you guys?"

"It's a very long story," said Somkit.

Ampai slid off the desk and went to the door, checking that it was shut. She whirled around, scowling. "You brought a *fugitive* to our house?" she said sternly. "Do you know what could happen to all of us if the police discovered that you've been hiding him here?"

"What could I do?" said Somkit. "Just leave him on the streets? He's my best friend. You would've done the same thing."

"Not if it meant endangering everyone in this house. Everyone, Somkit! Think of all the kids! Where would they go? What would happen to them if we got arrested?"

"I know, but he doesn't have anywhere else to go. We were waiting for you to get back. I promised him that you'd help him get on a boat going south. That's his only chance. He's got to get out of Chattana."

Pong clamped down on the guilty feeling rising in his stomach. "It's not Somkit's fault. It's mine. I didn't give him any choice. And we've been really careful not to get in trouble."

"Oh, really?" said Ampai. "Is that why you were out in the city with that stupid disguise? Because you were being careful?"

"Ampai, please," said Somkit. "I know it was risky, but we had to go out to get these." He held up the bundle of copper wire and stack of tin. "I haven't told you this yet, but . . . I got it to work."

Ampai's anger melted away. "The sun orbs?"

Somkit smiled bashfully and nodded. "Just after you left."

"And it really works? You caught light from the sun?"

"Not just that," said Somkit, pausing for effect. "*Gold* light."

"Ha, ha!" cried Ampai, throwing her arms around Somkit and spinning him around. "I knew you could do it! And just in time for next Sunday, too!"

"What's on Sunday?" asked Pong.

Somkit looked at Ampai and raised both hands innocently. "I didn't tell him anything about it yet. But you should. He told you his secret."

Ampai nodded. "Fair enough." She checked the door to her office once more, then leaned against it with her arms folded. "We're planning a march across the Giant's Bridge. It's why I've been gone. I've been gathering more people to join us." She smiled at Somkit. "I've got them, too. At least a thousand. And I bet I can get a thousand more if what you tell me about your sun orbs is true."

Pong stared at her. "A march? Like a parade?"

Somkit snickered. "Like a protest."

"But what are you protesting?"

"A week from Monday the Governor will sign a new law," said Ampai. "It will raise the price of orbs by ten percent. Every color."

Pong thought about the poor people he'd seen agonizing over buying Violet orbs at the Light Market. If the orbs were ten percent more expensive, they would be out of their reach.

"But it's not just that he's raising the orb prices," added Somkit. "It's the *reason* he's raising them. He's going to spend that money on a huge new building project. A youth reform center."

"It's a jail," said Ampai. "For children."

Pong winced as if someone had punched him in the chest. A children's jail. Just thinking the words made him feel sick.

Somkit looked at him sorrowfully. "Namwon's full," he explained. "There's no room for the prisoners' children anymore. And there are whole packs of kids who run the alleys. They don't have any homes or families to take care of them. They'll probably end up in the 'reform center,' too. The Governor says it's for their safety."

Pong stared down at the floor. *Desperate people deserve our compassion.* Father Cham had gathered up children, blessed them, and found them families. But here, the Governor was going to catch them like dogs and stick them in a pen.

"It's monstrous," Ampai hissed, pacing in front of the door. "A jail? We don't need another jail. We need schools — decent ones. And hospitals, like they have on the West Side. The people won't stand for it, either.

They've put up with things this long because they're afraid of the Governor. It's not just because he controls the police. They're afraid he'll take away what little they have. They don't want to lose his light." She stopped pacing and turned to Somkit. "But now they have nothing to be afraid of! If we can show up on that bridge carrying our own orbs, it will show everyone — on both sides of the river — that we don't need the Governor, or anything he has to offer."

She reached into her jacket and pulled out a tiny notebook. "I've got almost one thousand commitments for the march next Sunday," she repeated, tapping the cover. "I know you can't make that many orbs in such a short time. But what could you do? A hundred? Two hundred?"

Somkit's proud smile drooped. "At this rate? Five? I can't overcharge an orb or it'll shatter. I have to use ones that are already faded. But it's going to take too long to wait for our Mud House orbs to fade out. We lose only one or two a day at most."

"Isn't there anywhere else to get faded orbs?" asked Pong. "What if you offered people money to buy theirs?"

Ampai considered this for a moment, then shook her head. "The money we have saved up is for food and medicine. Besides, I don't want word to get out about what

Somkit can do. The Governor has spies everywhere, and if he hears that we're looking for faded orbs, he might figure out what we're up to. Then he'll find us and shut us down for sure. If we're going to do this, we need to keep it a secret until the last minute."

"What about taking faded orbs from a recycling depot?" asked Somkit.

"No," said Ampai firmly. "No stealing. We have to do this honestly. Otherwise we'll prove we're just as terrible as the Governor says we are."

Pong listened to Somkit and Ampai run through one bad option after another. There was just no easy way to get the number of faded orbs they needed in time.

Somkit's face sagged, his hopes crushed. Pong had never seen his friend so disappointed.

"I think I've got an idea," said Pong suddenly.

The others stopped talking and swiveled their faces toward him. "Go on," said Ampai.

"What if we went through the city and found Violet orbs that were just about to fade, and we swiped them before the owners found out—"

"That's stealing," said Ampai.

"And we replaced them with good orbs from the Mud House without them noticing?"

"That's swapping!" said Somkit.

"We could get the faded orbs we need," continued Pong. "People in the city would get fully charged orbs that will last longer. Everyone wins, and no one needs to find out about it."

"Totally brilliant!" said Somkit, beaming.

"There's just one problem," said Ampai. "No one knows exactly when orbs will fade. If you know how old they are, you can guess about how long they'll last, but when they actually go out — poof!— they just go."

"I can tell," said Pong. When the other two looked surprised, he added, "Orbs make a different sound when they're close to going out. And they flicker, very faintly. I saw it happen tonight at the Light Market."

Ampai raised one eyebrow, skeptical. "I've never noticed that before. Somkit, have you?"

Somkit shook his head, bewildered. "No, but Pong sees things that other people miss. You should've seen him with these mangoes when we were little. If he says it happens, I believe him."

Ampai chewed on her thumbnail as she paced in front of her desk. "If we could have one hundred orbs — one hundred *Gold* orbs — for the march . . ." She jerked her head up at Somkit. "Can you even imagine the scene? To have the people of Chattana holding their own light? What a statement that would make!"

Somkit's face mirrored her excitement. "Once I get the orbs, I can start charging them right away. As long as we keep them turned off, they'll last until the march, and then —" His eyes landed on Pong, and he stopped. "Wait. What about Pong? What about his boat?"

Ampai turned to Pong. She looked at him a long time, trying to read his face. Her eyes traveled down to his bracelet-covered wrist. "What do you say? Do you want to stay and help us?"

"I . . . think . . ."

"Because if you stay, you're taking a risk. I will protect you as much as I can, but I can't promise for sure that you won't get caught."

Pong swallowed hard.

"What I can promise," she went on, "is that if you help us, I will get you on the fastest boat to the sea when this is all over. If we pull this off, you'll be free. You have my word."

Pong looked from Ampai to Somkit. Once again he found himself pulled like the tide, torn between leaving and staying. The new prison sounded horrible, but Pong couldn't believe that one march would stop it from being built. The Governor would do what he wanted, just as he always had.

The world is full of darkness, and that will never change.

But he couldn't get over the look of hope on Somkit's face. He owed his friend. For saving his life. For living out those years at Namwon alone. He'd left him once. He couldn't leave him again, not right now. What was one more week when he'd waited four years?

Pong nodded at Ampai. "All right. I'll do it."

She nodded back. "Get ready. We start tonight."

Chapter 28

Pong became a bat, sleeping all day with a sheet wrapped tight around his face like wings. He woke at dusk and got ready to go out into the city with Ampai to hunt down faded orbs. Because Somkit's work required the sun, the boys crossed paths only at the dinner table, which was breakfast for Pong.

"I feel so weird," said Pong, yawning over a plate of garlicky clams. "This new schedule makes me feel like I'm walking underwater. At the temple, we were up before sunrise and in bed by dusk."

"Yeah, but that was before you came to the sleepless city," said Somkit as he dumped a spoonful of bright chilis onto his food and stirred. Pong's stomach burned just watching him. "This place doesn't come alive until the sun goes down. Besides, you get to go around with Ampai." Somkit grinned, then whispered, "Admit it — it's fun, isn't it?"

Pong smiled back. It was fun. Despite his desperation to escape, he loved the nightly excursions with Ampai. Every night when he waited for her near the Mud House door, his pulse revved faster, like a boat motor warming up.

"You ready, kid?" Ampai would ask, not waiting for his answer before she slipped out into the alley. Pong didn't wear the Junior Patrol disguise anymore, just plain clothes. But he did keep the cap to cover up his still-spiky scalp.

"The best way to hide in Chattana is not to hide at all," Ampai told him as she led him along the gangplanks, over a bridge, and out toward one of the main canals. "If you act like you've got nothing to hide, people will believe you. Just follow me and do exactly what I do."

Pong swallowed down his fear of being spotted and soon learned to walk forward with purpose — not too fast, not too slow — and to never, ever look over his shoulder.

Over the last few nights, Ampai had taken Pong into every pocket of the city. Sometimes they walked, and other times she rowed him in her shallow-bottom boat. While Pong listened to the Violet lights hanging outside shops and homes, Ampai distracted the owners, chatting them up as she peeled her tangerines.

In spite of the tens of thousands of Violet orbs in the city, their work was going more slowly than planned. For one thing, they had to be choosy about where they went. They had the most success in the poorer sections of town, where Ampai had the most connections, and where it was natural for her to strike up conversations with people while Pong made his quick switches.

But the other reason they made slow progress was that Ampai had other work to attend to — her main work.

She was a stirrer of hearts.

"This'll only take a minute," she said as she rowed the little boat through the network of canals at the southern end of the city. Down here, the city blocks dissolved into rafts of houseboats tied loosely together. Pong watched the people on the decks of their tidy homes as they pulled up nets of glittery carp or sat in semicircles, playing card games. Every one of them waved to Ampai as they passed.

She tethered the boat to a small floating house bobbing up and down in the reeds. "Kla?" she called, stepping onto the deck. "Hey, it's Ampai. I've brought you some tangerines."

A man's deep voice floated out the open doorway.

"Tangerines won't help me," said the tall man sadly. "But come in, sister."

Pong followed Ampai into the little shack. It was sparsely furnished but swept as clean as a monk's room. Like most people, this guy Kla called Ampai "sister," but one look at them together and it was obvious they weren't even distantly related. He towered over her, a great beast of a man, as big as Yai but with an even thicker neck and arms that were muscular and brown from working in the sun. He took up almost the entire room all by himself.

When Kla raised his eyebrows at Pong, Ampai said, "My assistant. You can trust him."

She stood in the center of the dark room with her hands in her pockets. "How's your wife?"

Kla nodded at a sheet of cloth covering the doorway to the other room. His face sagged, and Pong was struck by how such a huge man could suddenly seem so small. "Not good," he whispered. "She needs me to be home to care for her, but I gotta work. I gotta go right now, actually. Two jobs working the docks just to keep us fed. It ain't enough to pay for a doctor, too, especially not the kind she needs."

He rubbed his enormous wrists and Pong noticed that he had a crossed-out tattoo. He had served time in

Banglad, the men's prison. Pong stared, awed and a little afraid.

Kla slumped on a stool in the corner. "I tried to get better work, but you know how it is."

Ampai glanced at his wrist and nodded.

The giant cradled his forehead in his hands. "What'm I gonna do? I can't get a decent job, not with a prison record. I can't earn enough to get us more light than that thing." He nodded at the single Violet orb hanging from the ceiling. "We can't cook food. Can't boil water. If it goes out, my wife — she'll . . . she'll be in the dark."

"We're about to change all that," said Ampai.

"You been saying that for a long time, sister. Nothing changes."

"It will this time. We're going to show the people that Chattana's better off without the Governor."

"Ha!" barked Kla. "You mean the man who saved us all? Who brought us into the light?"

"The Governor lit the city," said Ampai. "That's not the same thing. How many years has it been since you were released from Banglad?"

"Eleven."

"Eleven! Brother, you already served your sentence and still you're paying the price for *one* mistake. It's the law, but it isn't what's *right*. It's time that we showed the

Governor that he doesn't have control over what's right and what's wrong."

"And you think a bunch of people standing together are going to make him step aside?" asked Kla.

Ampai squared her shoulders. "This march that I'm planning isn't just to prove to the Governor that he can't dismiss us any longer. It's to prove it to *ourselves*. Don't you see that?"

Pong had sat through dozens of these visits with Ampai. He'd heard dozens of versions of these hopeful speeches. But now, as he watched her lift up the giant man using only her words, he felt something shift inside him. He rocked on restless feet, and his chest ached as if his lungs were no longer sitting quite right. Something beneath his rib cage strained and fluttered, bashing against the old walls around his heart.

"This time is different," continued Ampai. "We've got more people on our side than ever before. The march is less than a week away. I told you my goal: to get everyone that lives beneath the Violet and Blue to come out. He can't ignore us if we have that many people."

The giant looked up. "And you've got them?"

Ampai smiled. "I will. But I'm missing the dockworkers. The great elephants of men like you. I don't want any violence — on either side — and if you and your friends show up on the bridge and stand with us, the police will think twice about a confrontation."

The big man shook his head. "I dunno. You really think the Governor's going to change things just because a bunch of people stand on a bridge all at once? We're like little fruit flies to him."

Ampai's eyes glimmered in the dim room. "I've got something up my sleeve that will show without a shadow of a doubt that we don't need him." She threw Pong a wink. "We can change things forever, but only if there's enough of us. That bridge has to be full. Say you'll be there with me?"

Nothing in the shack had changed, but somehow the shadows seemed pushed to the corners.

Kla looked up at Ampai. "All right. Me and my crew'll be there."

Ampai flashed him a grin. "Good. And until then, this is for you." She reached into her pocket and pulled out a tangerine. She handed it to Kla. It was wrapped in a sheaf of money.

Tears brimmed at the lids of Kla's eyes, but Ampai whisked Pong back to the boat before he could thank her.

* * *

Even after Ampai rowed them back to solid ground, Pong felt dizzy, as if they were still bobbing up and down on Kla's house. They had more work to do, but he dawdled, hanging back in the shadows of a side alley.

"Hey, little guy," said Ampai, stopping to wait for him. "You okay? Hungry?"

"I'm not hungry," said Pong.

Ampai sauntered back toward him. "What's wrong, then? You're tired? It's not easy staying up all night, is it?"

"It isn't that," said Pong quietly. "It's just that . . . I just realized that we're really different."

Ampai grinned. She was in a good mood, and she was trying to pass it on. "It's true. You don't eat enough oranges."

Pong shook his head. He didn't want to joke or laugh this off. "No, I mean . . ." He took a deep breath and let all the words out at once. "You look at this city and you see everything that's wrong with it. And you want to fix it. I look at it and see all the same things, but . . . I just don't think it's possible to fix any of it."

Ampai tilted her head and raised an eyebrow, waiting for him to go on.

"When something's really broken . . . when it's bad," said Pong, "you can't fix it. You can't make it good."

Ampai's face softened, and even though she wasn't much taller than Pong, she leaned down to look him square in the eyes. "What are we talking about now? The city? Or a boy?"

Pong looked away. "I don't know what you mean."

"You're wrong," she said. "We aren't so different. We have much more in common than you know."

Ampai unbuttoned the left cuff of her jacket sleeve and rolled it up. She held her wrist out to Pong. For a moment, he thought she was about to show him a prison mark, but her dark bronze skin was bare. Instead, she hooked a finger up her sleeve and pulled down a thin, woven bracelet.

Pong stared. Ampai wore a bracelet just like the last one Father Cham had given him — red and gold braided together. The colors had faded a bit, but otherwise it was identical.

"But how . . . ?" he whispered. "Where did you get that?"

"The same place you did." Ampai glanced up at the buildings towering over them. "I was one of those babies born among the ashes of the Great Fire. Before the Governor came. They called us basket babies, the ones who floated downriver to Tanaburi. I grew up there, going to the village school, but I spent more of my time at the temple, studying with Father Cham. He was my teacher until I grew old enough to move to Chattana on my own."

Pong couldn't take his eyes off Ampai's bracelet. "I can't believe you knew him."

Ampai's eyes twinkled at the happy memory. "And, yes, he was old when I knew him, in case you're wondering." She nodded at Pong's wrist. "You have all those white ones. He gave them to me, too, though never as many as you have. They snapped off a long time ago. He'd always tell me things like, 'May you never get kicked by a donkey.'"

"And did it come true?" asked Pong.

Ampai tossed her hair back and laughed. "I've never even seen a donkey!"

Pong laughed, too. "That sounds like something he'd say."

"He didn't give out many of these, though," said Ampai, tapping her own red bracelet. "In fact, you're the first person I've met in a long time who has one. What did he tell you when he gave it to you?"

Pong started to answer, but the words wouldn't come. The image of Father Cham lying in the temple came back to him. Pong thought about how he'd demanded his freedom, how he'd disrespected his teacher. He didn't think he could talk without crying.

"It's okay," said Ampai gently. "You don't have to tell me. Do you want to know what my blessing was?"

Pong looked up at her. He remembered how Father Cham had told him that he'd changed the types of blessings he gave out. He'd stopped trying to alter the world with his gift.

Ampai placed her hand on her chest. "He told me, 'May your courage never falter.'"

Pong swallowed and steadied his breath. "Ampai, did you know that Father Cham died?"

Her eyes shimmered, but only for a moment before becoming steely again. "I did hear that," she whispered. She took Pong's hand. "Look, he gave you that bracelet because he believed you were special. He believed you were good."

"He believed everyone was good," whispered Pong.

Ampai squeezed his hand in hers. "He believed in you. He knew who you were, and he didn't think you were broken."

Pong shut his eyes. He tried to let what Ampai said settle in his mind. But he could only hear the same words he'd heard constantly over the years.

You were born in darkness . . .

. . . and that will never change.

The words still terrified him, but there was something comfortable about them, too. Father Cham had wished for Pong to find what he was looking for: freedom. And he would be free. He would turn his back on all this darkness, all this hurt, and finally get away from it.

He slowly pulled his hand out of Ampai's. Without meeting her gaze, he said, "We should go get more orbs before we run out of time."

Chapter 29

Nok stood in the ordering line, a row of glistening brown chickens turning on a roasting rack near her head. The heat coming off the Crimson orbs made her woozy. She felt as if she could close her eyes and not wake up for a week. Between working out at the spire-fighting gym during the day and searching the streets for Pong at night, she was almost worn out.

She stretched her stiff neck side to side. She hated her squeaky cot at the gym. She missed the light from her parents' room shining under the crack in the door. She missed her parents. She even missed her whiny little sisters. Nok was genuinely homesick, a useless thing to be in her situation. Even if she gave up and left the gym, she wouldn't be going home. She'd be going somewhere even less familiar — the mountaintop school. No, if home was what she wanted, she'd have to stick it out and finish what she came here to do.

Nok had walked every alley and floated down every canal in the entire city, some of them twice. There had been times when she thought she spotted Pong, only to get closer and find it was someone else. Once, in a crowded street, she had *felt* his presence. She knew he was close, but she never saw him. She wondered if Pong knew she was hunting him. Maybe he was tracking her, too, and that's how he stayed at least one step ahead.

She'd resorted to asking people if they'd seen him. She didn't like this method — it felt sloppy. But she was getting desperate. She could risk staying in the city for another day or two, and then she would have to go back to Tanaburi.

Nok stepped up to the front of the line, where an older woman was taking orders for roast chicken. The woman's hairnet tugged her painted eyebrows up, which gave her a look of permanent surprise. She greeted most of the customers by name and knew almost everyone's orders. Nok had learned enough about street markets to know that every market had a "Matron," a woman who kept tabs on everything that happened on her little stretch of canal. This woman with the painted eyebrows was definitely the Matron.

That made her the best person to answer Nok's questions.

When it was Nok's turn, the woman slid a bird off the roasting rack and started hacking it to pieces with a long butcher knife. "Whatcha want, sugar?" she asked. "Half a chicken or a whole?"

"Actually, could I just get a leg quarter, please?"

The woman froze mid-hack and gave Nok a stinky look before slicing off the bird's leg. Nok couldn't help being cheap — her money supply was dwindling, and she needed to make it last. The Matron handed Nok the meat in a paper box.

"Ma'am, can I ask you a question?" said Nok as she handed over her money.

"Hm."

Nok raised up on her toes a little. "I'm looking for someone. A boy about my age with a shaved head. He was a monk-in-training. His name is Pong. Have you seen him?"

The Matron slid another bird onto her cutting board. "Sugar, I run the busiest chicken stand on this canal. You think I'm gonna remember every Pong who comes along?"

Another woman, a younger version of the Matron, stepped out from behind the stall carrying a tray of raw chicken to add to the roaster. "Are you talking about Ampai's kid?" she asked.

"No, sorry," said Nok. "This boy is an orphan. Thank you, though."

As she turned to go, the younger woman added, "Because if you are, tell that boy to come around and listen to my orbs sometime."

"What?" said the Matron. "Whatcha mean 'listen' to orbs? Are they gonna tell you the weather or something?" She threw her head back and laughed.

"Very funny, Mom," said the young woman, skewering the limp chicken bodies onto the rack. "There's a rumor that this kid is going around town with Ampai. He gets real close to orbs, and . . . well, he listens to them or something."

Nok was suddenly wide awake.

"Oh, *ppth*," mocked her mother, sticking out her tongue. "Why would he do that?"

"Someone told me that the orbs whisper to him about the future," said her daughter. "Maybe he can listen to our orbs and tell me whether I'll ever get to move out and stop plucking dead chickens."

Nok's head filled with the memory of the courtyard at Namwon. She remembered the boy with sticking-up hair staring up into the mango tree, his ear pointed to the fruit. At the time she'd thought it was so strange. What kind of child listens to mangoes? Maybe the same kind who would listen to orbs.

"The person you mentioned," said Nok. "Ampai. Do you know how I can find her?"

The young woman scratched her cheek. "Hmm. I actually don't have any idea where she lives. But she does have an adopted nephew — a great big guy named Yai. I see him at the Hidden Market sometimes. I go there to get Mom's foot fungus medicine."

"Ay!" snapped the Matron, waving the butcher knife in the air. "Enough chitchatting! You think those chickens are going to pluck themselves?"

The young woman rolled her eyes. "All right, all right — I'm going." When her mother turned around, the young woman quickly grabbed another leg quarter off the cutting board and tucked it into a box. She slid it to Nok and winked. "On the house," she whispered.

"Thank you," Nok whispered back.

And she was thankful. She would need plenty of fuel for what she was going to do next.

Chapter 30

The sun had just set, which meant it was time for Pong's day to begin. The Mud House atrium was so dimly lit that he nearly tripped over his chair. They had taken most of the Violet orbs out of the atrium to swap them with faded orbs in the city. The tenants, who still had no idea what Ampai was up to, complained about having to stumble around, so Somkit made up some excuse about tinkering with the tinfoil cones. With the march only a few days away, he would only have to put them off a little while longer.

"Oh, man, I could sleep for weeks," said Pong groggily.

He sat across the dinner table from Somkit, whose day had just wrapped up. Both boys' heads drooped, their faces in danger of being washed in their soup.

"You think *you're* tired?" said Somkit. He flexed his fingers and arched his back from side to side. "Try sitting at a workbench for hours, pricking your fingers on a thousand copper wires over and over again."

"How many sun orbs do you have now?" asked Pong.

"One hundred and thirty-nine," said Somkit, yawning. "Our goal was just a hundred, but I figured that as long as you keep bringing me faded orbs, I'll make as many as I can. Ampai is telling everyone to bring a pole or a stick with them to the march. That way we can hang the orbs on them and carry them more easily."

"But Ampai is still keeping the actual sun orbs a secret?" asked Pong.

Somkit squeezed a lime over his noodles and nodded. "There's a big meeting Saturday night before the march. She'll tell everyone then. It should help convince anyone who's still on the fence to join us."

"Where's she now?" asked Pong. Usually Ampai would be in the hall at dinnertime, talking to everyone, quizzing the children on their schooling, or debating philosophy with the old scholars.

"She said to tell you that she had to go upriver to the woodworking district, and she won't be back tonight." Somkit poured green syrup into his glass of fizzy water and sipped it. "She wants as many people from different pockets of the city as possible to be in the march."

Pong frowned down at his food. "How long will she be gone?"

"She should be back tomorrow." Somkit leaned over his bowl toward Pong. "Don't worry: she hasn't forgotten about getting you on a boat."

"Are you sure? She hasn't mentioned anything about it since we first agreed."

"She's just busy with the march — that's all," said Somkit. "But she'll keep her promise. She's working on getting you a border permit. You'll need it when you get to the sea. If you have one of those, the shore patrol will wave you past, and they won't check anything or ask any questions."

Pong looked at Somkit skeptically. "That sounds illegal, doesn't it? I thought Ampai didn't break any laws."

Somkit shrugged and slugged a big gulp of soda. "It's *almost* legal. And Ampai will stretch the dumb laws. She knows the difference between what's the law and what's right. That's why so many people follow her."

"Is that why you follow her?" asked Pong.

Somkit grabbed a knot of noodles with his chopsticks. "Nah, I'm just here for the food." After a few seconds of chewing, he wiped his mouth with his napkin. His eyes stayed down on his bowl as he talked. "When

I got out of Namwon, I didn't have anywhere to go. I didn't know what to do. I found some other kids living on the street, and I hung around with them for a while, but it was . . ." He lifted his eyes to Pong's. "Do you know what happens to kids on the street who can't run and can't fight?"

Now it was Pong's turn to look down. He didn't want to know. This is what had haunted him all those years in the temple. He should have been there with Somkit when he got released. Whatever Somkit faced, they should have faced it together. Instead, his friend had to go through all of it alone.

Somkit took a big breath and let it out the side of his mouth. He reached for a shaker of spicy salt and dumped half of it into his bowl. "I got lucky, you know? When Ampai found me, I was stealing food. If she hadn't come along, I think I'd be back in jail by now. Worse, maybe."

Pong had learned enough about life on the East Side to know that Somkit wasn't exaggerating.

"She brought me here," Somkit went on, "gave me a home, gave me food. I mean, that would've been enough. But she did more." He glanced up at the remaining Violet orbs swinging overhead, cradled in his reflective inventions. "She made me feel like I can do anything. Like I have something to give."

Pong watched his friend stir his noodles from one side of his bowl to the other and back again. If Ampai hadn't found Somkit, and he were still living on the street, Pong would never have forgiven himself. And Ampai was right — Somkit *could* do anything. Right now he was doing something no one except the Governor had ever done before.

"What?" said Somkit, his mouth full of food. "You're looking at me funny."

"You know something?" said Pong with a smile. "There was a time when we were little and you made me promise that I'd keep my mouth shut and stay out of trouble. And now you're the biggest loudmouth I know, and you're planning to march against the Governor."

Somkit grinned. "Yeah, well, when I run my mouth, I do it with charm. Makes all the difference." He pushed his chair back and let out a thunderous burp that made the little children on the other end of the table jump. "Sorry," he said to their mothers with a wave of his hand. "Soda. Does it to me every time. So, Pong, since Ampai's not here, maybe you can take a break. What do you say, should we head out and try to find us some dessert? I'm thinking —"

Somkit went quiet and stared past Pong. Pong turned around to see what he was looking at. Yord and

Yai slunk in the back door and hurried up the stairs, darting secretive glances over their shoulders.

"What do you think they're up to?" asked Somkit, narrowing his eyes.

"Can't be good," said Pong. "I really don't like those two. I just can't understand how Ampai puts up with them."

"Yai's mother was Ampai's friend. When she died, Ampai promised she'd look after him. I guess Yord just comes along for the ride. They are pretty useful at certain things. They can get anything you need on the Hidden Market, like medicine and stuff, so Ampai looks the other way when it comes to them skimming off the top."

"What do you mean, skimming?"

"You know. Whenever they go out to collect money for our cause, I'm pretty sure that Yord keeps some for himself."

Pong nodded. "A finder's fee."

"Wish he'd find himself a new gig," grumbled Somkit. "I hope Ampai will finally dump them after the march. She always tells me that everyone deserves a chance to do good things, but sometimes I think she's too trusting". He turned to Pong, rubbing his stomach. "So what do you say? Fruit market before it closes? Durian's in season."

Pong made a face. "No, thanks. I'm still waking up." *And I don't want to smell like a dead bat,* he thought.

"Suit yourself. I'll be back in a few."

Somkit left through the door under the stairs. Pong cleared their dishes away and then started to head back to their room. He paused on the steps. Somkit had said he made 139 sun orbs.

Pong counted up the nights that he and Ampai had gone out into the city. Pong had collected a total of 151 orbs. Where were the other twelve? He hurried upstairs into Somkit's room and pulled the curtain partway so that he was shielded from view but could still see Ampai's office door. He could hear Yai and Yord inside, shuffling their feet and sliding boxes across the floor.

The door to the office swung open, and the two men stepped out. Yai had his satchel slung over one shoulder. One of Yai and Yord's main jobs for Ampai was to deliver the donations she collected from her friends all over the city. Bandages and ointments, vitamins and creams — anything that was too expensive or hard to find.

But something was up. Yai didn't let his satchel hang over his back like usual. He cradled the bottom of it with one hand, like a lady carrying an expensive purse. Whatever was inside, it wasn't cotton bandages. Pong held his breath and listened. As the men passed Somkit's room and started down the stairs, he heard it: the soft *tink-tink* of glass on glass.

Pong scowled. Those crooks were taking the faded orbs.

Ampai hadn't told them what the orbs were for, but they must have figured out where she was keeping them. What were they going to do with them?

He waited until the men were down the stairs and out the door before grabbing his cap and following them.

Yai and Yord didn't head for the usual neighborhoods that would be on a supply delivery route. Instead, they snaked along the canals that led deeper inland, toward the metals district. Pong kept a good distance behind, thankful that Yai's hulking body was easy to track in a crowd. They passed through industrial neighborhoods, where the orb buzz was drowned out by the sound of clanging hammers and the whir of saws.

The men hooked around a rusty warehouse and turned onto a walkway suspended above a sludgy canal. The stink of sewage, mixed with boat paint and machine grease, wafted up from the thick water. People crowded the walkway and clustered around the shops perched above the sludge. Unlike the other alleys, where the vendors had big orb-lit signs and played music to attract customers, the vendors here had no signs at all. Everything was designed to be packed away quickly or abandoned.

This must be the Hidden Market. Somkit had told Pong about it: a place where you could get anything, as long as you had the cash. Pong tracked Yai and Yord to a rickety table squeezed between two other vendors. The crowd of shoppers provided a screen so he could watch them.

Yai opened his satchel. Just as Pong suspected, it was packed full of orbs.

A young couple timidly approached the table. Yord smiled like a toad and waved them closer. "Trust me, kids, these are as fine as any orb you'd buy in the Light Market, and I'll give 'em to you at half the price!"

Yord held up one of the orbs and flicked on the switch. As the couple leaned in closer, he quickly turned it off again. "I have to keep them switched off so I don't attract too much attention," he said with a slick smile. "Or else I'd be swarmed with customers. But don't worry — I'm saving this deal just for you."

Now Pong understood what Yord was up to. Most of the orbs that Pong had swiped on his nightly runs with Ampai still had a little bit of light left in them. They usually faded completely by the time they got to the Mud House, but some would last a few minutes more as long as they were kept switched off. Yai and Yord must have taken those, and now they were selling them here, to people who had no idea the orbs would go dead any minute.

Pong clamped his back teeth together. That poor couple was going to get swindled if he didn't stop them. He started forward, but then stopped cold. Through the metal-tinged air, he caught a whiff of something very different. It was a smell that pulled him downriver, up a mountain, and back through time to almost two weeks ago. It was the smell of lemon blossoms and fresh-scrubbed wood.

Pong whirled around, searching the mass of shoppers. Strangers bumped into him and shouldered their way past. He scanned their faces frantically, but he didn't see any other kids his age, and certainly no girls with a bob of black hair and sharp black eyes. But the scent of lemon and teak still lingered.

She was here.

Pong forgot all about the poor couple with Yai and Yord. He wove back down the walkway and ducked behind a stack of crates, breathing hard.

She couldn't be here. Could she? He remembered the look on Nok's face when he leaped from the edge of the cliff. At the time he thought it was a look of pure hatred. But now he wondered if he had read her wrong. Maybe that had been the look of someone determined to get her revenge.

What if she had somehow figured out that he had come back to Chattana? It seemed impossible. But what if it wasn't? If he could find Somkit by accident, maybe Nok could find him on purpose.

Pong's breath was coming fast, even though he was standing perfectly still. He had an overwhelming urge to run straight to the Mud House and hide. But he couldn't go back now. In fact, he couldn't go back ever again.

If Nok Sivapan was really on his trail and he went to the Mud House, she'd track him straight there. Back to Somkit and Ampai and everyone else.

If he was caught, he wouldn't be the only one in trouble. Ampai could be put in prison for hiding him. Everyone who depended on her would have no one to help them. And Somkit? Pong shuddered to remember what he'd told him about life on the street. Without Ampai, where else would he live? Pong would not do that to his friend, not again. He had helped them as much as he could. It was long past time for him to go.

Pong waited behind the crates, sniffing the air until he was as sure as he could be that Nok was nowhere near. Then he pulled his cap down to his eyebrows and hurried back the way he'd come. He waited in the shadows of a side alley he knew Yai and Yord would pass on their way home. When he spotted them coming, he leaped out into their path.

"Well, lookie here," sneered Yord. "It's the Junior Patrol. What can we do for you, little golden boy?"

Pong stared back at them, willing his voice to be confident and steady. "I know what you've been doing with Ampai's orbs."

Before either of the crooks could shut their surprised jaws, he added, "And if you don't want her to know what you've done, you'll get me what I need."

Yord smiled slickly. Blackmail was something he understood. "What's your price?"

"A boat," said Pong. "And I want it tonight."

Chapter 31

Nok kept her head down as she passed the men and women strolling along the quiet West Side canals. No one seemed to take much notice of her, but she kept catching whiffs of the greasy sewer smell from the Hidden Market coming from her hair. Any bad odor was noticeable here, where the sidewalks were swept hourly and lotus blossoms floated in the clear water below.

She wished that she could have showered and changed, but there wasn't time. Her message couldn't wait.

Nok had followed the clues she'd picked up from the young woman at the chicken stand, circling closer and closer to Pong's whereabouts. It took her a while to find the Hidden Market, but once she arrived on that grimy canalway, she had spied two men — one massive, one short — hawking orbs on a rickety table.

She had seen these men before, on the night she had gotten lost. They had been walking with a woman that night. The woman must have been Ampai, and this big guy must be her nephew. Nok could tell they were up to something funny. They were too happy to sell, and their customers were too desperate to buy.

Nok didn't see Pong with them, but she knew he was there. It sounded impossible, but she could *feel* his presence as surely as if he stood right next to her. He had to be close by. So she waited and watched the two con artists, hoping that if she followed them, they would eventually lead her to Pong's lair.

That's when she overheard a very disturbing conversation.

"Those are the guys," said a woman's voice. "The big one is Yai, and the one with the smashed-up nose is Yord."

Nok didn't dare turn around to see who had spoken. She held very still and listened.

"The ones who came and talked to you?" asked a man.

"Yes. They're helping Ampai," the woman answered. "We're supposed to gather at the Giant's Bridge on Sunday after the sun goes down. They said to bring a long pole or a stick."

"A stick?" said the man. "What for?"

"I don't know," answered the woman. "But they said to keep that part quiet. They said they don't want word getting back to the Governor about any of it."

"And you're sure this is really going to happen?"

The woman lowered her voice so much that Nok had to hold her breath to hear. "I've heard that a thousand people might be there! Can you imagine what the Governor will think when he sees us? I just hope we all have the courage to go through with it."

Go through with what? Nok wondered. A thousand people? And why would they be gathering sticks or poles unless it was to use them as weapons? Nok shivered all over. She turned the words around and around in her mind, trying to make sense of them, but she kept coming to the same conclusion.

She had uncovered a plot to attack the Governor.

Nok's pulse raced. The two con men she had been watching packed up their things and slipped into the crowd. Should she follow them to see if they led her to Pong's hideout? Or should she hurry to tell someone what she had just overheard?

She was so close to Pong that she could practically smell him, but in her heart she knew that the plot she had just learned about was more important. The right thing to do was to abandon her hunt and report what she'd heard. Once she realized that, her mind was made up. Nok always did the right thing.

Besides, if Pong was involved with Ampai, then when the authorities arrested her, they'd capture Pong as well. Two fish in one basket, all thanks to her.

Nok now hurried along the clean sidewalks, turning to take the shortcut through the botanical gardens to her house. The garden paths were empty of visitors. Along the walkways, hundreds of paper lanterns swung from the branches of orange trees, with more nestled in the reeds at her feet. Gold orbs cradled in folded paper cups floated among the lotus below. It was like walking through the blackness of the sky, surrounded by thousands of stars.

Nok's footsteps slowed. The last time she'd walked the gardens at night, the twins were still babies. Her mother had taken them to visit relatives, and her brother was sleeping over at a friend's house. Nok and her father had had a rare night alone, and he'd brought her to the gardens as a treat.

"When my father was a little boy, his family's farmhouse was right here," he had told Nok, sweeping his arm over the gardens. "There was no West Side back then. Just fields and fields of sugarcane."

"Your dad was a farmer?" asked Nok. "But I thought he had a big important government job."

Her father smiled. "That came later. You see, the Great Fire never crossed to this side of the river, so families like ours weren't nearly as devastated by it. When the Governor arrived, he needed people to help him. The West Side families designed factories to make glass orbs and constructed the motors powered by them. My father built the very first Charge Station, which saved the Governor time that he could devote to running the city. As a reward, the Governor made him the Commissioner of Finance. It could have all gone very differently for our family if he'd been born on the other side of the river."

"Mama says people on the East Side live like fish trapped in a puddle when the tide goes out."

Her father nodded sadly. "That's true for a lot of them, yes."

"They should be like the people over here," said Nok. "If you work hard and follow the law, good things happen to you. *The law is the light, and the light shines on the worthy.*"

Her father tilted his head at her. "Where did you hear that?"

"School," said Nok. "We're learning the Governor's proverbs."

"Ah, of course," he said dully. "I'd forgotten that one."

Nok didn't see how. That same proverb hung on the wall at the prison where he worked. But this was before she was old enough to learn that her father actually spent as little time at the prison as possible.

He cleared his throat and cleaned his glasses. "Sometimes things aren't as simple as they teach you in school."

"What do you mean?"

"Well, sometimes light shines on the worthy. But sometimes it just shines on the lucky ones. And sometimes . . ." He looked over his shoulder at the East Side, glittering like a rainbow across the river. "Sometimes good people get trapped in the dark."

Nok slipped her small hand into his big one. "I don't understand, Daddy."

"I don't quite understand myself, I'm afraid." Her father squeezed her fingers and sighed, his breath fogging his spectacles again. He took them off and cleaned them with his shirt. When he spoke again, he sounded like a schoolteacher, scolding himself. "It doesn't matter, sweetheart. Things are the way they are. There's not much we can do to change it."

As the memory faded, Nok shook her head side to side. She loved her father so much, but even though she hated to admit it, she was also a little ashamed of him. How could a man who had been the warden of a prison — who was the *Law Commissioner* — be so wishy-washy when it came to what he believed? Why did he have such a hard time seeing right from wrong?

Nok gripped her staff and started walking again, but this time she took a sharp turn out of the gardens.

The law is the light.

And right now that light was in danger of being snuffed out. Her father couldn't help her now. She needed to go to someone who would understand how serious this was. Someone who would know immediately what to do.

A soft rain began to fall as Nok arrived at the tall wooden gates. A guard materialized from the shadows.

"Stop right there," he called. "Who are you?"

Nok set her staff on the ground and bowed deeply. "My name is Supatra Sivapan," she said, using her formal name. "I am the daughter of Commissioner Sivapan, and I have an urgent message for the Governor."

Chapter 32

Pong was surprised at how steadily he walked as he wove through the crowds along the canal. He expected that he'd be jittery or in a hurry, but he was able to keep a calm, even pace. No one looked at him as he passed. Apparently, he'd mastered the art of walking unseen just when he wouldn't need it any longer.

He headed for the agreed-upon meeting place — a thin dock on a canal lined with butcher shops. The thick traffic in the canal moved slowly. Pong's stomach fluttered for a moment with the worry that Yai and Yord wouldn't be there, or that they wouldn't have been able to get him a boat in time. But when he looked up, there they were, standing beside a beat-up pink water taxi.

Pong frowned. He'd been hoping for something less noticeable, but it was too late to request an exchange now. Yai stood on the dock with one foot resting on the rim of the boat, holding it still. Yord stood beside him, his eyes darting to the people in the crowd. Pong hurried their way, wanting to get this part over with as soon as possible.

Yord grinned when he saw him. "Well, then, we're all settled, Junior." He looked down at the water taxi. "We even put some fresh water and bananas in the front for you. All the comforts of home."

"Wait," said Pong. "What about a border permit?"

Yord's grin melted into a sneer. "You think those things grow on trees?"

"How am I supposed to get out to sea in a pink taxi with no permit?" asked Pong.

"Just keep your head down," said Yord. "You'll figure something out. You'd better get going. Enjoy the beach, little guy."

Pong fumed at the oily man but climbed into the boat without arguing. Yord was right. He couldn't waste any more time.

He pulled his cap lower over his brow. Teenage taxi drivers were common, so at least he wouldn't look too suspicious. He just hoped that no one flagged him down for a ride. Yai tossed Pong the keys.

Pong started to thank him before deciding that he didn't owe those slimeballs thanks for anything. Besides, he had bigger worries — he had to figure out how to drive a boat.

Pong put the key into the ignition and turned it. The taxi's Jade orb winked on, and the motor sputtered to life. With a worrisome rattle, the taxi lurched forward, nearly crashing into a boat stacked high with papayas.

"Sorry! Sorry!" said Pong, easing back on the throttle. He steered away from the papaya boat, over-correcting and turning sideways in the canal. Grannies in their canoes shook their fists at him and pushed him away with the tips of their paddles.

Pong cut the motor off and wiped his forehead. This was not the speedy getaway he needed to make. He'd have to wait until he floated out to the river, where he'd have enough room to get the hang of the taxi without killing someone. He drifted along with the grannies, pulling his oar slowly through the inky water while his heart raced like a speedboat motor.

The boat-choked canal grew wider, and the dark band of the Chattana River opened up before him. Across the water, Pong saw the faraway firefly lights of the West Side. A fresh breeze of cooler air blew over him, and a gentle rain began to fall. Good, that would make it easier to get away without being noticed. He turned the key and slowly — controlled this time — motored out into the main channel. *Time to say goodbye to Chattana forever*, he thought.

He turned the taxi boat south and cautiously ventured into the slower flow, staying close to the eastern bank. He passed a small temple on the shore, where it was forbidden to go fishing. Fat carp schooled so thick they formed writhing mats of silvery scales on the surface.

The back of Pong's neck prickled with that familiar itchy feeling of being watched. He wanted to believe that he was just imagining it, but the feeling stayed. He squinted, trying to see the shore through the rain. Someone was walking across the temple grounds toward him a little too fast to be an ordinary temple visitor.

Pong gripped the throttle and tried to push it forward, but it jammed. He looked over his shoulder. The person was still approaching. They were close now, but he couldn't see who it was through the screen of raindrops.

Pong jiggled the slippery throttle. "Come on, come on, come on . . ." He felt gears grinding beneath the controls, but nothing would engage.

He was starting to reach for the oar when something heavy and bony slammed into him from above, knocking him down into the bottom of the boat.

"What the —?" Pong struggled out from under a

tangle of wet limbs and staggered to his feet. His stomach rolled up in a crest of panic, and then back down again when he finally realized who it was.

"Somkit!" gasped Pong. "What are you doing here?"

"What am I doing?" shouted Somkit. "What are *you* doing? You're running off! Without even a word to me about it!"

"Shh!" said Pong. The soft drum of rain muffled their voices, but they were still close enough to shore for people to hear them. "How did you know?"

"You weren't at the Mud House when I got back, so I went looking for you. My buddy from the motor repair shop said he ran into Yai and Yord at the junkyard. He said they were picking up a boat for a kid. So of course I put it all together." Somkit looked down at the taxi with mild disgust. "Good thing it was hot pink or I never would've found you."

Pong tugged at the edges of his cap. This was all going so badly. "Ugh, I should've known Yord wouldn't keep quiet about it."

"Well, it's a good thing he didn't!" Somkit was shouting again. "Otherwise I wouldn't even know you were gone until tomorrow. Were you even going to leave me a note? Anything?"

"Keep your voice down!" hissed Pong. They were still

in the thick of town. Pong took hold of the throttle and waggled it uselessly.

"Oh, for crying out loud," huffed Somkit. "Haven't you ever driven a boat before? Move over, move over."

He shoved Pong back into a seat and wedged himself at the controls, the wheel in one hand, throttle in the other. "Man, this thing is a real piece of crap. It's going to sink before you get to the sea. You know that, right?" Somkit finally rammed the throttle forward, and the taxi leaped through the water so fast that it nearly threw Pong over backward.

Under Somkit's skilled hand, the taxi zipped past the other boats, flying across the water. When they were far enough from the riot of traffic and out of earshot of anyone on shore, Somkit cut the motor off.

"Please," begged Pong. "You've got to go back to shore and let me go. I've already wasted so much time...."

Somkit crossed his arms over his chest. "Taking five minutes to say goodbye to your best friend is a waste of time?"

"Ugh, you don't get it! Tonight, on the street, I'm sure that I saw — well, not saw, exactly, but —"

"The march is just three days away," Somkit interrupted. "We've been working so hard on it. And you're just going to disappear?"

A hot bubble of shame rose in Pong's chest. He was leaving again. Running away — again. But couldn't Somkit see that he had no choice? "Is that all you care about?" Pong shouted. "That stupid march?"

Somkit looked stunned.

"That march is your thing, not mine," said Pong. "I was just helping because I owed you a favor. But I'm not going to stick around and put myself in danger for something so — so useless!"

"You don't really believe that," said Somkit quietly.

"How do *you* know what I believe?" said Pong. "You think we're best friends and you know me so well, but you've got no idea. You don't know what I've done, and you don't know who I am!"

Somkit scowled. He picked up the oar and jabbed the wide end of it into Pong's chest, hard enough that it knocked him backward into a seat.

"Hey!" gasped Pong, rubbing his chest.

Somkit stood over him, his face a jumble of sadness and rage. "Don't you tell me I don't know you. I know you better than anyone else does. Better than you know yourself."

Pong swallowed, too stunned to speak. The sudden *zhum!* of an orb motor closed in on them from the starboard side. The little taxi rocked on tall waves, and the boys were temporarily blinded by a Gold spotlight shining through the raindrops.

"Stop and get your hands up!" demanded a voice, tinny and amplified by a loudspeaker. "In the name of the Governor, you're under arrest!"

Chapter 33

The guard rolled back the heavy gate and motioned for Nok to follow a maidservant standing behind him. "She'll take you to the Governor's receiving room," he said.

Nok blushed, suddenly realizing the late hour. "I — I hope I'm not keeping His Grace up too late, but this is an urgent —"

"You aren't keeping him up," said the maid curtly. "His Grace works late into the night and is up again before dawn. The man has far too much to do to be asleep at this hour."

Nok nodded and followed her down the path leading to the Governor's house. Jasmine hung from wooden trellises lining the walkway. Tiny Gold orbs the size of cherry pits sat nestled in the blossoms.

Nok straightened the front of her tunic, wishing that she'd changed her clothes before coming. She imagined what her mother would say to her, showing up at a place like this wearing a spire-fighting uniform, but it was too late to worry about that now.

The maid led Nok into the house and up a short flight of steps to the second level. Everything inside was built from dark wood, polished to a gleaming shine. It was so plain and austere, very different from most West Side houses, with their gaudy furniture and show-off decorations.

The maid stopped at a door at the end of the hall and turned to Nok. "Put that over there," she said, eyeing Nok's staff and gesturing to a nook outside the door. Nok nodded and leaned it against the wall.

The maid swung open the door. "Your visitor is here, Your Grace," she said with a bow.

Nok swallowed a surge of nervousness and bowed to the Governor, keeping her eyes down until she heard his deep voice say, "Welcome, child. Please come in."

Nok walked forward. The maid stayed behind, standing at attention near the open doorway.

The Governor sat at the center of a long table, a neat stack of papers near his elbow. A faint ribbon of steam curled above the teapot and single cup of tea set before him. "Good evening, Miss Sivapan. I hear you have a message for me."

Nok knew it wasn't polite to stare, but this was only the second time she'd seen the Governor this close. He looked exactly as she remembered him.

Nok's mother often said that she wished she knew the Governor's secrets of youth. His face was smooth and unlined, though he must be much older than her parents. Nok knew he had come to Chattana as a grown man, and that was almost forty years ago. But she knew nothing of his life before that. Even though her schooling focused on the Governor's teachings and his deeds, she had never been taught when he was born or where.

Some people claimed that he was a holy man who had come down from the mountains to save the city in its darkest hour. His strict and humble lifestyle made that story believable — after all, someone so powerful could easily have used that power to make himself extravagantly wealthy. Instead, he lived plainly, like a monk. But now that Nok saw him up close, she didn't think he was much like a monk at all. Something tense hid behind his calm face, like a spring pressed into a tight coil.

Nok suddenly remembered what her father had told her years ago: when the Governor rose to power, the first thing he had built wasn't a temple, but a jail.

She felt a chill, even though the windows were open to the warm night. She dipped her head and fixed her gaze on the table in front of her. "Your Grace, I apologize for disturbing you, but I have important information that I felt couldn't wait."

"By all means," he said, waving her to the chair across from him. While Nok took the seat, he raised the teacup to his lips and took a small sip. "It must indeed be a matter of great importance if you felt the need to come to me directly."

Nok caught a hint of amusement in his voice, like a grown-up talking down to a little kid. She held her chin up. "Yes, Your Grace, I believe it is."

She kept her words slow and measured as she told him about Pong and about her quest to find him that led her through the city. She left out the details of lying to her parents, skipping instead to her trip to the Hidden Market and all that she'd heard there.

"I'm sure these people are planning some scheme that would bring you harm," she said, leaning forward in her seat. The Governor was listening to everything so passively. She wanted him to take her seriously, but now that she was saying everything out loud, she realized that she didn't have as much information as she thought. She knew there was a plot, but she didn't know exactly what they were doing.

"Your Grace, I — I urge you to take up the matter

as quickly as possible and send police right away to investigate."

The Governor set down his cup and folded his hands on the table. He smiled, looking a little embarrassed for her. "I thank you for your concern, child, but, you see, I already know about this."

Nok sat back. "You — you do?"

"Yes," said the Governor coolly. "And you're right. The woman you mentioned — Ampai — is indeed planning something. But it's not a plot to hurt me physically. She is planning a march along the Giant's Bridge."

"Are you sure, Your Grace? Perhaps that's their cover story for what they're truly planning. From what I heard, it sounded so —"

"I have a spy who works with her," interrupted the Governor. "A man named Yord. He lives in the building with her followers, a place called the Mud House. He's told me everything." The Governor took another slow sip of tea. "This woman, Ampai, has been working tirelessly over the past year to rally the poor to march against me. She will try to carry out her plans this very weekend."

"March against you?" asked Nok. "You mean a riot?"

"Oh, no," said the Governor, his lip turning up in the slightest of smirks. "She is determined to make it a peaceful march. She has ordered all who follow her to bring no weapons and even asked them to sign pledges against violence."

Nok suddenly felt as though she'd shrunk in her chair to the size of a toddler. What a fool she was! A peaceful march. She'd been so sure that she'd uncovered a sinister scheme, but now that she remembered all she'd overheard in the Hidden Market, a march made perfect sense. She'd let Pong go again, and had come here and embarrassed herself, all for nothing.

"Your Grace, I am so sorry . . ." she said, hanging her head.

"It's all right. Things like this happen from time to time," he answered, not seeming to understand what she meant by her apology. "When you have been in power as long as I have, you learn that these little ripples of trouble are unavoidable. It has been almost forty years since I brought my light to Chattana. The people have grown forgetful of what it was like before. But I remember."

The Governor's voice quieted. "When I first came here and saw the suffering and ruin, it nearly broke my heart. A once-great city flattened, and the people digging in the mud like dogs. I could hardly bear it." For a moment the tightness in his face unwound. His eyes held a trace of that heartbreak, as if he were seeing all that suffering for the first time.

"I wanted to leave. It seemed impossible that the city could ever get back on its feet again. But I knew I had the power to make things better." He held his hand palm up on the table and looked down at his open fingers. "The people were desperate for a leader, for someone to tell them what to do. I vowed that I would give them what they needed and that such destruction would never happen again."

The more the Governor spoke, the more his face hardened back into that noble image that Nok knew so well from pictures in textbooks. She heard a faint buzzing sound, like a mosquito flying in and out of striking distance.

"It was my destiny to bring Chattana back to the light," he said. "Every day since that first day has been a struggle to keep order, to keep the darkness at bay. Not just the darkness of the night, but the darkness in people's own hearts. But it has all been worth it. Forty years later, there have been no fires, no wars, no disasters. And I intend to keep it that way. This Ampai woman talks of fairness and compassion, but she forgets that those things are meaningless without the rule of law." He set his teacup down on the table and twisted it so that the design lined up with the teapot. "These little disturbances have cropped up before. I have always dealt with them quietly, but this time I realize that the best way to teach the people a lesson is to punish them."

Nok raised her chin slowly. "Punish them? But you wouldn't punish them for a peaceful march."

The Governor's eyes swung to meet hers, and for a moment Nok was afraid she'd said something wrong. She racked her brain, recalling her school lessons. But no, she hadn't made a mistake. There was no law against a peaceful demonstration.

"Do you know who these people are that this woman is gathering?" the Governor asked. Without waiting for an answer, he said, "Former convicts, the uneducated. The very lowest level of our society. Do you really think that their only intention is to walk peacefully across the river?"

Nok thought about the con men she'd seen selling orbs at the Hidden Market. She doubted they had good intentions. But what about their poor customers? What about the people she had seen begging? Nok didn't believe they would turn violent.

She blinked, trying to see things clearly. "I — I don't know what their intentions are, Your Grace. But the law . . ."

The Governor clenched his fingers into his palm. "Yes?"

Nok swallowed. She felt momentarily lost, as if she were supposed to repeat something she'd been taught in school but didn't know what it was. She said the first words that came to her. The ones that felt true. "The law is the light. Don't we all have to follow it?"

The Governor's dark eyes flickered. All the amusement drained out of them, and this time Nok knew she had said the wrong thing.

"The law is a light that shines on the *worthy* and punishes the *wicked*," he said crisply, repeating one of his proverbs word for word.

He kept his eyes on hers and inclined his face slightly. "Speaking of the law, does my Commissioner, your father, know that you're here?"

A chill crept down the back of Nok's arms as she shook her head. "I wanted to come here right away," she said. "Thinking you were in danger, I didn't want to delay."

"How considerate of you," he said, though it didn't sound like a compliment. "I have known your father a very long time. It was his father, your grandfather, who did so much to help me in those early days. Oh, yes, your father and I go back very far. He once represented one of the finest and most noble families in Chattana."

Nok swallowed at the word *once*.

"Everyone is entitled to make a mistake," said the Governor. "But no one escapes the consequences of their errors, and your father has made many. It started when he married that woman."

"You mean my mother," Nok whispered.

"No," snapped the Governor. "Not *your* mother. You are not the daughter of your father's wife, as anyone with eyes can clearly see."

Nok winced. It was a shock to hear someone speak her family secret out loud, like hearing a bad word you knew but never said. Was it really so obvious? Had she been fooling herself all this time, thinking that no one noticed the truth?

"Your father's wife — the mother of your siblings — came from a common family," he went on. "It was quite a scandal when they married. She had no money and no connections, but at least she abided by the law. Not like your birth mother."

Nok held her breath as the chill spread from her arms to the rest of her body.

The Governor didn't seem to notice she'd gone stiff. He spoke without emotion, as if they were chatting about something ordinary, like the weather or the fishing report.

"Your real mother was a criminal. I don't know how

your father met her. Some people are just drawn to the wretched, I suppose. Some time after they began seeing each other, she was caught robbing a man. Your father tried to get me to pardon her and hush it all up, but I refused. I sent her to Namwon, and that's where you were born."

Nok's teeth chattered. She hugged her arms in tighter.

Born in Namwon.

It couldn't be true.

The Governor flicked his fingers open and closed absentmindedly. Each time his hand opened, Nok's eardrum flexed from the pressure change. A pea-size ball of light formed in the Governor's palm, then went out as he curled his fingers shut.

"After your real mother died in childbirth, your father and his wife wanted to adopt you. They must have realized it would be easier to keep the truth a secret with you under their care. Against my wishes, they brought you into their home and raised you as their own. I suppose she must have forgiven him.

"However, I did not," he went on. "But I felt I owed him a debt because of all that his family did for me in those early days. I let him keep you on one condition: that he take the job as warden of Namwon, so that he would never forget the price of turning away from the law. For a while I thought that everything had worked out for the best. I had heard you were growing up to be a good, upstanding student. But now I see that I was right about you from the start."

Nok couldn't listen to any more of these lies.

They must be lies.

She couldn't have been born in a prison.

Nok had to get out of the room. She placed her hands on the table in front of her to steady herself. As she rose from her seat, the Governor reached out and grabbed her left wrist, pinning it to the table.

"Have you still got that scar?"

Nok stood frozen.

He twisted her palm up and pressed his fingers down on her wrist. "I heard it was quite a bad burn." He still held the little ball of Gold light in his other hand. "They tried to hide what you were," he snarled. "But they can't erase your true nature. I can tell that you sympathize with Ampai and those dark forces moving against me. I'm troubled by this but not surprised. Not at all."

Suddenly, the Governor squeezed the light into his fist. The air between them wavered and crackled like static. With a disgusted huff, the Governor let go of

Nok's wrist and sat back in his chair. The light was gone from his hand.

The skin beneath Nok's left sleeve tingled. She fumbled with the cuff and pulled back the fabric.

The scar tissue on her arm glowed. The tiny ball of light the Governor had held a moment ago seemed to be floating beneath her skin. It swam back and forth like a flickering minnow. Nok gasped as the light rose to the surface, blazed brightly for a moment, and then faded. The light was gone, but it had etched something onto her wrist that had never been erased, just hidden for years: the indigo ink of a Namwon tattoo.

The Governor gave a short nod to the maid standing at the door. "Send a message to this girl's father and tell him to come retrieve her."

Nok bolted from the table and ran for the door, but two servants blocked her way. Another stood behind them holding Nok's staff. It didn't matter. She was shaking too hard to use it.

"Lock her up," the Governor told the guards. "Treat her well, but keep an eye on her. I don't want her to run off before her parents see what she's done to their good name."

Chapter 34

Pong had never imagined that the first time he set foot on the West Side of Chattana, it would be under arrest. The police officer who'd picked them up on the river — a man named Winya, with a round belly and a thin mustache — had marched them through the quiet jasmine-lined walkways with hardly a word. The same was not true for Somkit.

He'd jabbered on, asking again and again to speak with some other officer — a man named Manit. Pong wished his friend would shut up. Surely they'd meet every police officer they'd ever want to see once they got to the station. But to Pong's surprise, they weren't taken to a police station at all but to some sort of stable.

Officer Winya slid open the stable door, and a sour whiff of hay billowed out of the dusty building. Barred stalls lined the walls, and a wide aisle ran down the center. The stalls were all empty and scrubbed clean, though the strong odor of animals meant they must have been in use not long ago.

"So you see, sir," said Somkit in a voice sweet as palm sugar, "we were just testing that taxi out so we could fix the motor. Ask Officer Manit — he'll vouch for me."

Winya grunted and swung open a stall door. He motioned with his thumb for the boys to file inside. "I told you, he's busy," he grumbled. "The Governor called a big meeting for all the senior officers. I'm not gonna go disturb him just because some street rat wants me to. When he gets out, he can come deal with you." Winya swung the door shut and locked it. "Then we'll see who's telling the truth."

"Oh, I assure you, officer," said Somkit. "I always tell the absolute —"

"Knock it off," snapped Winya. "Manit might be an old softy when it comes to you hoodlums, but I know better. You're lucky I brought you here and not straight to the jail. If I hear one peep out of you"— he held up the keys and jangled them in Somkit's face —"I'll be locking you up where you really belong."

He stomped back down the aisle, hung the keys on a peg on the wall, and went out. The stable door slid shut behind him.

"Now what are we going to do?" whispered Pong.

"Relax," said Somkit. "Once Manit gets here, I'll talk to him and everything will be fine."

"A senior police officer?" asked Pong. "That doesn't sound fine to me."

"Manit's different. I know him, and he's a good guy. Trust me, he'll do the right thing and let us go."

Pong couldn't imagine this, but his friend sounded so sure. Somkit began pacing the stall, practicing what he'd say to Manit when he came. "So, as you can see, we didn't steal the taxi. It's an old junker, and we were just . . ."

While Somkit paced, Pong looked around the stable. There were no orbs inside, just the dim moonlight shining in through the slatted windows near the ceiling. It felt like a long time since Pong had been in a room with no orb light at all. The shadows seemed richer here, as if they were made of more colors.

As his eyes tracked the room, he realized that the shadows across the aisle held a deeper shadow, one that moved ever so slightly. He held still and watched. The dark shape shifted slowly. Two black eyes glimmered at him unblinking, like an owl's.

Pong's breath snagged in his throat. He'd know those eyes anywhere.

Nightmares of Nok had haunted him ever since he

had escaped her in Tanaburi. Most days he'd woken up in a sweat, unable to shake the image of her towering over him, dragging him back to prison. And now, finally, here she was. Pong waited for the same wave of panic that had plagued his dreams, but instead he felt a strange numbness. Maybe he'd known all along that she'd catch him eventually.

Slowly, he stepped up to the bars of his stall. Nok must have known he was looking at her, but she kept her head tucked under her arm, like a pigeon using its wing to shelter from the rain. Finally, she lifted her head again and the moonlight hit her face.

Pong took a step back. Had he made a mistake? Was that really Nok? Shadows pooled under her eyes. She stared at him flatly, as though she didn't know, or care, who he was. She couldn't look more different from that confident, defiant girl he'd last seen on the cliff's edge. The girl sitting slumped over a few yards away looked like the most miserable creature he'd ever seen.

That should have been satisfying. Instead, an uncomfortable feeling wormed its way between Pong's ribs.

And now he realized that Nok wasn't just watching him from the shadows. His first thought at seeing her was that she was there to gloat over his arrest. Why else would she be there? But curiously, she sat on the floor of a stall just like theirs, also locked behind a door.

Somkit had noticed her, too. He stepped up beside Pong, just as confused. "What's going on? Do you know that person?"

"That," whispered Pong, "is Nok Sivapan."

Somkit gasped. "*Sivapan*? As in the warden's kid? As in the one who's been chasing you? But why the heck is she locked up in here?"

That was Pong's question exactly. It made no sense. "What are you doing here?" Pong asked her directly. "Don't these guys know who your father is?"

Nok's eyes shut and opened again slowly. "They know who I am," she rasped in a voice that sounded shredded and wobbly from crying. She sat with her left arm cradled gingerly against her stomach. Pong noticed a dark crust of blood stuck to her cheek that trailed from a gash on her temple.

"Hey, who did that to you?"

"Will you knock it off with the small talk?" hissed Somkit, suddenly frantic. He pulled Pong close and whispered, "We've got bigger problems! With her in here, we'll never be able to talk our way out of this. She'll tell Manit who you are, and then he'll have no choice but to take you in. We've got to get out of here!"

Somkit gripped the bars of the stall door in both fists. His arms trembled as he twisted and pulled. The wooden bars creaked but didn't budge.

Pong snapped out of his numb state. Somkit was right. He wouldn't just sit and wait to be taken away, especially not with Nok there to watch.

He rattled the stall door, testing the strength of the hinges. They'd never break it open. He reached through the bars and felt the lock with his fingers. "Have you got anything we could pick this with?"

Somkit made a sour face and shook his head. "Not even a snip of wire." He mashed his forehead to the bars, scanning the stable. "Hey!" He pulled Pong close to him. "See that stick? We could use it to try to get the keys!"

Nok's staff stood propped against the door of the stall next to them. The police must have taken it away from her.

Pong glanced at Nok. He didn't want her to see what they were doing. But the girl was lying down on her side, one arm tucked under her chest. She wasn't even looking at him anymore.

"Okay, let's hurry!" he whispered.

Pong's neck scraped against the wooden bars as he jammed his shoulder between them, groping for the staff.

His finger brushed against bamboo. The staff wobbled back and forth and then fell toward him. Somkit caught it inches before it clattered to the ground.

"Phew!" he whispered. Nok still didn't stir.

The boys slid the staff under their stall door. Pong picked it up and stuck it out between the bars, angling for the peg on the wall. "Here, you hold the end so I don't drop it," he told Somkit.

Together the boys aimed the staff at the ring of keys hanging on the peg. It took a few tries, but finally Pong was able to use the staff to flip the keys off the wall. They landed on the floor with a soft jangle.

"You did it!" whispered Somkit. "Now use the stick to drag them to us."

But before Pong could do anything, the front door swung open and the light from the porch orb flooded inside.

"All right, boys," said Officer Winya as he stepped into the stable. "The meeting's almost over, and—" Winya stopped mid-stride and stared at the boys. His eyes traveled down the length of the staff to the keys on the floor. "Hey, what's going on here?"

Pong yanked the staff back inside the stall with him. Somkit hid it behind his back, as if Winya wouldn't notice a five-foot-long bamboo pole sticking up in the air.

Winya snarled and picked up the keys. "I knew it," he said as he walked toward their stall. "You street rats are coming with me."

Pong's pulse throbbed in his jaw as he watched Winya unlock their stall door and step inside.

Somkit held Nok's staff out in front of him. "Don't — don't come any closer!"

Winya narrowed his eyes.

"Oh, crap," muttered Somkit.

The officer growled and rushed at him.

"Oh, crap!" Somkit swung the staff out with miraculous timing. Winya ran straight into it, groin first.

"Oof!" The officer doubled over, clutching himself.

Somkit whacked the staff over Winya's back, sending him to the ground. He looked at Pong, his face almost as shocked as Winya's. "Now what?"

Pong scooped up the keys from where Winya had dropped them. The guard rolled onto his side, moaning.

"Come on!" Pong pulled Somkit by the arm out of the stall and swung the door shut behind them. He quickly fumbled with the keys until he got the right one and twisted it, locking Winya inside.

"Let's go, let's go, let's go!" called Somkit, dropping the staff and running for the stable door.

Pong ran after him a few steps, then looked back

over his shoulder. Nok lay on the floor of her stall with her face pressed to the bars.

Pong expected to feel a surge of hatred for her. This was his moment to get even. She was locked up, and he was free, and she deserved every bit of it.

Nok looked up at him with flat, resigned eyes. Pong knew that look. It was hopelessness.

The space behind his rib cage flared with that old familiar heat.

Ignore it, he told himself. *Ignore it and run!*

But even as he thought those words, his feet were turning his body around and taking him back to Nok's stall.

"Hey!" cried Somkit. "What are you doing?"

Pong stopped in front of Nok's door. He glanced at Winya, who puffed for breath as he struggled to get his feet under him. Pong's hands shook as he tried a key in the lock.

Twee! Winya's whistle trilled. *Twee! Twee!*

"Pong!" called Somkit, stomping his feet like a toddler. "We have to go!"

Nok sat up and held on to the stall bars. "What are you doing?" she whispered.

"Getting you out," said Pong, trying another key and failing.

Nok blinked. "Why?"

Twee! Twee! Winya blew the whistle over and over. Outside, Pong could hear men's voices shouting and boots pounding.

Click! The last key on the chain opened the lock, and Nok swung out of the cell, tumbling onto the ground at Pong's feet.

Somkit hurried back to Pong and grabbed his arm. "We are going *now!*"

It was too late. Four men in uniforms of the Governor's guard filed in through the stable door.

"Grab them!" gasped Winya, pointing to Pong and Somkit.

Pong still clutched the keys in his hand, searching frantically for some way to escape. No good. There was only one door.

"You kids!" shouted a guard. "Hands on your heads! You're under arrest."

Pong dropped the keys. He'd ruined their only chance to get away.

Nok swiped her staff from the ground and stepped forward, standing between Pong and the guards. She stared at Pong strangely, as though she couldn't get her eyes to focus on him.

"Hold on to something," she said quietly.

Pong and Somkit both grabbed onto each other before realizing that wasn't what she meant. They let go and gripped the stall bars on either side of them.

One of the guards pointed to Nok. "You there! Put the staff down! You're coming with us."

Nok stood with her feet planted wide, holding her staff in front of her with both hands. The posture was the same as that day she faced Pong at the cliff's edge, but this was a very different girl. Her hair stuck out in all directions. Her breath came fast and irregular. She looked wild and dangerous, like a wounded creature. The armed guards exchanged wary looks.

The first guard took a cautious step forward.

Nok twisted her shoulders, as though winding her body up.

She took one deep inhale through her mouth and held the staff up high.

"*HA!*" She brought the end of it down hard onto the stable floor.

Pong shut his eyes. Silence smothered the room. A hard pulse of air blasted over him, rippling through his clothes. The ground shook like an earthquake. He heard men's voices crying out, their words muffled by the intense pressure in his head.

His ears popped and he opened his eyes.

Somkit still clutched the stall bars. "What . . . the . . . heck?"

All four guards lay on their backs on the floor, twitching like fish in the bottom of a boat.

Somkit suddenly leaped to life and grabbed Pong and Nok by their wrists. "If we stay in this barn one more minute, I'm gonna kill both of you! Let's go!"

Chapter 35

Nok gripped the bench in the back of the speedboat as it rocketed across the water. She felt hollowed out and dizzy.

She must be in a state of shock. How else could she explain sitting silently on the seat of a stolen police boat while other police boats chased right behind?

It was just before sunrise, that rare time when there was hardly any traffic on the river. Nok watched the boy named Somkit as he expertly shifted gears, weaving around the choppy sections of current as if he knew exactly where to expect them.

He was the one who had stolen the boat. Somehow he'd known a secret way to jump-start it without any keys. He seemed completely at ease behind the controls, as if he'd driven this boat a dozen times.

Pong sat beside her on the other bench. She had barely looked at him since they'd run away from the stable, and she couldn't bring herself to look at him now.

Search orbs reached across the dark water toward them.

"They're coming up behind us!" Pong shouted to his friend.

"You guys hold on!"

Somkit gunned the motor as he made a sharp turn upriver. The sky had lightened just enough now that he could cut the boat's headlights, but they still had the Jade glow of the orb motor to worry about. Unless they could cut that off, they'd be easily found.

Somkit headed for the thick pillars of the Giant's Bridge. It was the only bridge that spanned the entire river, one of the last remaining structures from Chattana's wondrous past. According to Nok's history books, it was named for the giants who helped build it.

She had never given the bridge much thought before, but now that she was looking at it from underneath, she marveled that anyone could have lifted those colossal stones. Only a giant would have had the strength to sink the massive pillars there, in the deepest, swiftest section of the river.

Somkit expertly steered the boat to the north side of the bridge, trimming the motor to match the speed of the current. The orb behind the boat still glowed, but not as much as before, and the pillar would help hide them. The only thing to do now was wait.

Nok's eyes traveled up the pillar. Elephants had been carved into the base. Above them danced celestial maidens whose lovely faces had been worn away by a hundred years of rain. Nok felt like them, faded beyond recognition. Without looking, she ran her fingers over her left wrist.

Who was she?

She was not Nok Sivapan — that was certain. Nok Sivapan was perfect.

The girl sitting in the stolen police boat was the daughter of a criminal. She'd been born in a jail.

Trees drop their fruit straight down.

That was true, wasn't it? After all, she had attacked the police. Run from arrest. Assisted a fugitive. In the past few hours, she had entered a backward world, where nothing was the way it should be. And there was one thing that was wrong most of all: the boy she'd been hunting had found her first. He had had her locked behind bars. That was his moment for victory, his chance for revenge, and he had let her go.

This, more than anything else, shook Nok to her core. He let her go.

Why?

The police boats drew closer, their motors buzzing like a cloud of hornets. Pong and Somkit exchanged nervous glances.

Nok could call out right now. She could turn the boys in. It might redeem her enough in the eyes of the law that she'd be forgiven for the other bad things she'd done that night. Nok parted her lips. She took a deep breath.

He let me go, she thought. *He let me go.*

The search orbs pivoted away. The buzz of the motors faded. The police had turned to search elsewhere. Somkit and Pong both let out heavy, relieved breaths.

Nok shivered and shut her eyes. The person she once was had truly and completely vanished.

After the sound of the police boats faded entirely, Somkit pressed the throttle forward again. "I'll take us a little farther upriver, someplace where we can hide this boat. I'll figure out how to send Manit a message so he can come get it."

"And you really think he'll forgive you for taking it?" asked Pong. "Somkit, you're going to be in so much trouble. I don't think you'll be able to talk yourself out of it this time."

"Maybe," said Somkit, chewing his lip. "But if anyone

will understand, it'll be Manit. The thing I'm more worried about is what'll happen to —"

He turned and scowled at Nok. He motioned for Pong to come closer. The two boys whispered together, glancing over their shoulders at her. Nok knew what they were arguing about.

"You don't have to worry about me," she said.

Somkit glared at her. "Oh, sure. Like you won't run home and tell your daddy everything the first chance you get."

Nok looked behind them, at the Gold lights of the western shore winking off with the rising sun. She tried to imagine walking in the door of her house and joining her parents and siblings at breakfast. Would they look her in the eyes or turn their heads in shame? Nok didn't want to find out. Now she understood what her mother had meant about gossip cutting like a knife. If anyone learned the truth about her — where she'd been born, who her real mother was — her family would never recover. No amount of spire-fighting trophies could overshadow that. They had been right to want to send her away.

Away.

That's where Nok wanted to go now. But where to? She couldn't picture herself at a cheerful country school in the mountains any more than she could imagine going back to her parents. For some reason, the image of the library in Lannaburi came to her — the one with all the old books. It was quiet there. A person could get lost among the shelves for a long time.

"I won't be running home," she said finally.

The boys exchanged a look. Nok didn't know or care what it was about.

Somkit gripped the wheel and turned them north. He sliced the boat through the dark-green water, maneuvering into a quiet canal on the East Side. Somkit and Pong hopped out and began tying up the boat.

"Where are you going to go now?" Pong asked her.

But Nok had already slipped away, melting into the shadows without a sound.

Chapter 36

Pong and Somkit hurried for the Mud House, using the rising sun to guide them east.

Pong kept sneaking looks at his friend, who wore a deep scowl. "I know you're mad at me."

Somkit snorted and scowled deeper. "Why would I be mad at you?"

"Because I let Nok Sivapan out of that stable."

Somkit coughed and rolled his eyes. "If she runs back to her daddy and you wind up in Banglad prison, *then* I'll be mad at you."

If that happened, Pong would be mad enough at himself for both of them. But something inside him told him that it wasn't a risk. If Nok had wanted to turn him in, she'd had plenty of chances to do it. He didn't know why or how, but something about her had changed.

He still didn't understand what she'd done to get locked up. He'd asked her several times during their escape, but she had barely spoken a word to him. Whatever had happened to her had sealed her shut, like an oyster at low tide.

"It was the right thing to do," he said to Somkit.

"Yeah, yeah. It's like I always said: you just can't —" Somkit coughed again, this time so hard they had to stop walking.

"Are you okay?" asked Pong. "Am I going too fast?"

Somkit shook his head, trying to catch his breath between coughs. "The air . . . it just seems like I can't get . . . enough . . ."

The air did seem chalky, as if it were full of dust. A breeze blew over them, filling Pong's nostrils with a scent he hadn't smelled since he left Tanaburi.

Burning wood.

In the east, where Pong had thought the sun was rising, a black column of smoke rose above the rooftops. That was not the sunrise. It was a fire.

The people along the canals had noticed it, too. Some pointed, horrified, while others hurried indoors, which at least made it easier to get through the streets. Pong tucked one arm around Somkit, who was coughing continuously now, and pulled him down the walkway. Pong kept hoping that they would turn away from the pillowy clouds of smoke, but their path to the Mud House was taking them straight for it.

Around the next corner, they were nearly knocked down by a group of people running in the opposite direction.

Somkit grabbed the arm of one of the women running past. "Auntie Mims!" he gasped. "What's happening?"

The woman lowered the rag she held over her face. "Somkit! My goodness, what are you doing? You've got to get away!"

"Please!" said Somkit, coughing out the words. "Tell me. . . . What . . . happened?"

She looked over her shoulder fearfully. "The Mud House is on fire! Everyone is fleeing for their lives. We've got to get away and hide ourselves before the police come!" Auntie Mims took Somkit by the wrist. "Come with us. We have to find a safe house, but I don't know where to go." She looked around, frantic and confused. "I was supposed to have more people with me, but I lost track of them!"

Somkit pulled back from her, holding his hand over his face. "But what about . . . Ampai?"

"She's back there!" said Auntie Mims, nodding in the

direction of the Mud House. "She's helping get everyone out. She told us all to hide!"

"I have to . . . go find her!" said Somkit. He doubled over, gasping for air.

Pong put his hands on Somkit's shoulders. He had to get his friend out of the smoke. "You go with Auntie Mims," he told Somkit. "You know everyone at the Mud House, and you can make sure they all get to a safe hiding place. I'll go find Ampai."

Somkit shook his head, coughing violently.

"Go on — they need someone to help them!" said Pong, shaking him gently. "We'll meet up with you at the safe house!"

Finally, Somkit relented. The old woman gave him her rag and they disappeared into the crowd. Pong took the hem of his shirt and covered his face, pushing against the flow of people streaming away from the Mud House.

He arrived to find the alley in chaos. While some people ran past him in a panic, others herded closer. The sight of orange flames flicking out of the third-story windows stopped Pong in his tracks. He felt hypnotized. Billows of smoke poured out, rising and rising, like a black tower building itself into the sky.

The sight had drawn a crowd of onlookers. They kept their distance, forming a half ring around the entrance to

Mark's restaurant. Pong pushed his way past them and ran to the front door.

"Ampai?" he called.

He got halfway across the dining room when someone grabbed onto the back of his collar and yanked him to a stop.

It was Mark. His glasses were streaked with grease and he held a wet rag over his nose.

"What are you doing?" he shouted. "Don't be a fool! You can't go in there!"

"But I have to find —"

Pong couldn't get the words out before his throat closed up. The black smoke hadn't found its way down to the lower floors yet, but the air tasted gritty and poisonous. It burned Pong's nose and mouth when he breathed.

As Mark dragged him back to the door, he heard a horrifying sound coming from the floors above: the sudden crack of splitting wood.

Mark pulled him out the doorway, into the alley. Pong gulped down the semiclean air. "Where . . . is . . . Ampai?" he gasped.

"Still inside," said Mark.

"Someone has to . . . get her out!"

"She'll come." Mark nodded confidently. "There are still people in there. Once they're out, she'll come."

As he spoke, a cluster of people staggered out of the building. Their faces were shiny and streaked with black. Pong looked past them into the restaurant. A flash of olive green darted back into the kitchen.

"Ampai!" he called.

"She said she's checking . . . the building," coughed out a woman who'd escaped. "To look . . . one last time!"

"Someone give me a hand!" called a teenager. He held the arm of an elderly man who stumbled at the doorway.

Pong took the old man's other arm and helped guide him away from the Mud House. Together, he and the teenager gently set him onto the street.

"Hang on, grandfather," said Pong as the teenager ran off to find help. "We're going to get you to a safe place."

The old man clutched Pong's arm weakly. "I couldn't stand up. . . . My legs wouldn't work," he wheezed. "I was ready to die, but someone picked me up and carried me down the stairs. . . . I thought it must be a giant, they were so strong!" His eyes watered and he smiled faintly. "It was Ampai. . . . Can you imagine? A little woman like that . . . carrying me like a baby?"

"What happened?" asked Pong. "How did the fire start?"

"I don't know. We were sleeping," the man said

hoarsely. He gazed up in horror at the flames coming out of the Mud House. "It's happening all over again. . . . I never thought I would see fire again. . . . Never!"

The teenager came back with two men who helped the old man to his feet and carried him out of the alley.

Pong turned back to the Mud House. The roof was now completely swallowed by the clouds of black smoke. The flames roared higher, leaping from one window to the next. The snap of wood and crash of breaking glass grew louder. As Pong watched the building burn, he thought of the Great Fire. He couldn't imagine what it must have been like to see every building on the East Side engulfed in flames like these.

He wanted to run away, but he couldn't go until he saw Ampai. If she was doing one last sweep to check for stragglers, she should come out at any moment. He didn't take his eyes from the door to Mark's restaurant.

"Finally!" called a woman in the crowd.

"Oh, thank goodness!" shouted another as the rest of the crowd cheered.

Pong craned his neck, looking for the olive-green jacket, but the crowd was cheering something else.

A horn blasted from the canal behind the Mud House, announcing the arrival of two stocky Fire Control Authority boats. Armed with water cannons and massive hoses, they shot thick streams of canal water up into the third-story windows.

The flames danced defiantly, and at first it seemed that the hoses were no match for them. But slowly, the black smoke gave way to gray steam. The fire retreated from the windows.

For a moment, the Fire Control boats caused even more chaos. The wind shifted, and the alley filled with clouds of gritty steam from the doused fires. People ran in all directions, afraid that the police would be the next to arrive on the scene. Through the fog, Pong caught sight of what he'd been waiting for: that flash of dusty green. Ampai's jacket.

With a wave of relief, he stumbled forward with his arms over his face, searching for the restaurant entrance.

Finally, he spotted Mark kneeling on the ground outside the front door.

"Mark, are you okay?" he said, trying to pull the man to his feet.

Mark looked up at Pong, tears streaming from his eyes.

"What? What is it?" cried Pong.

He looked down and saw the green fabric at Mark's feet. Mark reached down and gently brushed Ampai's hair off her face. Pong braced himself for the worst, but she wasn't burned. Her cheeks were sooty, but otherwise she just looked asleep.

"Ampai!" Pong shouted, shaking her arm. "Let's get her out of here! Mark, we have to take her to a doctor!"

"No good," sobbed Mark, shaking his head. "No good — she's gone. It must have been all the smoke. When I got to her, she was already gone."

"What?" gasped Pong. "No, she can't be." He reached down and took her hand. It was still warm, but limp in his fingers.

"Oh, Ampai . . ." he whispered.

Two officers from the Fire Control Authority stomped toward them. "Sir, is there anyone else inside the building?" one asked Mark.

Mark looked up at him, dazed. He shook his head. "No. She got them all out. Every person. She was the last one out."

Pong folded his other hand around Ampai's fingers. Her sleeve fell back, revealing her bare wrist. The red bracelet that Father Cham had given her so many years ago, the one that matched Pong's own, was gone. He shut his eyes and remembered her smiling at him and telling him with a wink what her blessing from the old monk had been: *May your courage never falter.*

"He was right," whispered Pong. "It never did."

Chapter 37

The warehouse was too warm. Sandalwood fans flick-flacked in front of sweaty faces, barely stirring the hot air. Pong guessed there must be more than two hundred people crammed in with them.

Mark stood at the front of the big, open room. Beads of sweat rolled off his forehead and onto the bridge of his nose, making his glasses slip down.

"Poor Mark," Pong whispered to Somkit. "He looks like he's so nervous, he's about to throw up."

"Yeah, he doesn't do so well at talking in front of a big group," said Somkit flatly. "That's what Ampai was so good at."

Now Pong wished he hadn't said anything. Somkit sat with his knees drawn up to his chest, with the same faraway look on his face that he'd worn for the past day and a half. At least he was talking now. Somkit hadn't spoken a word when he found out about Ampai. Pong wanted to reach out and pat him on the shoulder, or pinch his arm, or do something, *anything*, to break through that wall of silence. But he knew Somkit would only shrink away, back inside himself.

Mark raised his hands, and after a minute, the chatter settled down. He swallowed and cleared his throat a couple times. "Friends, friends . . . please give me your attention. I want to start by thanking you for getting here tonight. I know there are many more of us who were afraid to leave their safe houses for this meeting."

After the fire, the people of the Mud House had scattered across the city. Pong and Somkit had been hiding in Mark's sister's apartment, squeezed in with her parents and four children. The police had searched the Mud House neighborhood for the residents, but they had no idea that Ampai had built up such a wide network of safe houses, or that she had friends all over the province. For anyone who needed help, her name had become a key that would unlock doors and hearts up and down the river.

The Governor had ruled Ampai a criminal, guilty of the most severe crime: starting a fire. Reports said that the blaze had begun in her office, in the early hours of the morning, and that the medicines and chemicals that she stored there caused it to burn quickly out of control. But no one on the East Side believed for a moment that Ampai had anything to do with the fire. It must have been an accident.

But Pong wondered about Yai and Yord, the only other people at the Mud House who had access to Ampai's office. The two men had disappeared after the fire and not come back. Could Yord have started it? But why would he do such a thing?

Mark adjusted his glasses and continued. "I went back and forth on whether we should meet at all, but I felt that we must come together, if only to pay our respects to our dear sister."

There was a forlorn murmur in the crowd, and many people bowed toward the makeshift memorial at the front of the room. A strand of tiny Violet orbs hung over a charcoal portrait of Ampai. Bouquets of flowers and a dish of tangerines flanked the drawing.

"First, we must take care of some important business, and quickly, too," said Mark. "Now, I am no replacement for the leadership of Ampai, and I'm in no way trying to take over —"

"You're a good man, Mark!" shouted someone in the room.

"Yes, her right-hand man!" said another.

Mark nodded solemnly. "I served her as best I could

to the very end. And now I feel that it's my responsibility to determine how we will go on without her. As you all know, she had many plans that should have come to light in the next few days, starting with the march on the Giant's Bridge tomorrow night. But now we must ask ourselves: What do we do? Do we carry on, or do we abandon those plans?"

"Abandon them?" called a shocked voice from the crowd. "After all her work? How could we?"

A woman with a baby slung over her chest in a fabric sling stood up. "She wouldn't want us to do it now. Ampai cared about the march, but she cared about *us* even more. It's too dangerous to put ourselves out there. Even speaking her name out loud right now is a risk."

"So we won't use her name," said a teenage girl. "Don't forget, the march was never about Ampai. It was about the children's jail. That 'reform center,' as the Governor likes to call it. What happens to me, or my brothers and sisters, if that thing gets built?"

"It'll get built anyway," said a man, standing up on the other side of the room. "Think about it. If a march was all it took to stop the Governor and his rich friends, someone would've done it already!"

Worried murmurs passed through the crowd, and dozens of heads nodded in agreement.

A burly man in a sleeveless shirt stood up near the front of the room. When he turned around, Pong recognized him as the dockworker Kla. His booming voice hushed the room.

"I'm gonna be there on that bridge. Ampai saved my wife's life when no one else would help us. According to the Governor, we brought her sickness upon ourselves just because we were poor. But Ampai believed we weren't bad people . . ." His words trailed off, but then he squared his muscled shoulders. "But this isn't just about her. And it's not just about the children's prison, either. It's more than that. I'm marching 'cause it's time we stand up and say we won't be treated this way. We deserve respect, no matter what side of the river we live on. No matter what color orbs swing over our heads!"

A cluster of brawny men stood up near him. "And all the dockworkers feel the same!" one called. "We'll be next to Kla on the bridge, every one of us!"

"Hear, hear!" shouted the others.

"Please, please!" called Mark, struggling to be heard over the clamor. "Please, everyone, sit down and be quiet or we'll never get anything done!"

The warehouse settled into an agitated whisper.

A man with a scar over his cheek and an educated

accent stood up. "My friends, there is something we should think about. I, too, believe in what Ampai was trying to do. But I will remind you of her plan — her *entire* plan." The whole room seemed to lean toward him. "I'm sure that Ampai told you what she told me. She knew that it wouldn't be enough to march against the Governor. We had to have some sort of advantage over him. Ampai told me that she had a secret strategy that she'd reveal at this meeting. She promised me that when the people of Chattana saw it, they would immediately join her side and abandon the Governor. But I've talked to everyone who worked with her. She didn't tell anyone what this secret weapon was — if she ever actually had it in the first place."

The room was quiet. People looked down into their laps. Even the dockworkers had no response to this.

"The point of the march was to inspire the whole city to join us," said the educated man. "But we can't do that simply by marching. It sounds like a noble and brave thing, but without some plan to back it up, it leads nowhere."

"The guy's right," said another member of the crowd. "The Governor is too powerful. The people are either afraid of him or in awe of him. And don't forget: we need him. Without the Governor, this city goes dark. After what I saw at the Mud House, there's no way we're going back to using fire."

In the crowd, more people were agreeing with the educated man. They all murmured the same thing: the Governor was too powerful. This was too dangerous.

Pong's eyes traveled around the room at the faces going slack and resigned. He looked up at Ampai's portrait. All her hard work, what she'd given her life for, was turning to smoke. Is this how a dream died? On the lips of reasonable people?

Pong nudged Somkit, who had drifted a thousand miles away. "Hey," he whispered. "Didn't Ampai tell anybody else about your sun orbs?"

"What does it matter?" mumbled Somkit. "They're all destroyed now anyway. All that work, burned to ashes or melted. I should've known. Nothing in this city changes, and it never will."

Pong was shocked to hear those words come out of his friend's mouth. "You don't actually believe that," he whispered.

Somkit bent lower, curling in on himself. "What do you know about what I believe?"

Pong grabbed his friend's arm and shook him, hard. If he'd had an oar, he would've whacked Somkit over the head with it. "You have to snap out of it! I know you're sad." Before Somkit could respond, he added, "*More* than sad. Heartbroken. So am I. What happened to Ampai was the worst thing that's ever happened, and maybe you'll never get over it, and maybe I'll never get over it, either, but right now you can't just sit here. Come on, Somkit." Pong shook him again, more gently this time. "I know you. And this isn't you. Ampai wouldn't want you to be like this."

Somkit lifted his eyes to her portrait. He looked back at Pong.

"Please," said Pong. "Tell them."

Somkit nodded. He uncurled himself slowly and sat up a little straighter. "I know what Ampai was planning," he said, too quiet to be heard. He cleared his throat and said it again. When the other conversations in the room didn't die down, he cupped his hands around his mouth and shouted, "I know what Ampai was planning!"

Two hundred heads swiveled to look at him.

Mark blinked behind his glasses. "Somkit, you know this secret of Ampai's?"

"Yes," said Pong. He stood up and hooked his hand under Somkit's armpit. Before his friend could protest, Pong pulled him to stand beside him. "We both do. We were helping her with it."

"Well, come up here, boys," said Mark. "Come on, don't dawdle. All these people are waiting."

The crowd sitting on the floor scooted aside to make a narrow lane for the two boys to reach the front of the room. Pong suddenly felt tiny and embarrassed.

"Your lantern," he whispered to Somkit. "Show them."

Somkit had one small sun orb tucked in the cloth satchel hanging from his shoulder. It was the only one left, just a little lantern that he'd rigged together and kept at the Mud House back door in case of emergencies. After the fire, Pong had made sure to grab it so none of the police would find it.

Somkit stood with his hand on his satchel for so long that Pong thought he was going to refuse to show it. Finally, he reached inside and pulled out the sphere of glass. He twisted the copper contacts together on the top of the orb, and a beam of soft Gold light shone out from his hand.

Everyone in the room gasped.

"*Gold* light!" said a voice in the crowd.

"You stole that?" said another.

"No," said Pong loudly. "He made it. Somkit, tell them what you did."

There was a hush of wonder over the room as Somkit explained how he had used the faded orbs to collect light from the sun. He was nervous and went into way too much technical detail, but he must have been clear enough, because when he was finished, awed whispers rippled through the crowd.

"That light is impressive," said the educated man. "But don't forget what the Governor can do. He makes all the light in our city! We could never outshine him in a hundred years!"

"The point wasn't to outshine him," said Pong. "The point was to show him —" Pong shook his head and started again. "The point was to show *yourselves* that you don't need him. You don't need his light. You don't need his laws. You can do it without him."

He tried to say the words exactly as Ampai had said them during their nightly missions together, but somehow it didn't sound the same coming from him. Ampai had believed those words down in her core. Pong realized now that it wasn't Ampai's words that people had been willing to follow — not her words: her heart.

Somkit straightened up and squared his stance. "It doesn't matter!" he shouted angrily. The crowd quieted. "It won't work anyway. Every orb I made except this one burned in the fire. Along with everything else." He grimaced and looked down at the lantern in his hand. "It took us days to gather up enough faded orbs just to do this. The march is tomorrow night. That means we have one full day of sunlight. We'll never get enough orbs in time."

The giant Kla stood up again, towering over everyone around him. "I've got a faded orb for you. Our only light went out last night. My wife and me are in darkness. But I'd rather give that empty orb to you than have a thousand new ones. It's yours."

"I have one that just went out tonight!" called a voice at the back.

"And me!" cried another. "I brought it to take to the recycler, but you can have it!"

An older woman leaned on a cane and stood up. "The people of this city are heartbroken. We would give anything to honor the memory of our beloved sister. If we all work hard and spread the word quickly, I know we can get you what you need."

Pong looked at Somkit. "What do you think? There's no reason to keep all this a secret anymore."

"But what about my rig?" said Somkit. "The catcher, the sun juice jar. All of that was destroyed in the fire."

"Hey, Somkit!"

They turned to see the guy from the motor repair shop with the short-long hair standing up at the side of the room. "You need any help? I got a crew that'll lend a hand." He nodded at the other guys from the shop, who sat around him. "And any supplies you need, I'll get them for you. I'll pay for them out of my salary if I have to."

Somkit looked at the portrait of Ampai, then back to Pong. "Okay," he said. "I guess we should get started."

The crowed hummed with nervous energy.

"All right, all right, everyone, calm down," said Mark, trying to hush them. "You have all heard the arguments presented tonight. Ampai herself would never force anyone to be a part of this if they didn't want to. If you choose to bow out, no one will hold it against you. But clearly, if there is a time to finish what she started, we cannot wait. Those who will join the march tomorrow, gather with me at the south side of the building. Thank you, everyone."

And with that, the crowd stood up to take their sides.

Chapter 38

There," said Pong, rising up on his knees and arching his back. "One hundred and eighty-six. That's even more orbs than you had before."

Somkit sat back on his heels and rubbed the bridge of his nose. "When I close my eyes, all I see are copper wires and glass spheres."

They sat in the back bedroom of Mark's sister's apartment. The morning sunlight had just begun to shine through the tissue-paper screen covering the window. In front of them, orbs of every size were arrayed in tidy rows along the wall, largest to smallest. Pong and Mark had stayed in the warehouse all night, receiving the faded orbs that people brought in from all over the city. Somkit had taught a team of Short-Long's friends how to rig up the orbs and sun juice collectors so they'd be ready to start charging at daybreak. Soon they'd take the catchers and jars up to the roof and lay them out on tar paper to soak up the sunlight.

Pong felt woozy. Sunup was usually his bedtime. But he was relieved that his friend seemed to have turned a corner. He'd lost himself in the work and was acting more like the old Somkit now.

"Do you think people will still come?" asked Pong, standing up stiffly. "I mean, not just the people we know, but everyone else Ampai signed up. Remember, she thought she could get a thousand people to march?"

"Hmm. More like nine hundred and ninety-nine, actually."

"Huh?"

Somkit wiped his grease-stained palms on his trousers and stood up. He reached into his pocket, pulled out a piece of paper, and handed it to Pong.

"What is this?"

"Border permit. And I got you a boat to go with it. Don't worry, it's not a pink taxi. It's a fast boat with a souped-up motor." Somkit pressed his thumb to his chest. "The souping-up done by yours truly."

Pong flipped the permit from front to back. He looked at it for a moment and then held it out to Somkit. "Thanks, but I'll take it after the march is over."

Somkit pushed the permit back to Pong. "You're not

marching," he said firmly. "You can't be on that bridge tonight. There might be police there. If they start checking people, you'll get taken back to prison."

"But what about you?" said Pong.

"They can't arrest me for walking with my friends."

Pong nodded to the rows of orbs. "What about for making light?"

"That's not illegal. Yet." Somkit's smirk turned serious again. "Come on, man, you know it's not the same. Even if they did arrest me, it would be for a little while. If they get you, it's forever."

Pong studied the permit again. It was true. If he stepped out on that bridge, he might as well turn himself in at the police station.

"I know you wanna be there," said Somkit, "but you've done a lot already — more than you had to. It's the perfect time to leave the city. With the march going on, the police will be distracted." He swallowed and added, "If Ampai were here, she'd tell you to go."

Pong nodded. So this was it. He was really going.

Somkit twisted his mouth side to side, the way he did when he had something to say but didn't want to say it. This might be the last time Pong would ever see him. If Pong wanted to tell him anything, he had to do it now.

"I'm sorry," he blurted out.

"It's okay," said Somkit. "Like I said, hopefully all the people who promised to march will still —"

"No, that's not what I mean." Pong took a breath. "I'm sorry that I left you behind at Namwon."

Somkit's mouth froze mid-twist. "Huh?"

"When I escaped, I left you alone to fend for yourself. I wasn't thinking about you or how your life would turn out without me. Honestly, I wasn't thinking about anything, really." Pong's words spilled out faster than he intended. "I got out, and you had to stay. That wasn't — that wasn't fair. I hated myself for that. I wouldn't blame you for hating me, too."

Somkit stared at Pong, one nostril crinkled, his upper lip curled back, as if he were trying to locate the source of a bad smell. "What the heck are you talking about?"

Pong was slightly annoyed. It was hard enough to say all of this. Somkit didn't have to make it harder.

"The day I escaped," he said with a sigh. "I left you behind, and —"

"*You* left *me* behind?" Somkit shook his head. "You didn't leave me. I'm the one who set that whole thing up, remember?"

Pong blinked. "What?"

"You mean all this time you thought *you* managed that escape all by yourself?"

Now it was Pong's turn to be confused. "Well, I . . ."

"You honestly thought that it was a coincidence that I had you help me gather up those durian rinds just when the guards happened to not be watching?"

Pong blinked again, trying to remember that day: Somkit's weird coughing and his funny raised eyebrows. He had forgotten about it until now.

"But you never told me. . . . We never talked about it. . . ."

"Come on, man, we couldn't talk about it in front of the guards. I gave you the sign!" Somkit did the funny eyebrow-cough again, meaningfully. A smile tugged at his lips. "And all the time you sat in the basket, you think I didn't know exactly where you were? I put the lid on and clamped it on tight so it wouldn't fall off! I watched the trashman pull up to the dock and put you on the boat. I stayed close by the whole time to make sure that none of the guards got suspicious and nobody stopped you from going."

"You . . . did all that?" said Pong.

Somkit frowned darkly. "I did. And I regretted it. I didn't think about how serious it would be for you to run away from Namwon. It wasn't until after you were gone that it hit me that if you ever got caught, you'd go back to jail forever." Somkit looked up at Pong and bit his bottom lip. "You just seemed so miserable. You weren't yourself anymore. You wanted out so bad. I know it doesn't make sense, but I started thinking that if you stayed, you'd die there. I thought I was helping you. All those years you were gone, I wondered what happened to you. I dreamed that maybe you made it across the border or down to the sea. But when you showed up that night in the canal and I saw your tattoo, I realized that what I did was curse you. You're going to be on the run for the rest of your life. I'm the one who needs forgiving, not you."

Pong stood frozen, not knowing what to say.

There was a knock on the wall, and then Mark appeared in the doorway. "All right, Somkit, you ready? The guys are here to take everything up to the roof."

Somkit looked at Pong, then back at Mark. "Um, give me just one more minute and I'll come with you."

Mark nodded and left.

Somkit looked down at the border permit Pong held in his hand. "I guess we both have things to be sorry for. Does this make us even?"

"I don't know," said Pong. "There's one thing I don't think I can ever get over. . . ."

Somkit's brow lifted, worried.

"You making me sit in a basket of rotten durian rinds," said Pong.

Somkit grinned. "It was that bad?"

"I threw up on my own crotch. Twice."

Somkit threw his head back and laughed. He elbowed Pong in the side and then put his arm around Pong's shoulder. The boys hugged, a brief and awkward embrace.

Later, as Pong made his way to the boat waiting for him, he wished he'd given Somkit a proper hug goodbye.

But it was too late now. There was a current pulling him south, and he couldn't fight it anymore, even if he wanted to.

Chapter 39

Mr. Prapan put his hands on his desk and stretched
his spine left, then right. It had been a long day
for him. On the corner of his desk were two stacks of
papers that he still had to transcribe into his border control notebook before he could leave for the evening. One
stack represented all the people who crossed the northern border out of Chattana province that day; the other
stack was for all of the people who had come in. The second stack was twice as tall.

Prapan leaned over his desk and looked out his little
square window. He sighed gratefully. There was only one
person left to process, thank goodness.

"Next!" he called.

A girl who couldn't be much older than twelve or
thirteen approached his window. She set down her bag
and walking stick, then slid her passport through the slot
under the glass.

"Good afternoon," said Prapan, opening the document. "Where are you off to today?"

"To Lannaburi, sir," replied the girl without meeting his eyes.

Prapan looked past her, into the waiting room. "Are you traveling by yourself?"

The girl kept her head down so her short black hair fell over her cheeks. "Yes, my mother and siblings went on ahead of me. They're meeting me at the ferryboat station."

Now she did look up at Prapan, and he noticed that her eyes were red and puffy, as if she'd been crying. She fidgeted, rubbing the fabric of her left sleeve between her fingers. The whole situation was a little suspicious, but the girl's passport was in good order, and she'd been approved to cross the border before. Besides, Prapan wanted to go home already.

He had started to flip through her papers when his coworker slid into the chair beside him. Everyone in the office called her Shorty.

"You still here, Prapan?" Shorty asked, smacking her chewing gum. "Time to shut down for the day, don't you think?"

"Tell me about it," said Prapan. "We had so many

people crossing into Chattana today! More than we've had in months."

"Really? What for?"

"Well, they all gave different reasons, but I can tell what they're actually here for because they're all wearing black armbands." He lowered his voice a bit. "They're going to the city. For that march."

Shorty's eyes widened, impressed. "Really? But I heard that woman who was leading it — Ampai — was killed."

Prapan nodded. "In that fire. So sad. Can you imagine if it had gotten out of control? Could've been like the Great Fire all over again."

Shorty let out a slow whistle. "Hard to believe. But the people are going to march without her?"

"Guess so." Prapan shrugged and kept flipping through the girl's passport. Flip, stamp. Flip, stamp.

Shorty scratched the back of her head. "Are *you* gonna go to the march?"

Prapan paused mid-stamp. "Are you kidding? I don't want to get in trouble. If I got arrested, I'd lose this job! Then what?"

"Aw, you wouldn't get arrested for walking across a bridge," said Shorty, leaning back in her chair. "As long as you don't cause any trouble, there's no law against it."

"Not *yet*, anyway."

"What's that supposed to mean?"

Prapan leaned toward Shorty and said quietly, "At the central office this morning, I overheard that the Governor is cracking down. After the fire, he's got no choice. He's changing the law to make marching a crime. If anyone shows up on that bridge, they're going straight to jail."

Shorty leaned back, shocked. "But can he do that?"

"Aw, you know that he does whatever he wants," said Prapan, stamping the last page of the passport. "And we just have to make do and keep on living. Now — hey, where'd she go?"

The girl who'd been standing at his window was gone. Prapan leaned over the desk and called into the waiting room. "Miss? Excuse me, miss?"

"Now, isn't that odd?" he said, sitting back down. "I didn't even hear her leave."

Chapter 40

Pong was getting a late start out of Chattana. After staying up all night to help with the orbs, he had slept for a few hours. He had jolted awake, sweaty and anxious to get going, but then had to wait for Short-long to meet him in a safe place with the boat. By the time he had started up the motor, it was already late afternoon.

Pong turned up the speed, trying to follow the instructions that Somkit had given him. It wasn't too complicated, thank goodness. This was a long-tail boat, designed with the motor, orb, and rudder all attached to the same long pole. Pong could sit at the back of the boat and operate everything all at once. It was terrifying at first, but at least there was hardly any traffic on the river to worry about.

He was ready to get pulled over by police boats at any moment, but so far he hadn't been stopped. In fact, he hadn't seen any police craft on the river at all, which was peculiar. Somkit was right — the police had their attention elsewhere.

Pong passed the city limits, passed the last Charge Station, and zipped by the sleepy riverside villages. His boat rounded one bend in the river, then another. It was dusk now, nearly night. The river narrowed and the banks rose higher, growing into dark limestone cliffs with sides too steep for the jungle to cling to.

The river curled to the right, then back to the left, and Pong gasped. He jerked the boat's tail up in surprise, cutting off the motor. The boat slowed and glided to a stop. High above him loomed the mountain of Tanaburi. He'd completely forgotten that he'd have to pass it on his way to the sea.

The cave mouth above was a yawning black chasm. Somewhere inside sat the Buddha statue, waiting for the rays of the next day's sun. Pong stared at the ledge where he'd jumped to escape from Nok. That was two weeks ago, and yet it seemed so much longer.

Pong's eyes traveled up the mountain to the place where he knew Wat Singh sat nestled in the jungle. Pong had thought about his teacher many times in the past weeks. He had accepted the fact that Father Cham had passed on, but here in the shadow of the mountain, Pong felt the loss all over again.

He clicked off his headlights and slid off the boat's seat, lowering himself to his knees. The water had stilled and the boat swayed gently. Fireflies began to wink on and off in the air around him. Pong put his hands together and did something he hadn't done since he'd left the temple: he prayed.

Pong waited to feel the presence of Father Cham's spirit. After all, the monk's blessing was finally coming true. Pong was about to get the one thing he'd always longed for: freedom.

A few more miles and he'd reach the sea. No more hiding, no more fear.

But Pong felt nothing. The river stretched ahead and behind him, empty. Tree frogs peeped loudly from the banks, but their song was too mechanical to be comforting. Pong felt completely alone. This wasn't right. It shouldn't be like this.

He raised his left wrist, pressed the red braided bracelet between his fingers, and shut his eyes. He took a deep breath. "Father Cham," he whispered, "I'm about to fulfill your wish. I'm going to get what I've been looking for." He held his breath. Still nothing. Pong sighed and opened his eyes.

The night had gone completely black.

Pong blinked, looking all around him. It didn't

matter if he closed his eyes or opened them. All he could see was darkness. Had the night really come on so quickly? Where were the fireflies? Even when he looked up, he couldn't see any stars.

Nervous, he felt his way back to the boat's rudder. He was about to turn on the motor when he saw a swirl of white hovering where the river should be. Pong gasped and stumbled, falling onto the boat's seat.

The white swirl glowed. It flowed like smoke, but looked solid, like the strands of a silkworm web. It thickened as it whirled into a shape that floated in the darkness. Pong's pulse beat fast in his ears, and goose bumps ran down the backs of his arms.

The white wispy shape formed the body of a man. The man lifted his bald head. It was Father Cham. Decades had been lifted from the monk's face.

He was a man of middle age, with no stoop to his shoulders and fewer wrinkles, though he had the same cheerful smile. Pong realized that he must be seeing through some sort of window into the past. His heartbeat slowed as he watched, trying to pay more attention than he ever had in his life.

Father Cham faced Pong but stared past him, into the distance. Pong was so turned around that he couldn't tell which direction was which. But he thought that

Father Cham looked north, in the direction of Chattana. The monk's smile disappeared, and his face filled with sorrow and worry.

Pong turned to follow Father Cham's gaze and saw a pulsing orange glow hovering on the northern horizon. He knew he was seeing another vision from the past: the Great Fire.

A speck of white floated through the darkness out of the north. The little white shape drifted toward Pong. As it passed his boat, Pong looked down, and the white mist swirled into the shape of a baby tucked into a basket. The basket floated to Father Cham and stopped at his feet. He knelt beside it, his eyes full of tenderness and pity for the bundle inside.

Another white wisp of a figure stepped out from the darkness. He also wore monks' robes, but he was much younger than Father Cham — a fresh-faced monk-in-training.

He bowed to Father Cham, who drew a braided strand from his robe and tied it around the young man's wrist.

Father Cham whispered a prayer that echoed softly in the black night: "May you bring the light back to Chattana."

Father Cham finished tying on the bracelet. The young man turned around.

His face was calm, but his eyes burned with a cold intensity that Pong immediately recognized.

It was the Governor.

Pong stared, trying to understand what this meant.

He remembered what Father Cham had told him the day before he died: *There was a time, before I learned my lesson, when I did grant the types of blessings you are talking about. I wanted to use my gift to help people, to wish away all the pain and suffering in this world.*

The figure of the Governor glided past Pong without looking at him. He walked north, toward Chattana. Father Cham watched him go out of sight, his face full of hope. But after a long moment, the monk's expression turned to disappointment and then despair. He sank to his knees and covered his face.

But it was arrogant of me to think that I could fix the world with one wish. And my gifts went awry.

Pong shook his head in wonder. So this is how the Governor got his magic. The man had indeed brought light back to the city, but at a terrible cost. Without meaning to, Father Cham had brought sorrow to the very people he'd wanted to protect.

The wispy spirit of Father Cham rose to his feet. His face was still sad, but he wasn't broken. He gazed north.

More tiny bundles of white floated down from the

direction of the city. They glided past Pong like glowing lotus blossoms, cooing soft as kittens. Father Cham gathered each luminous baby to him and gave them bracelets. But now his blessings were of a different type:

"May you find wonder in everything you see."

"May your thoughts be clear."

"May others learn kindness from you."

The babies swirled taller and became older as time spun ahead. Then they, too, glided away, some going south, others north, east, and west. Soon the darkness was filled with the glow of men and women who carried the blessings of Father Cham with them.

Pong watched the monk — who had aged now, into the wrinkled version that he remembered so well — as he blessed a little girl.

"May your courage never falter."

The girl grew and grew, but this time she didn't stop getting taller as she grew older. Soon she was a giant, almost as tall as the mountain. A cool breeze blew from the south, ruffling her long hair. When it passed over Pong, he breathed deep. It smelled sweet and sharp, like tangerine peels.

Pong craned his neck back to see the spirit of Ampai towering over him. She flipped up the collar of her jacket and grinned down at him. Tears filled Pong's eyes as he watched her turn north, following the trail of the orange-scented breeze. She walked the path of the Governor, toward the city, covering a hundred yards with every stride.

Pong gazed after Ampai until she disappeared. When he turned around, the darkness was empty except for Father Cham. The old man now looked directly into Pong's eyes. Slowly, he glided toward the boat.

Pong's heart began to race again. The old monk reached out a white hand and touched the bracelet on Pong's left wrist. He didn't say anything. Instead, he looked at Pong, waiting for him to speak first.

Pong swallowed and said, "May I find what I'm looking for?"

Father Cham nodded and smiled.

How Pong had missed that smile! "You want me to find what I'm looking for," Pong said, his voice crackling. "And I will. That's why you're here, isn't it? Because I'm so close. I'm looking for my freedom. It's what I've always wanted."

But Father Cham's reaction wasn't what Pong expected. He rubbed the side of his nose and tilted his head down, pretending to be very interested in the bilge at the bottom of the boat. It was the same exasperating thing he'd done back at the temple when he disagreed with Pong but wanted Pong to figure out why for himself.

Pong sighed. Even after death, the old man could be extremely frustrating. "But that *is* what I want. I want to be free — of course I do. Who wouldn't want that?"

But even as he said it out loud, Pong knew it was only half of what he longed for.

He shut his eyes and saw all the days of his life winding back through time, like a river, leading to the one place he had never wanted to think about again.

"Namwon," Pong whispered. "I thought if I escaped and ran away I could find someplace better. I thought the world outside would be different."

Even here, in the presence of his teacher's spirit, Pong felt those old words of the Governor hissing in his ear. *The world is full of darkness, and that will never change.* But now that Pong had learned the truth about the Governor and where he came from, the words didn't hold the same power as before. They seemed thin and flimsy. Pong waved his hand in front of his face, as if brushing away cobwebs.

"The world wasn't what I wanted it to be," Pong went on. "Not Chattana. Not even Tanaburi. I thought if I ran far enough, I could find that perfect place where life is fair and everything is good. But even if I make it to the sea, even if I go all the way to the end of the world, I'll never find a place like that. It doesn't exist."

Pong opened his eyes. Father Cham leaned toward him, his face held taut with expectation. Pong knew that whatever he said next would be important, and it needed to be true.

"You can't run away from darkness," Pong whispered. "It's everywhere. The only way to see through it is to shine a light."

Father Cham shut his eyes and smiled. He tilted his face to the sky, a gesture of relief and joy.

"Oh, Father Cham!" cried Pong, reaching one hand out for the old man. But the monk swirled away from him, like the smoke of a candle. The white mist vanished and the night lifted, and Pong found himself alone on the river.

Chapter 41

Nok hurried back through the city, racing against the fading light. She'd finally managed to get a seat on the last passenger boat of the day coming back to Chattana. Now her trip north would be delayed, and she'd spent too much of her money, and on top of all that, she'd left her passport at the border.

She'd have a lot to overcome when she finally got back on the road. But for now she had to get to the Giant's Bridge.

The border control agents had said that Ampai had died in a fire only hours after Nok's visit to the Governor. It couldn't be a coincidence. Especially not since the Governor was using that fire as a reason to crack down on the people.

A few days ago, Nok never would have believed that the Governor would be capable of something like this. But now her entire world had shifted. Nothing she had been told — about the Governor, or the law, or even herself — was true.

She tapped the skin on her left wrist for the hundredth time that day. She was still reeling from the shock of learning about her birth, but hearing about Ampai had shaken her out of it.

A woman had died.

What if more people died? Or got hurt? Or went to jail? The Governor had said he was going to punish the people for standing against him. Nok had to get to the bridge and tell someone. The people had no idea they were walking straight into a trap.

Luckily, the walkways in the city had thinned out. In fact, as Nok approached the Giant's Bridge, the canals and alleys were almost completely empty. It was eerie, but she didn't have time to wonder what was going on. She hurried to the bridge, which was also quiet. Usually, there would be tourists admiring the view and vendors selling umbrellas or cold drinks. But this evening, only a handful of people stood at the rails, silent and watchful, like animals before a storm.

When she reached the bridge's midpoint, Nok halted. At the far west end, a man paced, cleaning his glasses on the hem of his shirt, again and again. Everything that she'd planned evaporated at the sight of him.

"Daddy!" she cried, dropping her staff and running to him.

He looked at her, his eyes wild and confused. "Nok?" He caught her in his arms and pulled her into his chest. "Nok! What are you doing here?"

Nok had been determined to run away from her family forever, but now that she was in her father's arms, she couldn't let go of him.

"We have been worried sick about you!" he said. He really did look ill. His clothes were mismatched and rumpled, and there were dark bags under his eyes. He held her out at arm's length. His glasses sat crooked on his nose, but he didn't bother to straighten them. "What's this? What happened to your face?"

Nok touched the wound she'd gotten when the Governor's guards threw her into the stable. "It's nothing, Daddy. Just a scratch."

He hugged her tight again, as if he worried she'd run off. "We heard you never showed up at the school in Tanaburi. We tracked you to your spire-fighting gym, but they said you packed up and left yesterday. Where in the world have you been?"

"Oh, Daddy," Nok whispered, closing her eyes.

"Sweetheart, you can tell me," he said, pushing the hair off her face. "Whatever it is, you can tell me."

"I — I've made some mistakes," said Nok, her voice cracking as she peeled her left arm away from her chest. She pushed her sleeve up to show her father the tattoo that was now visible on the surface of her scarred wrist. "I guess we both have, huh?"

Her father gasped and took her arm in his hands. He rubbed his fingers over the scars and across the tattoo. "But . . . how?"

"I went to see the Governor." She pointed to the ink letters. "He did this with his powers."

Nok's father's mouth distorted into a frown and he looked over his shoulder at the West Side with contempt. "How dare he!" he said through gritted teeth. "And did he . . . did he tell you everything?"

Nok nodded. "Yes, everything," she whispered. "I'm sorry."

"Sorry?" Her father cupped her face in his hands. "Nok, what do you have to be sorry for?"

Nok's tears pooled on her eyelids and ran down, soaking her father's fingers. "I just — I think I've messed everything up."

Commissioner Sivapan pulled his daughter close and wrapped his arms around her. "Oh, sweetheart, you haven't messed up anything. You are perfect, so perfect, do you know that? I remember when you were born.

The moment I saw you, that was my first thought: she's perfect."

"No, I'm not," said Nok, crying. "I tried to be, but I'm not."

Her father held her by the shoulders. His own cheeks were wet with tears. "You are to me," he said firmly. "You're right, though. I have made mistakes. Many mistakes. But you were never one of them. I realize now that my biggest mistake was keeping the truth from you." He looked down at the ground and let his breath out slowly. "Years ago, when I was a lawyer, I had an affair with a woman who worked in the coffee shop below my office. It was wrong, and I nearly destroyed our family by doing it." He raised his eyes quickly to Nok's. "I'm sure you feel ashamed of me. You've every right to be, but you mustn't be ashamed of her. She was a good woman with a good heart."

Nok shook her head. "She was a criminal. A robber."

"She was struggling," said her father. "And she had no family to help her. She worked very hard, but it was never enough. One day, a customer left his wallet at the shop, and she took it. I guess she was too proud to ask me for money." He tilted his head down and nudged his glasses with his shoulder, but they didn't straighten. "She was arrested and taken to Namwon. When I finally found out where they took her, I begged the Governor to release her, but he refused. That's how you ended up being born there."

"And she died," Nok whispered.

Her father nodded sadly. "The Governor allowed us to take you out on the condition that I take the job as warden. Of course I said yes — I would have done anything he asked if it meant I could keep you." He took Nok's hand in his and rubbed the scarred tattoo. "I never regretted that you were born. I only regret how I handled it. I never should have lied about who you were."

"But you did it for Mother," said Nok before correcting herself. "I mean, for your wife."

"She *is* your mother, and she loves you more than you can understand." Her father closed his eyes a moment. "I hurt her very badly, but that was my fault, not yours. Somehow she found it in her heart to forgive me. When you were born, she wanted to adopt you right away. She has loved you like her own daughter ever since. Why, right now she has a search party out looking for you. She went to Tanaburi herself to try to find you. When she learned you weren't there, she was beside herself with worry!"

"But our reputation . . . the family . . ."

Her father sighed and looked behind him at the

orderly teak buildings of the West Side. "Your mother is trying to do her best for her children. She is just trapped by the rules we live by. We all are." He tried straightening his spectacles once more before pulling them off in frustration and shoving them into his shirt pocket. Without the foggy glass screening them, his eyes looked bright, washed clear by his tears. "The rules are wrong, Nok. We never should have used them as an excuse not to do the right thing. We love you, and we're proud of you. That's all that matters."

Nok sobbed. Her father hugged her tight to him, and she pressed her face into his shirt. He smelled like their kitchen and her mother and her siblings and himself all mixed together. She had the sudden strange wish that she could fall asleep right there, and he would pick her up, the way he used to when she was little, and carry her home and tuck her into bed.

Nok's cheek rolled against her father's chest pocket, crunching the glasses. They both sniffled and laughed as he took them out and cleaned them on his now-damp shirt. "These old things. I've got to get —" He stiffened as he put them on again.

Nok followed his gaze and noticed how many more people had begun to crowd around them.

"We have so much more to talk about, Nok, but now

is not the time," her father said in a low voice. "I need you to go home for now and wait for me there. This is not a safe place for you."

Suddenly, Nok remembered why she'd come back to Chattana. She wiped her face dry with her sleeve. "Daddy, I have to tell you something. There's going to be a march on the bridge tonight. It's going to be peaceful, but the Governor wants to shut it down. He's going to try to arrest everyone."

Her father leaned back, shocked. "How do you know that?"

"Dad, you have to stop him! It isn't right!"

Her father shook his head. "Nok, the Governor came to me not even an hour ago and asked me to change the laws so he could do exactly as you say."

"And what did you do?" asked Nok, holding her breath.

"I — I didn't know what to do, honestly." He looked down at his sagging socks. "I'm not good at being the Law Commissioner, Nok. A good Commissioner would have had a clear answer for him right away. I should have been able to quote from an important book or bring up some lesson from history. But for some reason, all of that flew right out of my head. The Governor is so sure of himself. The more he talked to me about this march, about the law, the more confused I became...."

"Oh, Dad ..."

"But I just couldn't do it. I knew that if I did what he wanted, I would never be able to hold my head up in front of my children. So I told him no."

Nok squeezed his hands tightly in hers. "You did the right thing!"

"Maybe. But it doesn't matter. He fired me."

"What!"

Her father nodded. "And some other Commissioners, too. I'm actually lucky not to be in jail myself. The Governor is going to change the law anyway. He is losing his grip on the city, so he's squeezing his fist even tighter. That's why I want you to go home right now. Things are about to get very dangerous here." He pointed discreetly to the people standing around them. "You see all of them? They're undercover police. I worry that the Governor himself will come out with his personal guards. I don't know what he'll do. I'm afraid of him."

Now Nok realized why the men and women on the bridge had looked so odd. All their clothes were the same, as if they'd pulled them out of the same costume trunk. Nok glimpsed the tip of a staff peeking from beneath the jacket of a man who stood close by.

A soft, rhythmic drumming drifted toward them from the east. It grew louder, then louder still. After a moment, Nok realized what it was: the footsteps of hundreds of feet.

The police on the bridge gathered like a shoal of fish and began shedding their plain clothes costumes.

"All right, things are starting," said her father. "You must go home, and — Nok! What are you doing? Stop!"

Nok broke through the line of police. She scooped up her staff and ran, her black hair swishing behind her, straight into the mass of marchers.

Chapter 42

Pong dug the boat's propeller into the water, willing it to go faster as he sped northward. His rib cage ached, like he hadn't taken a deep, full breath in a very long time. That box inside his chest had come down and crumbled away, and he could feel his heart beating between his lungs — a hot, fluttering thing.

It was a strange feeling. Not new, exactly. He'd felt this way before, years ago. Before he'd met the Governor, before anyone had told him that *the world is full of darkness, and that will never change.*

Those words had kept him locked up for so long. Now Pong understood what sad, cruel words they were. If you believed them, then the only way to make sense of the world was with courts and judges, rules and jails. Those were the things that kept a city orderly. They kept people in line. But by themselves, they did nothing to make the world better.

Father Cham had known that. Even after his mistake with the Governor, he'd never given up trying to make a better world. Not with wishes or with magic. He had fanned the embers of people's hearts and sent them out into the world to do extraordinary things.

Pong remembered what Father Cham always told him: "You have a good heart." For the first time, the words didn't seem like a lie or a mistake. For the first time, Pong believed them.

He took another deep breath, both excited and terrified to share what he'd learned about the Governor's secret connection to Father Cham. He would tell Somkit and Mark. Together, they would find a way to speak to the Governor. Pong would share the vision he had on the river and explain that Father Cham would never have wanted things to turn out this way. The Governor would listen if Pong invoked Father Cham's name, and Pong could show his own bracelet as proof.

But would he ever get to the bridge in time? The boat's tail was as far in the water as it could go, but he was still moving too slowly. Pong couldn't even see the lights of the city yet. At this rate, the march would be over and done by the time he reached the city limits.

He cut off the motor and lifted the pole out of the water. Oh, why didn't he know anything about how machines worked? He slapped the side of the motor with the heel of his palm in frustration.

"Ah!" he gasped. A sharp pain shot through the tender flesh below his thumb. He rubbed the bruise as he felt along the smooth case of the motor with his other hand. A squared-off bit of metal stuck out on the side.

It was a switch. Pong flipped it and started the boat up again. This time, a second, larger orb kicked on, nearly blinding him with the strength of its Jade light. The motor whirred even louder than it had before.

Pong lowered the boat tail back into the water. The boat shot along the surface of the river like a rocket from a bottle. *This* was what Somkit had meant by souped-up!

The wind blew fast on Pong's face, wicking the last tears out of the corners of his eyes and flinging them into the dark river. He gripped tight to the boat's tail, hoping that when the time came, he'd know what to say, and that he'd have the courage to say it.

ok held her staff close to her chest as she squeezed
through the flowing crowd, searching each face that
passed her. There were so many people. They walked
shoulder to shoulder, filling the entire bridge, and still
more poured out of the city. There must be thousands!

Frustrated tears pressed at the corners of Nok's eyes.
She'd been so wrong about everything and everyone, but
there was one person she'd gotten wrong most of all.

"Please, excuse me?" she asked the people shoulder-
ing past her. "I'm looking for a boy named Pong. Do you
know him?"

"Pong?" said a girl carrying a Gold orb lantern. "He's
over there."

Nok gasped, but the girl pointed to a teenager with
long hair. "A different Pong," she said as the girl continued past.

This was going to be impossible. She didn't even
know his last name.

"Do you know a boy named Pong?" she asked again and again. "Any of you? He's a boy my age, with a shaved head."

"Oh, great," grumbled a voice behind her. "Just what we need."

Nok spun around to see Somkit standing among a cluster of people holding poles with Gold orbs swinging from the end. He eyed Nok spitefully as he worked on an orb for a woman holding a baby in her other arm.

"There," he told the woman, twisting two copper wires attached to the orb. "The contacts just weren't touching. It should be fine now. Anyone else? No, all of yours are on. . . . You look good. . . . You're good to go."

The other people marched away from him, but he stayed where he was, glaring at Nok.

She watched the orb-carrying marchers with astonishment. Only now did she realize how odd it was that one in every dozen in the crowd carried the same Gold lights. She pushed past them to get closer to Somkit. "Where . . . ? How did you get so many Gold orbs?"

"We didn't steal them, if that's what you mean," grumbled Somkit. "We made them."

Nok didn't understand, but she didn't have time to ask him to explain. "Is Pong with you?"

Somkit scowled deeper. "Why do you care?"

"Please, this is important," she said, putting her hand on Somkit's arm. "I want to help him."

Somkit wrinkled his nose, as if he were trying to decide whether to believe her. "You can save your good deed," he said finally. "Pong's not here. He left town this afternoon."

"He left?"

"Yeah. Now, will you let go of me?" He yanked his arm away from her.

Nok took a half step back. Somkit still glared at her like he hated her guts. "Well, that's good to hear," she said, "because every police officer in the city is on the other side of this bridge, and if they catch him, he'll go to jail for the rest of his life."

Anxiousness rippled over Somkit's face. "Why every officer?"

"They're planning on arresting everyone who marches tonight," said Nok, keeping her voice low so she didn't cause a panic.

"They can't do that," said Somkit. "Look around. Nobody has any weapons. We aren't doing anything wrong! You can tell your daddy to send all those police home. We're here to make a point, not make any trouble."

"You don't get it," said Nok. "The Governor wanted my father to change the law so he could arrest you all.

When my father refused, he fired him and changed the law anyway. The Governor plans to put everyone on this bridge in jail tonight!"

Even as she said the words, Nok looked at the massive throng of people and knew that would be impossible. She also knew how determined the Governor was. A shiver of fear ran down her back. What if fighting broke out? What would he do?

"Listen, you need to get out of here," she said to Somkit. "I'm worried about what's going to happen. It's not safe for you."

He looked down at his orb and then out at the crowd. "I can't leave. We worked so hard for this. Look how many people actually showed up. . . ."

Just then, a gust of cool air blew over the bridge from the south. Somkit and Nok both breathed in deeply. The breeze smelled familiar to Nok: sharp and bright, like a tangerine. When Somkit turned back to her, the worried look was gone from his face.

He took another deep breath and nodded to her. "Look, thanks for the warning, but I'm not leaving. We're going to finish what we planned."

He brushed past her and ducked into the crowd heading toward the center of the bridge.

"Wait . . . please!" Nok turned around and wove

around the marchers, pushing her way through the gaps in the sea of bodies.

The flow of people pushed her up to the midpoint of the bridge, almost to the very front line of marchers. She searched for Somkit but didn't spot him anywhere. Ahead, the orb light glinted off the buttons of the police uniforms. But the officers hung back from approaching the crowd, as if they were waiting for something.

Behind them, Nok saw the shutters of the West Side windows swinging closed, one after another, shutting off all that pretty Gold light. Whatever happened on the bridge tonight, the people on the West Side didn't want to see it.

The throng of marchers had kept up a steady hum of conversation. Some had started songs that rippled through the crowd in waves. But now all the singing and talking stopped, replaced with frightened whispers running from the front line toward the back.

"He's coming!"

"I see him!"

"The Governor!"

Chapter 44

By the time Pong finally reached the city, his knuckles and back teeth ached from keeping them clenched so tightly against the vibrations of Somkit's supermotor. Clouds had moved in — the low-hanging ones that ran ahead of a big rainstorm. For a half second Pong hoped they would dump rain, keeping everyone inside and off the bridge, but the air still smelled dry. It wouldn't rain tonight.

The city lights reflected off the clouds, making it bright enough that he didn't need to turn on his headlights. He held the permit in his left hand as he steered with the right. He wanted to have it ready in case the police stopped him and asked questions. But he didn't see any police boats. In fact, there were hardly any boats on the river at all. Pong glided past an empty fishing pier. The docks and walkways along the riverfront were also deserted. Music played from the balconies of restaurants, but no diners sat at the tables. Had all those people gone to join the march on the bridge?

As Pong motored on, he realized why he hadn't seen any police boats on the way. Up ahead, every police craft in the city sat nose to stern, forming a barricade that spanned the entire width of the river. Pong cut his motor and stared, unsure what to do.

If he wanted to get to the bridge in time, he'd need to be closer. It would take too long to dock his boat at this distance and walk through town. He took a deep breath and turned the motor on at half power. Slowly, he puttered closer to the barricade.

Pong expected the police boats to be full of officers, but they bobbed silently in the water, anchored in formation.

"Hello?" Pong called. "Is anyone here? Hello?"

No one answered him.

Pong turned and motored down the line, his eyes searching the hulls of all the boats. The night Somkit had jump-started Manit's speedboat, Pong had taken note of the officer's license plate. Now he hoped Somkit had found a way to get Manit's boat back to him.

He found it, bobbing empty, tethered to a big double-decker cruiser. "Please!" Pong called up to the cruiser. "Is someone there?"

The cruiser's spotlight snapped on and swiveled toward him, shining directly into his eyes. "Hey! You in the long-tail boat!" called a woman's voice. "Nobody passes! You gotta either dock or wait till morning."

"Please let me through," called Pong.

"What do you not understand about *nobody passes?* Now, get outta here!"

Pong shielded his eyes against the blinding orb light. "Please!" he called again. "Is Officer Manit here? I need to talk to him!"

"Yeah, yeah," said the officer. "You and every other bony street rat in this city. You can hit him up for a handout some other night. Now, scram!"

The spotlight swung away from him. Pong groaned. He was running out of time. For once he actually wanted the police to pay attention to him, and they were telling him to buzz off.

He ran his trembling fingers around and around the frayed bracelets on his left wrist. Suddenly, he remembered what Father Cham had said about never removing his tattoo.

What if someday you need it?

Pong took a deep breath. "Wait!" he shouted up at the boat. "I'm a runaway! From Namwon Prison! I'm turning myself in!"

There was a pause, and then the spotlight blasted back onto his face. Pong squinted and held his left arm high. He pulled up the bracelets, showing the blue mark on his wrist. "I escaped, see?" he called up to the boat. "I'm turning myself in, but *only* to Officer Manit! You better go get him. Right now!"

"Uh . . . uh . . ." stammered the woman. "Okay, don't move! Stay right there . . . in the name of the law! Manit!" she called out. "Manit, you gotta get up here!"

Pong heard the thunking of feet hustling to get belowdecks, followed by a double-thunking rising up the stairs.

"All right, all right, calm down," said another voice behind the spotlight—a familiar voice this time. "Wait a second—Somkit's cousin? What the *heck* is going on?"

"Please," said Pong, lowering his hands. "I really have to talk to you."

Manit stepped down onto the back platform of the cruiser and held out an open palm. Pong tossed him the line from the long-tail boat, and Manit pulled him in closer. He gave Pong a hand up, hauling him onto the platform beside him.

"It's okay. I got this," Manit called over his shoulder

to the other police officer. "Go get onto the transport boat next to us and wait for me there. I'll bring the prisoner with me in a minute."

The other officer nodded and climbed over the deck rail onto a smaller boat bobbing beside Manit's.

Manit stared down at Pong's left wrist, shaking his head. "Is that . . . ?" His eyes wandered up to Pong's half-inch-long hair, and he smacked a palm over his eyes. "Oh, you have got to be kidding me. The monk? The convict that everyone's looking for?"

Pong nodded. "That's me."

"Where the heck is your cousin?" Manit demanded. "Where's Somkit?"

"That's why I need your help," said Pong urgently. "I've got to get to him, and I can't do it unless I go through this barricade."

"No, he's not there," said Manit, shaking his head. "He left the city this morning. I gave him a permit so he could get out of town easily."

"You mean this one?" Pong held up the paper in his hand.

Manit's jaw dropped open. "What the . . . ? He was supposed to use that to lie low for a few days! I told him that it wouldn't be safe for kids like him to be hanging around the city. Things are about to get dicey around here."

"What do you mean, dicey?"

Manit looked over his shoulder, then lowered his voice again. "The Governor has got the police and his own personal guards going out to meet the marchers on the Giant's Bridge. They're supposed to arrest them all, but I don't think they're prepared for how many people will be there. I just did a sweep by the eastern shore, and the whole place is empty. They can't arrest that many people! The jails won't hold them all. So I don't know what they'll do, but I've got a bad feeling about it."

A knot of worry pulled itself tight in Pong's stomach. "Officer Manit, Somkit is *with* the marchers. He's going to be on the bridge tonight, probably right in the thick of things."

Manit shook his head, confused. He started to ask Pong more questions, but then they heard the faint sound of music. Pong and Manit both held still and listened. Voices, thousands of them, sang together. Pong recognized the melody. It was a popular love song, but they had changed the lyrics.

"Take my hand, oh, brothers, sisters, take my hand and walk with me . . ."

The voices were faraway but growing closer. Beating

drums accompanied them. No, not drums — the sounds of thousands of marching feet.

Pong turned back to Manit. He rubbed a thumb over his tattoo, hoping that his gamble had been worth it. Otherwise, everything was about to go disastrously wrong.

"Do you know what Somkit told me about you?" said Pong. "He said you always did the right thing. If that's really true, then I need your help. I have to get to that bridge. After that, I'll turn myself in to you, and you can take me to Banglad. I swear."

Manit looked down at Pong's wrist. "It's no good. You can't stop anything tonight. The Governor himself is going to be there, and you can't stop him. None of us can."

"Please. Just get me to the bridge and let me try. I'm the only one who's got a chance."

Manit grimaced. The sounds of the crowd grew louder and louder. "How can you be so sure?"

Pong ran his finger along his red-and-gold bracelet. "I just have a hunch."

Manit sighed. "Take a seat," he said, climbing the steps to the bridge of the cruiser. "Kid, you're lucky I believe in hunches."

Chapter 45

Nok held tight to her staff with sweaty palms. What should she do? Leave? Join her father on the other side of the bridge? This felt like a test she hadn't prepared for.

The line of police parted, and the Governor stepped out in front of them, flanked by the armed guards of his estate. Like the police, they carried long wooden staffs at their sides. Daggers swung from their hip belts.

The people fell silent as the Governor walked forward. He wore a pristine white robe that pooled in silky puddles at his feet. If he was shocked to see so many Gold orbs in the crowd, he didn't show it. The look on his face was calm, in control. He scanned the marchers coolly for a long moment. Nok didn't think anyone around her was even breathing.

When the Governor finally spoke, his voice reverberated across the silence. "Citizens, I don't know who has persuaded you to gather here in defiance of the law, but it is time to end this foolish escapade."

A short man wearing glasses and a waiter's apron stepped forward from the crowd of marchers. Nok caught sight of Somkit standing just behind him.

"Your Grace," said the man with the glasses. "We are marching within . . . within our rights. We have come bearing a message." He nodded to the crowd. "The people are suffering. For years we have lived in shadow, growing poorer and bearing impossible burdens put on us by your laws. We have come here to ask — to . . . to *demand* — that we have a say in the laws that rule over our lives. It's time for things to change."

The little man wasn't a confident speaker, though Nok could tell he was trying. His shaky voice seemed to give the Governor strength.

"If you are so concerned about the law," said the Governor, "then you should know that you are breaking it as we speak." He gestured to the guard on his right, who pulled out a sheaf of papers and held it high. The Governor pointed to the document. "I have decreed that any demonstration against me is a threat to our city," he called out. "And those who participate will be punished with the harshest sentence."

Worried murmurs rippled through the crowd. "The harshest sentence?" people asked each other. "What does that mean? Jail?"

The marchers rocked on their feet, but no one moved from their position.

The Governor stepped closer to the crowd, eyeing them with frustration, as if they were disobedient pets.

"Think about what you are asking for," he said to the crowd. "Do you really want to go back to the days before I came here, before we had order and light? Surely now you remember the dangers of fire. Or have you forgotten what it was like when the people of this city wallowed in ash and died in the mud?"

The Governor continued, recounting the horrors of the Great Fire. His deep voice rumbled. His cold eyes moved across the crowd, settling for a few seconds on one face after another. The people couldn't help but listen, mesmerized by his terrifying descriptions of those dark days. Nok was just as entranced as everyone else, but then he said something that broke her concentration.

"The law is the light, and the light shines on the worthy. . . ."

Those words again.

She had always found comfort in them, but tonight it was as though she were hearing them for the first time. And they didn't sound right at all.

Nok had been grasping for that light her whole life. She thought that if she were perfect in every way — if she were the best spire fighter, best student, perfect daughter, perfect everything—she'd be worthy enough for the light. But she'd gotten it all backward. So had the Governor.

Nok turned and looked at the people standing all around her. The orbs they carried shone softly on their faces, making it look as though the people themselves were glowing. It reminded her of what she had read in that book about the history of spire fighting: everyone has an ember burning inside them.

Nok unbuttoned the cuffs of her uniform and rolled her sleeves up to her elbows. Her scarred forearm, hidden from the sun for years, looked pale in the Gold glow of the orbs.

"Whoever stands against the rule of law," the Governor said sternly, "stands with the darkness. Citizens, I ask you to look at your own ranks. Criminals. Beggars." He sneered at the short man with the glasses. "Those who plot against me. Just look!" he cried, pointing to the shuttered western shore. "The law-abiding citizens of the West Side have shut their windows against you. If your cause has any merit, why do no people of worth stand with you?"

"They do!"

Everyone gasped and turned.

"They do!" Nok cried out again as she ducked through the front line of the crowd. She strode to the midpoint of the bridge, into the empty space between the Governor and the throng of people. Thousands of eyes stared at her.

"Nok!" cried a voice from behind the line of police. Nok's father rushed forward but was stopped short by the Governor's guards. "Let me go!" he shouted, fighting to free himself. "That's my daughter! Nok!"

Behind her, Nok heard the crowd whispering:

"That's the Law Commissioner's daughter!"

"Commissioner Sivapan?"

"Yes, yes — that's her!"

The Governor stood very still. Only his eyes moved, watching her like a cat.

Nok planted her feet. She swept her bamboo staff out in front of her slowly, making the motions that signaled the start of a spire-fighting match.

A collective gasp went up from the crowd behind her. The Governor's guards held their own staffs ready. Everyone knew what a skilled spire fighter was capable of, and the ones who had heard of Nok Sivapan knew just how skilled she was.

Nok looked into the Governor's cold eyes.

"Everyone on this bridge is worthy," she said. "And we've found our own light."

Without breaking her gaze with him, Nok bent down and set her staff on the stone at her feet. Slowly, she backed away until she'd joined the front line of marchers, who were all watching her in shocked silence.

"Hey. Hey, Nok," whispered a voice beside her.

She turned her head to see Somkit. He smiled at her and held out a Gold orb dangling from a string. Nok took it from him and held it up. Everyone in the crowd with orbs lifted them high.

The police exchanged confused glances and looked to the Governor for guidance.

He was seething. He raised his hands, and the tension on the bridge ratcheted even higher.

"You think you don't need me?" he said calmly to the crowd.

The icy confidence in his voice made Nok tremble.

"You want to return to the way things were before? So be it."

He swept one arm out to the east, over the rainbow lights of the city. His fingers spread wide. His arm shook. The air thinned and the temperature dropped. The Governor curled his fingers tight into his fist.

In that instant, every orb on the East Side of the river went dark.

Chapter 46

M anit cut off his headlights and motor and coasted up to the base of one of the bridge's stone pillars. "There's a ladder there on the side of the pillar. You see it?" he said, pointing to the crumbling carvings. "It doesn't go all the way to the top, but it almost reaches. If you can just climb the last few feet, you can swing yourself up over the side. I'll stay down here and make sure nobody sees you from the water."

Pong craned his head back to see the top of the bridge. "Okay," he said, swallowing down the dizzy feeling rising from his stomach. "Here I go."

He swung his arms and jumped from the boat onto the pillar, grabbing the ladder with both hands. The metal ladder had rusted, which made it easy to grip. He'd left his sandals in Manit's boat, and his bare toes clung to the rough metal. The bridge wasn't nearly as high as the cave ledge he had leaped from, but he still didn't want to look down. He climbed past the timeworn carvings of dancers, and he imagined them whispering to him. *Keep going,* they said. *Almost there.*

Pong slowed as he neared the top, rehearsing the words he planned to say to the Governor. He didn't have much more time to get them straight. Something was happening up on the bridge.

Someone was speaking in deep, rolling tones. It was the Governor. But what was he saying? Pong couldn't make out his words.

He climbed up faster.

The Governor stopped talking. Suddenly, a girl's voice cried out: "They do!"

The crowd above Pong gasped as one. Something had happened. What was it? The girl said something else, but it was too quiet for Pong to understand.

Pong had now reached the end of the ladder. He looked down. Surely Manit hadn't left him, but Pong couldn't see anything except the inky water beneath him.

He heard the Governor's voice again, briefly, and then he saw something he never imagined possible.

The lights of Chattana went out.

Pong stared, openmouthed, at the eastern shore. The entire shoreline had gone dark. Above him, the crowd on the bridge cried out, and then he heard anguished wails coming from the place where the city should be.

The sight sent a tremor of dread through Pong. He had to hurry.

The few orb lanterns that lined the bridge were still lit, and the Gold orbs that the marchers carried cast just enough light for him to see where he was climbing. Slowly, Pong rose up on his toes and reached for the bridge railing. Using all his strength, he hauled himself up.

Pong paused with his face peeking up over the side. There was enough light for him to see, but enough shadows to hide him. The crowd of marchers whispered worriedly. The Governor stood a few yards to Pong's left, just west of the bridge's midpoint.

The Governor held both arms raised. He pointed his hand to the lamps above the bridge. He clenched his fist, snuffing the lights out one by one.

Pong quickly swung his legs up over the rail of the bridge and dropped onto the stone. The Governor pushed his sleeves up to his elbows and raised his right hand out over the crowd.

"You have made your choice." The Governor glared at the crowd with cold certainty in his eyes. "You do not deserve my light!"

The air crackled. Pong's scalp tingled as his hair rose

on end. In the Governor's right palm, a huge ball of light began to swirl, as blindingly bright as the center of a star. It swelled, bigger and bigger. People in the crowd cried out, but the bridge was too packed for anyone to run. The Governor reared his arm back, as if getting ready to hurl the enormous mass of light forward.

Pong's heart sank. His plan wouldn't work. There would be no talking, no reasoning with this man. Not even summoning Father Cham's memory or showing him the bracelet would change his mind.

The bracelet!

Pong looked at the Governor's left wrist. Yes, there it was: something that no one else had noticed. Something that even Pong had failed to observe those four years ago, when the Governor had been only inches away.

A braided bracelet, identical to Ampai's, identical to his own.

May you bring the light back to Chattana.

Pong knew what to do. Shielding his eyes against the bright glare, he rushed toward the Governor.

Before anyone could notice him, Pong seized the Governor's wrist and held on.

Chapter 47

Pong's hand was on fire. A fire with no flames.

As soon as he grabbed the Governor's wrist, the raw light swirling in the Governor's right hand went out, throwing the bridge into darkness. A surge of energy pulsed out from the Governor and flowed into Pong's fingers. It was the strangest sensation: a burning without pain.

Pong kept his grip on the Governor as the Gold light flowed into his palm, down his left wrist and into his arm.

"What — what are you doing?" gasped the Governor, trying to pull away. But Pong did not let go.

The guards surrounding them started forward but then pressed back in fear as the tattoo on Pong's left wrist began to glow.

A liquid Gold light flowed, trapped beneath Pong's skin. The only place it could get out was through the letters of his tattoo. Thin lines of light streamed out of his prison mark. They shot out into the black night and reflected against the low clouds.

"*Pong!*"

Somkit rushed forward to help his friend. He grabbed onto Pong's right arm to pull him back to the safety of the crowd. "Ah!" Somkit gasped, looking at his own wrist in shock. "What's happening?"

Light flowed from Pong into Somkit's hand. The same streams of Gold light poured from Somkit's crossed-out tattoo.

The Governor growled like a beast and raised his other fist to strike Pong. As he brought it down, a streak of jet black shot out from the crowd. Nok flew to Pong's side and crossed her forearms in front of her, blocking the Governor's fist. In a classic spire-fighting move, she gripped his wrist in both her hands and twisted his arm back. And then she, too, gaped down at herself in shock.

Rippled beams of light shone out from the tattoo under her scarred skin.

The Governor cried out and shoved the children away from him. He tore himself free of their grasp and stumbled backward, out of their reach.

But even though they had let go of the Governor, the light coming out of them didn't fade. Nok, Pong, and Somkit held on to one another, confused and awed at the light that still shone from their wrists. For a long moment, the three of them stood alone, glowing like human lanterns on the dark bridge.

And then the crowd came forward. Gently, timidly at first, they put their hands on the children's shoulders. Then they reached for one another, holding hands, linking their bodies together. The gasps rippled through the crowd as one by one, each person felt the surge of light flow through them and burst out into the darkness. Even those without prison marks glowed softly, like paper lamps. The shouts of the people turned from shock to awe and then delight.

"Look at me! Oh, my goodness, look at *you!*"

"Can you believe it?"

"Look up, look up! I've never seen anything like this!"

The low-hanging clouds reflected the light that beamed from the bridge. The night was lit bright as daybreak, bright as their city. One after another, the guards on the west side of the bridge lowered their staffs. Some backed away and left. Others dropped to their knees in wonder, and a few joined the crowd and embraced their neighbors.

Pong stepped back from the crush of people, toward the bridge rail. A few steps away, the Governor stood staring at the mass of illuminated bodies. His face was twisted in fury. His chest rose and fell with angry breaths.

He raised his arm over the crowd just as he had before, when he'd snuffed out the lights of the city. He held his fingers outstretched and clenched them tight. When nothing happened, he did it again, and again. No matter what he did, he could not shut off the light that poured out of the people of Chattana.

Pong met his eyes. "This light doesn't belong to you," he said.

A voice shouted, "Nok!"

A disheveled-looking Commissioner Sivapan broke through the line of kneeling guards and grabbed his daughter. They embraced, and then he lifted her up in the air. They laughed as he twirled her around and around. She held both hands overhead, like a little child, sending dazzling streams of light up into the sky.

Pong turned and spotted Somkit's round face smiling at him from the crowd. Somkit held up his hand and flicked his fingers in and out of the beautiful beams. Pong smiled back.

As he took a step forward to join his friend, his body jolted to a stop. Two hands gripped his shoulders. The last thing Pong saw was the rage in the Governor's eyes as he yanked Pong toward him, and then hurled him over the side of the bridge.

Chapter 48

Years before, when Pong was a very small boy living at Namwon, every Sunday he and Somkit would sit by the river gate and watch an old man and his grandson on the riverbank near the prison.

The grandfather would slide his body into the water while his grandson sat on the shore with a basket. The grandfather would take a huge breath and then use the dock posts to push himself down under the surface.

Somkit and Pong would watch the grandson watching the water, waiting for the old man to come back up.

"What's he doing?" asked Pong once.

"Crabbing," said Somkit. "Down at the bottom, there are great big crabs crawling around in the mud."

They waited and waited, and still the man didn't come up. They kept waiting, but the man stayed submerged.

"Gosh, how does he know when he's got one?" asked Pong.

"He just feels around until one clamps onto his fingers," said Somkit.

And then, just when they were sure the old man had definitely drowned, he shot up to the surface, holding a gigantic black crab in his hands for the delighted grandson to put into the basket.

All Pong would think about was how terrifying it would be to be down at the bottom of the dark river, waiting to get pinched by the claws of scratchy-backed crabs.

That is precisely what Pong was thinking now as he sank through the dark water of the Chattana River. He felt a scratchy scraping of thick crab legs all over his back. And he was sure that before he drowned at the bottom of that great river, he was going to be crawled over by dozens and dozens of horrible crabs.

What an awful way to go.

The crab legs scrabbled down his neck and under his collar, and the last thing he remembered was those crab legs curling themselves into the back of his shirt and pulling up very, very hard, almost as if they were fingers.

And then everything went black.

Things were still black when Pong realized that he wasn't in the water anymore.

He was lying on muddy ground. He felt a heavy weight mashing on his chest. It hurt. His mouth was open and someone else's lips pressed against his, blowing into his mouth with breath that tasted like lemon cake. He heard voices all around him, watery and far away at first, and then sharpening into focus.

He heard Officer Manit. "Keep pumping his chest, Ms. Sivapan!"

He heard Mark. "Breathe into his mouth again, girl! I saw him come around!"

"Oh, man, Nok, you better back up because he looks like he's going to vomit right in your face!"

That was Somkit.

Pong slowly opened his eyes. Bright beams of Gold light danced in and out of his vision, making it hard to focus.

The first time Pong nearly drowned, he woke up to a chicken. The second time, he was saved by the wide-grinning moon.

And the third time, once his vision cleared, Pong found himself looking up into the black eyes of a bird.

Nok's hair lay plastered against her face. Her clothes were soaking wet, and water dripped off the tip of her nose. She leaned over him, worried. "Pong, oh, my goodness, say something!"

Pong swallowed. "After this I'm going to learn how to swim," he croaked.

The light-beaming crowd that had gathered around them let out a deafening cheer.

Nok smiled so big and bright that Pong felt it would outshine every light that had come before or after.

Chapter 49

Pong paced under the mango tree and looked across the river. The sun was just beginning to set over the silhouettes of the houses on the West Side, and the sky was a glorious wash of purple and orange.

He'd once promised himself that he'd never set foot in Namwon again, and yet here he was. They'd taken down the metal chain fences and the barred river gate. The sign over the entrance now read THE CHAM CENTER FOR EDUCATION. Namwon had become a school, modeled after the one in Tanaburi.

But even though Namwon was no longer a jail, Pong still had a hard time visiting. It was easier to change the name on the front door than it was to erase all the old feelings of being inside. Even the students, many of whom were former prisoners, wore the same uniforms as they had before, with new patches over the pockets. But

Pong made himself come twice a week — for no other reason than to walk out the door on his own two feet, rather than riding out in a durian basket.

Pong frowned as the sun set and the Gold orbs hanging in the mango tree flicked on. The last practice session at the spire-fighting gym should have ended an hour ago. What was taking so long?

"Hey."

"Ah!" exclaimed Pong, wheeling around. A face with sharp black eyes stared at him, inches away. He jumped back even though he knew immediately who it was. "You've *got* to quit doing that!"

Nok smiled. "Sorry. I've been doing the Nothing Step all day at practice. It's hard to remember that most people like to hear you walking up behind them."

"What took you so long to get here?" asked Pong.

"I stopped by the market to get this." She held up a big sack. The spiky skin of a durian poked through the fabric. "Not for you," she said when Pong held his nose. "It's for Somkit. Is he here?"

Pong nodded to the building that used to be the prison guards' quarters. "He's in class right now."

Nok set the bag down against the tree. "What class is he taking?"

Pong smiled. "No, he's *teaching* a class. About light

and energy and a bunch of other things I can't understand yet."

Through the building's windows, they could see Somkit, standing at the front of a room. He was holding up an orb light and drawing a picture of the sun on a chalkboard while his students took notes.

"Maybe he'll come to your school next and you can take the class from him," said Pong.

Nok rolled her eyes. "Oh, I'm sure he'd just love to be the one grading my papers."

Nok was enrolled in the prestigious Chattana Girls' Academy, across the river from Namwon. Now that classes had started, Pong didn't see her as often. She was busy with schoolwork and spire-fighting practice and helping her family. And he'd been busy, too. He and Somkit had started taking classes at the boys' school down the street from Officer Manit's house. Manit and his wife had given them a place to stay, and they walked them to and from school every day.

It was quite a change from living at the temple or the Mud House. And that morning, Manit had told them that he had started the paperwork to adopt them both. There had been lots of hugs and laughing after that, and Manit's wife had said, "Now you two will be brothers!"—not realizing that of all the many things that were changing in their lives, this would not be one of them.

Nok walked to the dock, where the river gate used to be. Pong watched her standing near the water for a while. Whenever he saw her, he remembered how she'd looked that night on the bridge, with the light streaming out of her arm.

The light that had flowed from the Governor to the people was gone now. It had beamed out of them into the dark all night, but by morning it had faded. The only evidence left of the spectacular event was that anyone who had once had a prison mark woke to find it gone.

The Governor had also disappeared by the next morning. It seemed that he'd lost all his powers — at least, some people reported seeing him trying to charge up orbs without any success. Others said they saw him fleeing the city, disappearing into the darkness of the forest.

Once the people learned of Somkit's sun orbs, everyone wanted one, which was how Somkit had found himself in the position of teaching a classroom full of grown-ups. But even so, people felt a little lost without the Governor's powers. They would have to use fire again — for cooking, at least. But how could they make sure it never got out of control? Which was better: being safe or having freedom? And did you have to choose?

Everyone in every pocket of the city was having to figure out new ways of doing things. Nok's father and Mark were working together to organize an election the next month. It would be the first election since the Great Fire. But there were still so many questions: How should they keep the peace in the city? Should there be new laws? If so, who should write them? There were still so many poor and struggling people living on the East Side. What was the best way to make sure they shared in the wealth and opportunities of their city? Even though few people missed the Governor, there had been something easy about having him answer all the questions for them.

Pong walked down to the river's edge to stand beside Nok, who watched the lights of the city coming on: one, by one, by one thousand.

"Wow, you can really see everything from here, can't you?" she said dreamily. "Though I hope that Somkit can figure out how to make the orbs glow with different colors. I think it's great that everyone can afford Gold light now, but I sort of miss the rainbow, don't you?"

Pong nodded. Then, after a moment, he asked, "Do you think we did the right thing?"

Pong already knew the answer to the question, but he

wanted to know what Nok would say. He was relieved when she rolled her eyes at him as if he were a silly toddler.

"Of course we did," she said. "Even my *mom* thinks things are better this way."

Pong caught a flash of emotion when Nok mentioned her mother, but it was too fast for him to tell what it was. She didn't talk much about her family, but from what Pong had managed to learn, it was at least as complicated as starting a new government.

Even so, Nok seemed happy. Every time Pong saw her, she seemed less weighed down. But right now, he could tell there was something on her mind. She was fiddling with a loose thread on her uniform, wrapping it around and around her finger.

She looked at him, then looked away. Finally, she blurted out, "I never said sorry. You know, for . . . for . . . everything."

The fingers of Pong's right hand wandered absentmindedly to his left wrist, the way they still did whenever he thought of his life on the run.

"I just wanted to say," continued Nok, "that I was wrong, and . . . and, well . . ." She grew quiet, then added, "My father said they're going to rename the Giant's Bridge. I told him they should name it after you."

Pong half smiled. "The Pong Bridge? I could get used to that."

Nok gazed back at him, her eyes serious and a little bit sad. "I told him they should name it the Bridge of Good Hearts."

Pong quickly turned his face away from her. He smiled, savoring her words. Then he looked down at his left wrist, bare now of any prison mark. All his bracelets had snapped off when the Governor had thrown him from the bridge, even the red braided one. At first, Pong was distraught. The bracelets were the only reminder he had of Father Cham. But right now he was struck with the thought that maybe he'd lost them because the blessings had all come true.

A fresh breeze blew across the water and riffled the mango tree leaves. Pong looked up at the ripe fruits, swinging beside the globes of glowing Gold glass. He remembered now why he'd been standing under the tree in the first place.

"Are you okay?" asked Nok. "I hope I didn't —"

"Shh, stand here . . ." Pong held her arm and moved her one step to the side. "Not here . . . a little more . . ." he said, shifting her one more step to the right. "There." He took her hands and placed them out in front of her, palms up. "Now, just listen . . ."

They stood like that for a moment, until they heard the soft *pop!* of a mango stem.

Nok gasped as a mango dropped straight into her open arms. She beamed delightedly at Pong.

He smiled back. "Trust me, that's going to be a really good one."

ACKNOWLEDGMENTS

I am so grateful for the many people who helped bring this book into the light. Thank you to my agent, Stephanie Fretwell-Hill, for guiding Pong and Nok to their perfect home and for being my partner along this publishing journey. I am so lucky to have you in my corner. Thank you to my wonderful editor, Andrea Tompa, who understood the hearts of these characters right from the start and who simultaneously kept her eye on the big picture and the tiniest details. I'm so proud to be working with you.

Thank you to Ji-Hyuk Kim for the dazzling jacket image; to designers Sherry Fatla and Hayley Parker for making this book so beautiful, inside and out; and to all the extraordinary team at Candlewick for everything you do for young readers.

Thank you to the many people who read this tale all along the way: To my writing comrades Aimee, Sean, Jason, and Andrew, thank you for cheering me on in those difficult first-draft days. Paige Britt, thank you for your wisdom and for being such a positive force in my life. Thank you to Anna Waggener and Lori M. Lee for reading and giving me such insightful feedback. Thank you so much, Dow Phumiruk, for your careful eye, your wonderful words, and your friendship. Thank you, Quincy Surasmith, for believing in this book and for making it stronger.

Thank you to my daughters, Elowyn and Aven. Every story starts with you. Thank you to my husband, Tom, for standing beside me every step of the way. I could never do this without your love and support.

I owe everything I have to my family, to those who came before me and sacrificed so much so that I could live this life. I am especially grateful to my father, Amnaj Soontornvat, the greatest storyteller I have ever met. His epic tales of growing up in Thailand could fill a library. Dad, thank you for all you have done for me. You are on every page of this book.

Most of all, thank you to my mother, Wilna Jean Gillespie, who filled my childhood with art and books. When I was ten years old, she told me a story about a convict, a policeman, and the difference between man's law and God's law. When I eventually read *Les Misérables* on my own, it changed my heart and made me want to be a storyteller. Thank you, Mom, for everything.